B O

END
OF THE
SIX

MATT RYAN

THE PRESTON SIX SERIES

Cover design by Regina Wamba | www.macidesign.com
Edited by Victoria Schmitz | Crimson Tide Editorial
Book design by Nadège Richards | www.inkstainformatting.com

BOOKS BY MATT RYAN

Rise of the Six
Call of the Six
Fall of the Six
Break of the Six
Fury of the Six
End of the Six

CHAPTER 1

EVELYN KNELT NEXT TO THE Alius stone and typed in the code. It'd taken her more time than she'd like to admit, but all it'd taken was one careless person conducting maintenance in a tower on Hector's world. What a hapless fool; entering the code out of routine, not checking for any bystanders.

Taking a deep breath, she clicked her shield on and readied herself to slow time. The stone hummed and the Preston forest turned. Gone were the oak trees, replaced with towering pines and a smattering of ferns. The smell hit her stronger than the sight. Pine needles, mixed with recent rain, and maybe a hint of ocean air.

She closed her eyes and slowed time. Recently, she felt she'd spent more time in *slow-mo*, as her mom called it, than she did in regular time. But with so much to learn, to prepare, and to find . . . regular time would take a millennium. Interesting enough, she didn't age while in her state of near suspended time. How many months would equate to a day for her? Not knowing the answer niggled at her mind. Other things took higher priority, she supposed.

She opened her eyes and spotted a trail; worn, with two deep ruts, leading into the woods. On either side of it, sat two large guns mounted on steel frames, the kind that sat atop old battleships. They had pivot points and were most likely autonomous, with every intention of killing her, yet they stood still. She'd expected something, but this seemed a bit on the crude side for such a high level race as the purge people. She slid her hand over the gun's gray metal as she passed them.

A few more guns peppered the forest as she scanned her surroundings. Maybe they weren't as prepared as she'd thought. The forest didn't have a single bullet mark and the ferns had grown up to the bases of the guns. Rust ran down some of the bolts.

She whistled as she skipped down the dirt path and spotted the asphalt road, overgrown with weeds. She sighed and hoped this wasn't some abandoned planet. She'd hate for the trail to go cold again. She didn't have the time.

Jogging down the road, she spotted the first series of houses and, to her relief, a group of humans.

The first few people didn't have embers hovering over their heads like the purge people always had. Yet the place seemed typical of the purge camps, with large vats of liquid sitting over fires, each one being attended to by at least one person. Steam trails hung frozen above. She'd seen a few camps like these—barbaric conditions. She hadn't given them much thought, but maybe she should. This would be the fourth such camp she'd encountered.

Passing through the camp, she popped her head through a

broken window; just a couple of men eating from a can. She pulled away and wished the smells would fade, but in the slow-mo world, they hung on like smoke from a burning tire.

Evelyn was disappointed with this location and ready to leave, when she spotted it. A man's embers danced above him, floating into the sky. It reminded her of the orange bits of light that would run up into the dark night after stoking a fire. It didn't matter what speed she was in, they flowed the same, always in motion.

Her heart raced, looking at the scruffy man. He looked so normal, but he wasn't. Of all the worlds and all the people she'd encountered, the purge people had a different genetic makeup—a magic all their own. For Evelyn, these embers were their call sign.

Creeping behind a shack, she released time and the sounds of conversations, wind in the trees, and the distant crash of the ocean came to life. She enjoyed the silence, but the vibrations of the living world were much more fascinating.

One of the few benefits of looking like a seven-year-old girl, meant no one took you seriously. If she kept her face simple and seemed to not have a care in the world, almost every society ignored her. She skipped past a few people and made her way near the scruffy purge man. He licked his dirty fingers and tossed a chicken bone to the pine needle-covered forest floor.

After a couple of agonizing hours, the man finally made his way to a shack, and came back out with a satchel tied to his belt. She'd seen these among them, but hadn't procured one yet. She thought about slowing down time and taking this man, but she wanted to see where he'd lead her.

After a thirty-minute stop at an outhouse, the man made his way toward the stone. She kept her distance, and the man didn't appear to care if someone was watching him. The anticipation of getting somewhere with one of these purge people excited her so much she felt her heart pounding.

The man slapped the guns as he passed them, then knelt next to the stone.

Evelyn slowed time down and moved in right behind him. She released and watched him type in the code and then slowed time down again just as he was turning around. He'd take it for a gust of wind, or whatever else his imagination might come up with to rationalize what he felt.

Behind a pine tree, she waited for the distinct sound of the stone working and then quieting. But it didn't hum. She peeked around the tree and the man's grimy hand closed around her neck.

He squeezed and growled. "Who are you, little girl. Why are you following me?"

Evelyn tried to speak, but the man's hand seized around her throat. She couldn't slow time, or even speak. How could this man have gotten his hand on her?

He let go of her neck and picked her up with both hands, shaking her by the shoulders. "You working with the daughter? She send you?"

Daughter? "I was just curious. Wondering what this place is. People disappear here."

The man laughed and set her down. "Even the daughter wouldn't send such a child. Go back to the village and remind those people to keep working, or they'll get a visit from the queen."

"Yes, sir."

He nodded. "Go on. Get."

Evelyn ran down the path. She had the code. It didn't matter what the man did or where he went. She knew the next place to go, and she couldn't stop the grin on her face.

She waited a half hour before returning to the stone.

END OF THE SIX

Rubbing her neck, she thought of the man. It wasn't the first time someone had manhandled her, and each time she'd been violated, a tinge of guilt seeped into her. Evelyn couldn't fail her people, and making stupid mistakes could quickly turn into catastrophic outcomes.

She typed in the code. Shield on, she counted in her head the precise time the stone would jump, and the nanosecond before it finished, she slowed down time. She had a bad feeling about this man on the other side.

The inside of an opulent house blinked into existence; she was surrounded by people pointing guns at her. Their brown and green clothes contrasted the white walls and shiny floor around the stone. Evelyn had never seen such a manmade surface molded right up to the stone. Even the Alius stone looked different, with smoother edges, a shiny surface, and three lines running down the side. What did it mean?

One thing of interest were the embers floating above each of the people. A few held small, round stones in their hands, ready to throw them. They had fear in their eyes.

Could this be the queen's house? After searching for so long, had she finally found her? This one person was the sole being behind all of the purge activities. She had created these terrible factories of ruin. And from what Evelyn understood, with the queen gone, the others would have no reason to continue.

Walking past the frozen men and women, she again resisted the urge to inspect them. Even she had limitations in slow-mo. An internal clock ticked away. She took the stairs, feeling as if the queen would be in the higher rooms, looking down on her world.

When she reached the top of the stairs, she stopped and glanced at the group below. All their connections were so strong, and their special embers floated up and swirled in a maelstrom above. Beautiful. What a unique race.

Past the stairs and down a large hallway, she encountered several more people, running away from the circle. Her arrival must have set off an alarm. She smelled fear on them as she passed.

Another staircase, covered in gray marble with red stripes running up them, led her to the next floor. Her breath stopped at the sight of robotic guns pointing at her. A flash erupted from one barrel, and then the next. Soon, all of the guns had flashed. These ones apparently worked. Thankfully, bullets traveled way slower. They hadn't even left the barrel yet and the sound wave spread out from them. The barrel did look rather large. What kind of bullets were they shooting?

At the end of the room, stood a set of twins holding stones. They were holding hands. The connections between twins were always fascinating and these two in particular had a strong connection. Their embers coalesced and mingled above. She didn't know why, but she thought this made them stronger in some way.

Evelyn stepped carefully around the twins and stood at the carved wooden door with symbols and diagrams around the edge. She took one of the twins and pulled him by the back of his shirt, until he fell into the door. It sent out an electrical bolt and struck the twin, transferring the bolt to his brother. She hoped it hadn't killed them, but was thankful they'd unwittingly dismantled the trap set for the door. She kicked the door in the rest of the way, spotting the queen.

Brilliance, amazement, and fear filled Evelyn as she took in the woman floating a few feet above the floor. Her golden connections shot out from her in all directions, as if the entire world loved her and she loved them back. It swirled around the center of her chest, instead of the top of the head, like everyone else. All of that was nothing compared to her fire. Other's had embers floating, but this woman had a bright flame, blasting from her head and shoulders, straight through the ceiling. This woman must command the heavens.

Tears fell from Evelyn's eyes and froze in the air as they left her cheek. How could she kill such beauty? She pulled out her mother's dagger and picked a spot to stab. She decided on her left eye.

The woman moved, lowering to the ground.

Evelyn thought she released time, and looked back to the twins to confirm she hadn't. Turning back around, she found the queen smiling, like a cat might with a cornered mouse. *How is this possible?*

"How did you do that? You don't have our gift," her angelic voice said, freezing Evelyn in her presence. Her gaze washed over her whole body. "You have more of it than any person I've ever seen in my life. You would create a soul stone worth millions, maybe billions of people. Who are you?"

Evelyn couldn't catch her breath. No one but her father had ever been in her time, and this woman's entrance into her space felt like the biggest violation imaginable. Her words glossed over her and her mouth moved, trying to find the words, like a preverbal child.

"Cat got your tongue?" The woman asked and walked closer. "I've seen the worlds, yet I have never come across a soul like you. Where did you come from?"

Evelyn thought about slowing time down again, yet there was nowhere to go, and no time left to slow. The woman had her in her clutches, all she had to do was squeeze. She'd made a terrible miscalculation about this queen. Attempting to gain control over the situation, Evelyn calmed herself and focused on the air around her. When all was quiet, the queen's intentions became clear; bits and pieces of her thoughts floated to her.

This woman felt an amusement and a curiosity, but mostly a hunger. She wanted Evelyn. She wanted to devour her. With more of her wits about her, Evelyn set to take what she wanted from the queen. She concentrated on getting into the woman's mind, her thoughts, and memories—anything she could pull from it before dispensing with her.

The queen tilted her head, feeling the intrusion—Evelyn didn't have time to hide it, and could possibly even damage her. The queen's thoughts poured into her. Secrets and desires. Regrets and determination. She hid something of great value. Evelyn grabbed the location of this before moving onto the one thing she'd searched all the worlds for. In a matter of a millisecond, she found it . . . sitting in the mind of this very woman.

It came as such a shock to finally have this information, Evelyn gasped and the queen took advantage of the momentary lapse, pushing her out of her mind with brute force. Evelyn screamed and grabbed her head. The woman had such strength, it made Evelyn feel like her mind was ripping in half.

The queen moved next to her in a flash, as if she'd moved through time and popped into Evelyn's space. Her gloved hand touched Evelyn's and they watched as the stone melted into her skin. Her shield did nothing to stop it and she braced for death. What came next, felt worse than death.

Evelyn's eyes went wide and she stared straight forward. Not able to control her body, or her mouth.

"You think you can get into my head?" The queen raged. "Now tell me, where are you from?"

"Earth." The word spilled uncontrollably from her mouth.

"Are there more like you there?"

"One more." Again, the answer spewed from her without her consent. She tried to control herself, but the commands wouldn't work.

What have you done to me? Evelyn wanted to ask, but she was no longer the master of herself and this woman played with her like a puppet.

"Two of you. Interesting. Show me the code to your Earth, tap it into my arm." The queen extended her arm.

Evelyn complied, even as she shook inside at the total loss of control. She wanted to scream and run from this woman before she answered another question.

"Is there another planet you know of, one I might want?"

"Vanar."

"Show me."

Evelyn showed her the code.

"Do you know how special you are?"

"Yes."

She laughed. "I'm sure you do. What are you, ten?"

"One."

She laughed again. "One year old? Remarkable. You and this other one might just be enough . . . I could go through a hundred planets and not get what you offer."

Evelyn screamed in her head and something snapped. She felt herself getting closer to her consciousness. She grabbed at the strands and yanked them.

"It's almost a pity to do this to you; like destroying a fine piece of art. Be happy in the knowledge you are serving a greater good. You are helping more than you can ever know." She held out both hands, each one holding a stone.

Evelyn knew if those stones touched her, she'd be dead. She screamed at herself, and while it didn't reach her lips, her finger moved. Then she flexed a muscle in her leg. With a newfound confidence, she dug deep into her soul and found the strength. Screaming louder than she ever knew possible, her voice erupted outward, sending a shockwave bursting from her. The sheer force collided with the queen's chest and sent her flying backward. As the queen slipped back into real time, Evelyn held her still in slow-mo.

Turning around, she ran toward the door. Jumping over the twins at the doorway, and past the guns. The same kind of round stones hung about a foot out of the gun now. Then down the stairs toward the Alius stone.

The group still stood around it, pointing their guns and stones to the center of the circle. She shoved each person to the ground and kicked away their guns. She glanced up, half expecting the queen to float down and suck her away to some terrible tower. But she never showed.

Evelyn typed in the code for Ryjack. She'd bounce around to a few locations to cover her tracks. She gave one last scan of the people laying on the ground and released time. The men and women scrambled to their feet and grabbed their weapons. The stone hummed. One large man, quicker than the rest, fired his gun. A black round stone flew out and struck her shield, deflecting and striking another man. He fell to the floor as the room changed.

A brisk breeze blew past her, carrying with it the terrible smell of a nearby grinner. She knelt, put in another code and jumped again, landing back in Preston.

She fell to the ground and looked up at the oak tree canopy stretching high above the Alius stone. Blood trickled from her nose, as the weight of her catastrophic mistake weighed heavily on her. The queen of the purge people still lived. She not only knew where they were, but she'd be coming. Evelyn saw many things in the woman's mind; nothing eclipsed her hunger for *more*. She wouldn't stop.

There had to be a way to fix this. First, she needed to warn Travis and tell him most of the truth. With her mom, she'd change how it happened. She didn't want her knowing she'd traveled to all these worlds. She had enough to worry about.

Either way, her encounter with the queen was meant to be . . . because she held the one thing Evelyn had been searching for her whole life.

CHAPTER 2

TRAVIS WALKED DOWN THE HALLS of his empty hospital and sighed, running his hand down the tiled wall. His finger squeaked over the surface and he stopped at the door.

"What are you doing here?"

He jumped and spun around. "Evelyn?" He didn't scare easy and this intrusion seemed egregious. Looking at the young girl's face, he knew she had something important to convey.

She took two steps forward and stopped like a soldier at attention. "I came to warn you. They're coming."

"Who?"

"The purge people. The magicians. Have you no knowledge of them?"

He didn't. "Tell me of these people and maybe it will spark something I've forgotten. I am rather old, you know."

Evelyn laughed and swayed, as a young girl might do, but

Travis had spent some time with her, and knew she was a genius, to put it mildly—a mastermind. Any meeting with Evelyn was more difficult to navigate than any he'd had with government officials or dignitaries. And the truth was, she'd helped his world come back from the brink of death with ingenuity and brilliant strategies. She'd even coded back most of the net. Travis's poll numbers shot to the moon once the more basic services were restored. All thanks to this little girl, that virtually no one in Vanar knew existed.

Didn't mean she wasn't without risk though. She had poured over all of Marcus's research and gathered such an astute knowledge of the systems he created, it became frightening to Travis. He imagined she could take away all that she'd given in a few strokes of her hand. In fact, if it wasn't for the glimmer of Poly that he saw in Evelyn she'd be downright terrifying.

"I don't have much time. Can we walk, like we used to?" Evelyn said.

"It was only a few months ago."

Evelyn smiled and extended her hand. "Feels like decades for me."

Travis gripped her child hand in his. Something seemed off about her, and if he didn't know her better, he'd guess she was nervous. "Have you been exploring again?"

"Maybe." Some of the shy little girl shone through and reminded him of Compry or Gladius as a child.

"You know there are worlds not suitable for you."

"I'm safe, no need to worry." She pulled at him and he followed. Evelyn glanced back at the doors Travis had been standing in front of. "You haven't gone in there, right?"

"No, ma'am, under strict orders." He saluted her, but the young girl charm had left, and her stern face asked the question again. "You know I haven't. Besides, you locked the doors."

She smiled and pulled Travis along faster. "Good. Can we take the trail?" The door slid open, revealing the outside.

"Sure." He didn't want to. He hadn't walked it since Poly had left. The trail was filled with bad memories, yet Evelyn skipped along the dirt path of her mom's tormented trail, swinging his hand in hers, as if she had fond memories. The screams still haunted Travis.

Down the path and around the stone wall, they neared the tree. "Who do you think made the stones?" Evelyn asked as she let go of his hand and sat under the tree.

"I suppose a greater being," Travis said, sitting down next to Evelyn.

"God?"

"No, a person I would suspect. Probably from a world much like ours, but highly advanced."

"I believe I've found them," Evelyn said.

"The stone makers?"

She nodded. "You are very difficult to read—so guarded."

"I like to think I'm cautious. Now why don't you tell me more about these stone makers?"

She ignored his question once again. "Did you know every human has a visible connection to the people their lives have touched?" She squeezed his hand. "It's almost like an aurora borealis you'd see in the sky. Normal folk like yourself can't see it the way I do, but I know you feel it; like when someone is watching you and you turn around. The more lives you touch, the more connections you have, and some are much stronger than others. Especially blood relatives."

"Like a mother and daughter." He wasn't sure where she was going with this.

"Precisely, which is why Marcus knew he couldn't grow me in a lab. I had to have that connection in order to be who I am."

"What are we doing here, Evelyn? You said you came to warn me about magicians?"

She smiled and looked down at her shoes. Taking a deep breath, she went on to tell him about an encounter she'd had with a *purge queen*, as she called her. With each sentence, Travis's eyes got wider. He couldn't believe what she'd done.

"Are they coming here?"

"Yes, but I don't know to which planet they will arrive first. It could be both at the same time, I'm not sure of their level of resources."

"And what do they want?"

"Us. They will take us and use us, until there is nothing left."

"There must be something we can do to stop them."

"Earth has a chance of delaying it, but there is something I found in her mind, something she had hidden very deep. And I think I got it without her noticing. I'm going to have the mutants get it for me, and I hope it's something that will help us all."

"HARRIS, WE'VE GOT A PROBLEM," Travis said into his Panavice, having said goodbye to Evelyn.

Harris arrived at his stone room, looking around for trouble. "What's so urgent?

"Why don't you tell me about these purge people?"

Harris's eyes narrowed and he walked closer. "Why exactly?"

"Because our little friend just gave them an invitation to Vanar and Earth."

Harris normally didn't have much expression, but he took

a few steps back and looked stunned. "Evelyn should know better. We can't defend ourselves against them, and Earth is in an even worse predicament."

"So you *do* know about them?" Travis recounted his talk with Evelyn.

"We should count our blessings she got out and was able to warn us."

"There's searching for a positive. How do you know them?" Travis asked.

"Julie told me about a world they visited. I hunted down Hector, the man they took from that world, and had a long conversation about these purge people. This is bad, she's probably just brought death to our planet."

"Good thing we have a resident expert on bringing death. What should we do?" Travis hoped for a viable answer.

Harris rubbed his chin. "Evelyn knew this was coming. She wrote some code onto a very dangerous program. A program we told you we destroyed."

Travis glared at Harris. "I hope you're kidding. And even if you have this tech, Evelyn is scared of their leader. The way she talked about them, it was as if they were magical."

"I don't believe in magic. These people have tapped into some kind of tech that is beyond us, or have some genetic mutation. They will have a weakness, and what Evelyn created, may be our only chance."

"This is dangerous, Harris; especially in your hands. Everything around you dies."

CHAPTER 3

THE LIGHTS WENT OUT, AND the carousel nearby slowed to a stop. The music that had been blaring with a mixture of rock and country folk tunes, stopped playing. People looked around, annoyed a power outage was ruining their time.

Poly had other concerns. Her daughter stood in front of her, next to a boy she could barely recognize as Julie and Lucas's kid. Evelyn kept a steady gaze on Poly, and her intelligent eyes held a patience most adults didn't have.

"Did you turn the power off?" Poly asked.

"No, *they* did. It's what they do in preparation. First, they kill the power. Next, they'll send in their machines, build those towers, like the one we saw in Chile with Hector. Then the cubes will emerge."

The speaker crackled to life with a static hiss and people turned to face it. A woman's voice came to life over the airwaves. "It is my deepest regret to inform you that although your lives seem important to each and every one of you, you're entire civilization is but a mere blip in time and space. I have a great need for you. Your lives, your essence, will push me on, and therefore, your existence will have meaning.

"Our culling will begin immediately. You may resist with all the vigor your world can muster, but none of it will matter in the end. Take solace in knowing there are many of you in existence, so no matter how far we reach, there will always be a *you* somewhere in the worlds. I thank you for the gift you are giving us. You matter more than you know."

"That's . . ." Poly said. "That's the voice from the video Marcus showed us."

"She's their queen."

The crowd rumbled with conversation and some laughter, thinking it a joke by someone who found the microphone.

"Evelyn, you're bleeding," Julie said.

Poly's daughter reached for her nose and ran a finger across her upper lip, extending her hand to study the blood on the end of her finger.

"Baby, what did you do?" Poly rushed to her, kneeling and staring at her little girl. She couldn't bear to lose another person in her life. "Evelyn, you can't go fast like that again. Your father—"

"I'm fine. I am learning my limits. Will was harder to find than I thought." Evelyn wiped the blood on her shirt.

"Let me help you." Poly pulled out a tissue from her purse and wiped the blood from Evelyn's face. She glanced back at Julie and Lucas. They both looked terrified. Even with Marcus long gone and dead, she couldn't shake the feeling of being on the run. Tears came to her eyes.

"It's okay, Mom. It's going to be over soon," Evelyn said.

"What have you done?" Julie asked, with more force than Poly liked.

Evelyn looked at the ground and checked her nose again for blood. She took a step back and held Will's hand, pulling him closer to her. "They want to take Will away from me," Evelyn motioned to Julie and Lucas, while keeping her gaze at the concrete floor.

"They want their child back, yes. You don't have to hold onto him like that," Poly said and reached for Will.

"No," Evelyn said and looked up.

Poly stumbled back at the fierce look in her eyes. "Baby, what have you done? You can tell us. We can help."

Evelyn looked down again. "I'm sorry. It's hard with so many around us."

Julie walked next to Poly with a smile and knelt down. "Evelyn, we love you. We know now you're not going to hurt Will." But Poly heard a hint of a question in her voice. "So, why don't you tell me what you have to do with this attack on Earth?"

Evelyn took a deep breath and looked at Will. He tilted his head and then nodded. "They would have eventually found us, these purge people. They would have killed all of you. If I've learned anything, I know life is fragile, including my own. If I died before they came here, all of you would die. Marcus set in motion the plans to save this world for when they came." She raised her hands in the air and looked at the sky. "He wanted to save us all, and when he died, it was left to me to complete what he started."

"Evelyn, you can't be serious?" Poly said and the tears overflowed. She wanted to hug her, to pick her up. Hell, if she could, she'd run away from it all. There had to be so many worlds out there, where they could live and be safe.

"Mom, you saw what I built. It's done. It just needs a person to control it. Unfortunately, there have been many babies born since Marcus implanted the world with the bug and every second I wait, more are born and more will die."

"Are you saying you're going to save the world with some machine you and Marcus built?" Julie asked.

"Sort of, but I'll need Will to run the machine because I found out something exists that I need to collect."

"I'm not following you," Julie said. "You think we're going to let Will run some machine you and Marcus built?"

"Yes, we have to try. At the very least, it will distract them. Listen, there are going to be sacrifices on all sides. Plus, what Will does, is only the start of it all. The rest of you will need to do your own parts."

"What do you mean?" Poly asked.

"We need to kill their queen and take back our lives. Come on, I'll explain on the way."

CHAPTER 4

HANK TURNED THE KEY AGAIN, but the car didn't make a sound. The lights wouldn't turn on, and the radio didn't work. Even his cell phone and Panavice appeared to be disabled.

Gladius paced outside of the car, messing with her Panavice and taking the occasional glance at the flaming wreckage of a plane in the nearby field. After the wreck, they'd tried to get close, but the heat wouldn't let them. Even if they could, there was nothing left of the plane.

He turned the key again. "It's not working."

"I think my Panavice's emergency protection mode is working. Otherwise, this thing would've exploded on us."

"Good to know." Hank tapped the one in his pocket. "That could've been bad." He stepped out of the driver's seat and onto the asphalt road. The smell of burning plastic and rubber wafted by.

Behind them, the road led back to Gladius's potential factory for Snackie cakes. The other direction led to Preston. Hank didn't forget the conversation Gladius had started right before the car broke down and the message came across the radio. She'd wanted to leave Preston and his friends behind. She said they'd never be free otherwise, as death followed them. He hated hearing those words from her.

He sighed and sat on the hood. "We should get back to Preston."

Gladius stopped walking and looked down the road. "You're right. We need to warn Trip and the others."

He wondered how everyone would find each other. Poly had texted earlier, saying she and Evelyn were on a road trip. While Julie, Lucas, and their son were in hiding. He pictured Joey and thought about where he was and his heart sank. He slumped against the hood of the car.

Two friends were now gone. Maybe Gladius was right. Maybe dangerous things surrounded them, and an early death was inevitable. But the last thing he was going to do was leave his friends to take the fight on without him. "You know I'm going to have to help them," Hank said.

"I know."

"You with me?"

Gladius slid the Panavice in her pocket and walked to him. "Until the end."

Hank exhaled in relief. If she had demanded a different path, he didn't know what he'd do. "First, we go to Preston."

"It must be another ten miles down the road," Gladius whined. "It won't even matter that these things are coming here to kill us all, I'm going to die from feet-in-heels disease."

Hank pushed off the hood and jogged to the back of the car

and opened the trunk. He pulled a pair of sneakers out and presented them to Gladius. His dad had made him start carrying essentials around, in case of emergency.

She looked disgusted at first, but took them and kicked off her heels. "Better not take a pic of this," she said, looking dubiously at her feet as she slipped the sneakers on.

Hank laughed. "Can you jog?" He hated the way that sounded, but he truly didn't know if she was capable of a long distance run. He didn't know how capable *he* was.

"Oh please. You think you can keep up with me?" Gladius had her hands on her hips.

"It's a race then?"

Gladius rolled her eyes and pulled out a small pouch of Orange and chugged it down. Hank took off at a sprint. He knew he couldn't keep it up for long, and it was probably foolish to expend the energy when they had ten more miles to go, but sometimes a joke took sacrifices. Plus, he knew how competitive Gladius was.

He glanced back and stumbled when he saw she was right next to him, running backward. She passed him with a salute, then turned around to run ahead. Hank slowed down and watched Gladius further her lead. She didn't even look to be breathing hard.

In all, it took over an hour to get to Trip's front door. It was a good thing too, because Hank felt he might die if he had to go much further.

Hank bent over, breathing hard as Gladius knocked on the door. He would have told her she didn't need to knock, if he could say the words between his heavy breaths. He didn't think Gladius even broke a sweat. He on the other hand, had hip pain. He felt like an old lady, needing a replacement.

Trip opened the door, and Gretchen hovered behind him.

"Hey," Hank took a few breaths before the next word, "Dad."

"Gladius, Hank, what's going on?"

"They're coming. You guys didn't get the message?" Gladius said.

"Who? What are you talking about?" Trip asked.

"Come in, kids," Gretchen said and pulled the door open. "Hank, you look like you're about to die."

"Thanks," Hank said and walked into his dad's house. He nodded to Gretchen as he passed her. Gretchen and his dad had spent a lot of time together since Samantha's death, and even though Hank was happy for them, he couldn't shake the weird feeling he had.

Hank looked for the TV that used to be on the wall, or the radio that used to be in the corner. Both were gone. The only light came from a few candles around the house. "Where's your stuff, Dad?"

"Got rid of it all. It was just feeding us rubbish anyways. How many times can you watch about recovery efforts, or what happened to the beloved Zach Baker? Made me want to throw up."

"What's with the huge antenna out in the backyard then?" Gladius said.

Trip lit up with excitement and motioned them to Hank's old bedroom. "I installed something the government isn't controlling. A place where us radio jocks can spread the truth."

Trip opened the door to Hank's bedroom. Inside, sat a metal cage covering the entire room. A desk with various radio-like components sitting on it, a couple chairs, and a couch were the only things left in his room.

"What did you do to my room?"

END OF THE SIX

"You haven't been living here for over a year, son."

"You could have used the upstairs guest room. There's nothing in there."

"Hank, it doesn't matter," Gladius said. "There's an invasion coming. Trip, you remember that message Marcus played us, the one where the lady said she was going to destroy us, blah blah blah?"

"Yeah," Trip said and opened the door to the cage.

"It just played over our car radio, after our car died and a plane fell from the sky."

Trip rushed to the radio and flipped a few dials. He glanced back. "Get in here and close the door.

Hank ran his hand along the metal cage. "What have you got going on in here? What is this?"

"Faraday cage," Trip said and turned a dial. Static crackled through the speakers. "If someone knows what's going on, some handle out there will be broadcasting."

A voice came across the speaker. Hank heard the fear in it as he spoke. They all leaned closer to the speaker.

"I'm watching them now. There are these black cubes flying around the city in a swarm. The sun is setting and it's hard to see them clearly, but they look metal and definitely unidentifiable. They defy everything I know about aviation."

Trip pressed a button and moved close to a microphone. "Location?"

"Ah, somebody is out there. Minneapolis."

"What's happening?"

"I don't know. All the power went out and I see fires near the airport. The highways are clogged with cars and I see many people walking around. Call me crazy, but I think we got hit with an EMP. Wait, something's happening near the Mall of America. A much larger cube is hovering over the building.

"Oh my God. An explosion. It's collapsing to the ground, I can see the dust and debris in the air. The cubes are attacking. They are circling around the larger cube now. The larger cube is moving down, it's landed on top of the rubble. We're under attack. We're under attack. Someone needs to tell the military."

"Tell him to get out of there," Gretchen said.

"Minneapolis, you got a way to get out of there?"

"No, I'm on the top floor of a building and the elevators are out. Besides, I can't stop watching. The world needs me to report this. You recording?"

"Aye," Trip said.

Hank looked up at his old ceiling. A humming sound passed over the house and then another.

"You hear that?" Trip asked and stood. He squinted at the wall.

They rushed out of the room and out the front door. They each scanned the skies, searching for the source of the noise. Then they saw it. A black cube, flying over the house. Then a second one.

"Just like Minneapolis described," Trip said.

"How much you want to bet they're coming from the stone?" Gladius said.

"Let's get there then," Trip said.

"Cars are busted, we'll have to hoof it," Hank said.

"Come on, I've got a few bicycles. It's not too far." Trip ran to the garage.

"You ride a bike?" Hank followed behind his dad.

"I can."

Another cube flew overhead. "They must be setting up their invasion first. Julie told me these things tried to take her and the rest," Gladius said.

"We don't know what's going on at the stone. We might

be walking right into a trap," Hank said.

"Fine, we just check it out and see what's going on," Trip said. "Every second we waste, another one of them flying things comes into this world."

"Okay, but we're just *looking*," Hank stressed.

They arrived at the head of the trail. Setting their bikes on the ground, they listened to the sound of rustling trees and a constant humming.

Gladius looked to the sky as one flew over the treetops. "Julie said those things are drones; unmanned and performing tasks to some kind of code. They pull in people and then take them away to those towers. She went all nerd on me after that."

"We better keep quiet. I doubt these things will like us coming up on them," Trip said.

Hank walked behind his dad and into Watchers Woods. He glanced back as Gladius and Gretchen followed them in. He half wanted them to stay back with the bikes, but these cubes would be killing them all if they didn't stop them. At least if something unforeseen happened, they'd reach their fate together. He reached back and offered a hand to help Gladius over a log. She took it with a smile and hopped over, keeping her hand wrapped around his.

As they approached, the humming sound grew in volume, making the idea of sneaking up on the stone ludicrous. They could be yelling and not be heard. Hank wanted to tell his dad to stop, that they'd seen enough and could go back and create an actual plan.

They reached the charred part of the forest and Trip stopped on his own and knelt down. Hank and the rest kneeled down around him, but kept their attention on the spectacle over the Alius stone. A mist swirled around in the circle, like a smoky snow globe. The black cubes flew from it at a continuous rate. Flying in all directions.

It was much worse than Hank thought. Back at his dad's house, they were only getting a small fraction of the cubes emerging from the stone.

"Holy crap," Gladius said.

"How are we going to stop that?" Gretchen asked.

"I don't know," Trip said.

"We should get closer. See if someone is controlling the stone," Gladius suggested.

Hank got up first and took lead. He walked low as he approached the circle. The sound became so loud, he was tempted to cover his ears. Glancing back, he saw Gladius and Gretchen doing exactly that. He motioned for them to stay back while he walked closer. The cubes flew over him low enough that he could jump up and slap their underside as they flew by.

Trip moved up next to him, crouching low and squinting at the mist. He pointed and Hank followed his direction. Through the cloud, he spotted a man next to the stone, with his head low. His dad nodded in the guy's direction, and moved closer to the edge of the circle.

Hank wanted to tell him to stop, but the noise became so loud it blurred his vision. Cubes moved just a few feet over their heads, so both he and his dad were laying down by the time they got to the circle. Trip army crawled his way toward the guy at the stone.

Hank followed him in, watching as cube after cube appeared and took flight.

The man glanced back and spotted Trip and Hank. His red, disheveled hair and youthful appearance wasn't what Hank was expecting. He wasn't sure what he'd expected, maybe another

version of Arracks, or some alien, but this guy looked like a
scared young man, around his own age.

The man shook his head and took both hands off the stone,
as Trip reached out to grab him. The mist cleared and the
deafening silence struck Hank in the gut. Even though the
cubes stopped flying by his head, he stayed low.

"You can see me?" the man asked and glanced back to the stone.

Hank stood and sidestepped closer to the stone.

"Why couldn't we? You're right there," Trip said.

"This isn't right." He looked around, confused. Then he
lunged for the stone.

Hank had expected this and beat him to it, smothering the
stone with his body.

"Get off it!" the man yelled and attacked Hank. Trip pulled
the young man off and he kept screaming. "You don't know
what you're doing!"

"Stop it." Trip warned, holding him tighter. "Why don't
you start by telling me what you're doing here?"

"Set me down first."

Trip released him. The guy shoved both hands in his
pockets, then disappeared.

"Whoa, where'd he go?"

"There, I see his footsteps," Gladius said, pointing past them.

Hank spotted the footsteps and ran after him. His legs hurt
from so much use over the past couple hours, but he couldn't
let this man get away. He may be the entire world's salvation.
The bushes rustled and collapsed under the invisible man. Hank
leapt onto the spot and felt the man's body. He moved to his
arms and held them down as Trip got to him and lifted the
person up. He reappeared as quickly as he disappeared and
Hank held him tight.

"How'd you do that?" Hank asked, dragging the man back toward the circle.

"No, no, no . . . this isn't right." He shook his head. "Who are you people? You have to let me go. She won't be happy with this. It won't take long for them to notice this portal is closed." He looked terrified.

"Dude, we aren't letting you go." Gladius walked up to Hank and Trip. "And if you don't put a stop to all this crap, you're going to be in a world of hurt."

"Who are you people?" His face lit up. "Are you with the little one? The one she's after?"

"Who are you talking about?" Hank said, loosening his grip on the man.

"Evelyn?" Gladius said, then covered her mouth.

"You *do* know her."

"What of her?" Hank asked, keeping a hand on him. More to protect him from the blade Gladius held. He wanted this guy alive long enough to get some information from him.

"I don't know much, but there was a rumor of a little girl who took on the queen's entire fortress and escaped. It seemed too crazy to believe, but then every plan changed and all efforts were sent to this planet. That's never happened before, so it is assumed this is the little girl's planet."

"What does she want with her?" Hank asked and gave him a shake.

"If she's able to take on the queen, then she must have enough quintessence to send her to the next evolution."

"What's quintessence?" Hank asked.

The red-haired man looked to each of them. "I've never even seen another alien person. You look just like us." He gazed at the ground and ran his hand over his face. "I don't want to do this, believe me, but this is bigger than any of you. I do this to get closer to . . . ."

"To what?" Hank asked.

"Listen," he held up his hands, "it's all too much to explain, but know this, we want the same thing you do. We want this," he pointed to the sky, "to end. We want the feeding off other worlds to end. We've been waiting for you." He faced Hank.

Gladius moved close to him and brandished her knife near his face. "You better start making sense, or I'm going to get stabby."

The young man raised his hands, taking a step back. "Let me take you to my leader. She'll know what to do. She can help us. You can help us end this."

"Why don't you just tell us how to stop it?" Hank asked and pointed at the stone.

"You can't."

Hank glared at him. "We stopped you."

"Even if you stopped this one portal, more are pouring out with the reclamators. It's too late. There's no stopping it, unless we can stop her. There are a few of us in the resistance, but we need people like you. People like Evelyn."

"What's your name?" Gladius asked, taking on a slightly friendlier tone.

"Wes."

"I tell you what, Wes. Why don't you bring this leader to us, here, and then we can talk with her."

"No, she won't use that kind of portal. We have to hurry. They'll be here soon to see why the reclamators aren't moving."

"This is crazy," Gretchen said. "This guy could send us anywhere in the worlds. We could end up inside a glacier."

Hank glared at the stone and then back to Wes. "So your boss is aiming to stop all of this from happening?"

"Yes, she's been trying to stop the queen for a long time now. I don't think it's a coincidence that out of all the portals on this world, you happened to find mine. Any other one, and you'd be long dead by their keeper. This was meant to happen."

"I don't believe in fate," Gladius said.

"Fate doesn't give a crap what you believe." He glanced at the stone. "We need to hurry."

"Let's just say we agree to this—" Hank's words cut short as the stone hummed.

"We're too late. Run. Get out of here!" Wes yelled.

CHAPTER 5

POLY SHIFTED AROUND IN THE driver's seat. Sitting in the car next to Evelyn, and with Julie, Lucas, and Will in the back, shouldn't feel awkward. She checked the mirror again and made eye contact with Julie, before veering around another broken down car.

Evelyn had prepared in many ways, and the car had been one of them. She'd put protective cages around the *sensitive parts,* as she put it. Poly felt uneasy about everything Evelyn had accomplished. It was far too much for one little girl, and it had to have taken years of work. Poly suspected Evelyn slowed down time more than she ever imagined.

She glanced over to her daughter as she skimmed through her Panavice—another thing she'd protected for each of them. Poly thought she heard her humming, but it must have been the drone of the car. Although, she was sure she saw a small smile on her face.

"Take a right over here," Evelyn said, never looking up.

Poly turned down another dirt road. The car bounced over the washed out side of the road and rattled down the washboard ripples.

"Easy to hide a body in the desert," Lucas said.

"It's not much further, and I hope you aren't thinking of killing me out here, Lucas," Evelyn said.

"Nah, just an observation. Did you check the trunk for shovels, Poly?"

"Shut up, Lucas. That's my daughter you're talking about, and Evelyn isn't going to hurt us. It's those freaking cubes flying overhead we need to worry about." Poly glanced back and saw Lucas and Julie communicating to each other with looks.

"Why don't you just tell us what you want from Will?" Julie said.

"You'll see, soon enough." Evelyn straightened up from her seat and pointed ahead. "Look, you can see the top of it."

"Holy cow, Evelyn, what have you built?" Poly said, as the car crested over the hill and an enormous complex came into view. It looked like a giant steel ball sitting on top of a box. A few vehicles were parked around the structure and they looked like small toy cars in comparison.

"That is what Will is going to use to save the world," Evelyn said.

"What?" Julie leaned forward between the two front seats.

"I've set it up to work for either Will or I, and I think he should be the one to operate it," Evelyn said.

"It's okay, Mom. I want to," Will said. "This might save the world from the purge people."

"What does it do?" Poly asked.

"Let me show you when we get there." Evelyn bounced on the seat as she stared at the structure.

By the time they parked near the front door, it shaded them and what must have been a square mile behind them. Poly got out of the car and the rest of them followed suit.

A man walked out the front door with a rifle slung over his shoulder. He approached, and Poly grasped one of her blades, finding a nice kill spot on the man if needed. She squinted and the man looked familiar, but she couldn't place him.

"Evelyn," he said extending both hands. "So good to see you again."

"Hey, Derek, I brought some friends with me this time."

"I see that. Poly, Lucas, Julie, and this must be Will. How's it going, little man?" He held out a hand for a high five and Will left him hanging.

"Did she hold up to the electrical attack?" Evelyn asked looking up at the dome.

Derek lowered his hand and glanced back. "That she did. Only lost one backup generator."

"Wait," Julie said. "I know you. You were there with Samantha. You were her bodyguard."

"I was." He lowered his head. "Damned shame what happened. Afterward, I was a lost man, until Evelyn found me." He smiled. "She gave me something to work toward. Something I can do to right the wrong."

"The *wrong*? Our friend was killed by your boss. You should have protected her," Julie said.

"It weighs heavy on me every day. I liked Samantha, a lot," Derek said.

Evelyn turned to Julie. "People deserve a second chance. A past error isn't a guaranteed future failure."

"Thank you for that second chance," Derek said. Something in his pocket dinged. Poly gripped her knife and slowly exhaled as he pulled out a Panavice. "We have a cube on a deviated course, heading straight for us."

"Already?" Evelyn said. "Set in motion plan sixteen. We can't let them get into the globe."

"Aye," Derek said and punched the commands into his Panavice.

"What's going on, Evelyn?" Poly asked.

She was looking at the sky, searching in one area for something. "Looks like we drew their attention already. I doubt it's the queen, but somebody is in that thing." She pointed at a cube floating toward them.

"I'll take point," Derek said and ran toward the cube. He typed into his Panavice as he moved.

A clanking sound came from the bottom of the building. Poly turned to see the shiny, steel panels slide open and large guns come out.

Derek stopped about a hundred feet out and held his rifle up as the cube landed on the dirt road. The cube opened up and Poly remembered her ride in one of them. Each one could have carried thirty people, or much more if they stuffed inside.

Three people walked down the ramp and out of the cube. They wore long black coats and a black cloth covered most of their face and hair. Poly's heart raced as they approached Derek.

One of the people in all black walked forward as the other two stayed back. Poly strained to hear the words, but the wind had picked up and pulled the sounds away from her. Evelyn watched intently, not blinking.

"There, see that? The one in the back." Evelyn pointed.

Poly didn't see anything at first, but then watched as the one in the back threw something at Derek. Derek, quick to react, fired at the person; the bullets ricocheting off him. The object the man threw struck Derek and he fell to the ground.

"They've got shields," Julie said and pulled Will to the car.

Lucas kept an arrow on standby and Poly gripped a knife. They were too far away, but she imagined they would be coming for them next.

"Evelyn, get your shield up," Poly said, activating her own.

Evelyn didn't answer as she plowed through the screens on her Panavice. "Amazing," she whispered.

"We should get out of here. They're coming," Julie yelled and opened the car door. Lucas got into the driver's seat.

Poly looked back to the three men dressed in black. The wind whipped out their long coats, revealing satchels at each of their hips. Their gloved hands appeared to be holding something, as they walked steadily toward them. Poly glanced at the car and then the building. They could reach both if they left quickly.

"Evelyn?" Poly asked. "Evelyn, we've got to go."

"None of them are the queen," she said, looking just above the three men. "They have the embers, but nothing like her."

"Come on, they're coming." Poly took a few steps toward the car.

"I will stop them."

"We should run," Poly urged. If it had been her and Joey, she thought they would have a chance, but Evelyn was just a small girl, and these three were big men, who'd easily taken out Derek.

Evelyn typed a few more lines into her Panavice, then stowed it into her pocket. "We aren't running. If you want to sit in the car with Lucas and Julie, I understand."

Fifty feet away. Poly saw the eyes of the three men. The one in front didn't have the blood thirst in his eyes like she'd suspected; they held a curiosity. She moved closer to her daughter and splayed out three knives. They were designed by her and Travis and were an exotic type of metal that should penetrate any shield.

The two men behind the larger one stopped and threw two small balls into the air. Poly watched them fly above, until they touched. They exploded into a blinding light. She screamed and dropped her knives. Covering her eyes, she fell to her knees and heard Evelyn mumble something.

"I can't see," Poly cried out.

"You will, give it a second." Evelyn grabbed her and helped her to her feet.

The white light diminished and Poly felt for Evelyn at her side. She yanked out a few more knives and spotted the men walking toward them.

One of them yelled out, "Stop right there. Don't move, little girl."

Evelyn disappeared from Poly's side. A moment later, the three men fell to the ground.

"Evelyn?" Poly yelled.

Her daughter reappeared a few feet behind the men. "I'm fine."

"Did you kill them?" She eyed their bodies. None of them had moved yet.

"No, but they'll be out for a while. I want to study them. I want to study their tech. It's like nothing I've ever seen on any world. Something very strange has happened to their version of earth to allow them to make these things."

"What things?"

Evelyn slipped on a glove she had yanked off the large man's hand and pulled a black stone from the pouch dangling from his hip. "They're able to create these stones." She held the stone in the sky, squinting at it. "They have magic-like properties, and if we don't figure out how to stop them, they're going to plow right through this dome."

CHAPTER 6

POLY WALKED BY THE THREE men laying on the ground, seeing their chests moving with long, deep breaths. One snorted and Poly gripped her knife tighter. She didn't care so much about their magical golf balls, but more about how her daughter took them out. "How did you do it? I mean, what did you do to them?"

"I fought them. They were too slow," Evelyn said through a grin.

"How long are they going to be like this?"

"Not sure, they are unique." She looked at the men, then followed something Poly couldn't see up into the sky. "We better get them locked up. I think we could learn from them."

"They hit me with something," Derek said, feeling his shoulder.

"I thought they killed you back there." Poly was unmoved either way.

"I think the shield helped me out with a lot of it. What do you want to do with them, Evelyn?"

"Put them in the holding cells. Keep them separate and take all their belongings. I'll be there soon to inspect their contents. And Derek, wear gloves. I mean it, all of the people who handle them have to wear gloves. I don't think we can allow those stones to touch our skin."

"Aye." Derek spoke into his Panavice and several more people ran from the building to help him drag the men toward the front door.

"And make sure you strip them to their underwear before putting them in there."

"*That's* who we are fighting?" Poly asked, as the plain-looking men were carried off.

"Yes," Evelyn said. "I think they were scouts. Their queen is looking for me." She watched another cube fly by.

Poly sighed and glanced back at Julie and Lucas, standing in front of the car with the hood open. Will was buckled up in the backseat.

"That car won't start without me in it." Evelyn sighed. "I'm surprised at them. I thought they would be warriors, ready to defend this planet against the invasion. I mean, if I fail, we all die, including their little boy."

"Being a parent changes your priorities." Poly watched Julie and Lucas mess around under the hood. They looked to be arguing. "They are the bravest and best people in the world, Evelyn. They will do what is right for them, but they need to know what's going on." She turned to face her daughter. "What *is* the plan here?"

Evelyn looked back at the globe. "Sadly, we're carrying out Marcus's plan. He implanted the world with those nanobots for this very moment. I'm sure it was a selfish act, and I wonder greatly about what he'd have done once the world was catatonic." She faced Poly. "Will is going to use what I've built here to silence the minds of the world, so those cubes don't have a place to go. Don't you remember Hector trying to get us to do that in his world? He tried to teach us to clear our mind and go into a stupor. It's a way to stop them." She pointed to the sky and a distant black cube.

"We blew one of them up, if I remember right," Poly said. "Won't the armies of the world just destroy these things?"

"If they had time, maybe. But we just got sent back a couple hundred years, when they knocked out our power and electronics. We might have a few birds up there, but they will have tens of thousands of those cubes worldwide by now. We are going to be nothing but a crop for their queen to harvest, without this machine."

A cube flew overhead, as if on cue. "Can't you hack into them? Julie was able to shut one of them down for a bit."

"I've tried, and while I can get into some of their systems, there is another part on a completely different level."

"Above you?" Poly had thought her daughter had no limitations.

Evelyn laughed. "I wouldn't say above . . . different, maybe. It's like a person living in a two dimensional world for their whole life and then someone trying to explain the third dimension to them. They could never understand it."

"These people have another dimension?"

"Sort of. They have embers floating around them. These embers help in the construction, but I can't figure out how. It's another form of tech, more organic."

"We should have asked for help from Vanar. They have a magical level of tech as well."

"They know. I told Travis all about them. I wouldn't be surprised if they were facing an invasion as well." Evelyn looked at the ground and then back up to the globe. "They don't have this though."

"Hey," Lucas called out. "Car's busted."

"We better get inside. No telling when another one of these things is going to drop in for a visit," Evelyn said.

After some unheard deliberation from Julie and Lucas, they walked with Will toward the front door, keeping a leery gaze on the sky.

"They'll come around," Poly said, hating the idea of Julie and Lucas being scared of Evelyn. She wasn't going to hurt them; and if she truly wanted to, how much could they do to stop her? Poly had a terrible thought of Marcus's manipulations on Evelyn. What if he did something to her, put in a trigger of some sort that would switch and send Evelyn into a monster?

"Don't worry, Mom. After I save earth and get what I need from these people, everything will be as it should be. We will be able to live out a happy life." She smiled.

"What do you mean, get what you need from them?"

"These people could be a blessing. I think they have something we need. I'm not going to discuss it because I don't know if it's going to be possible. If it is . . . things could be better, happier even."

Poly didn't know if she could be happy without Joey by her side. She took a deep breath and felt tears building in her eyes. In all the happenings of the day, she just realized she'd not cried over him once the entire day. A feeling of betrayal spread over her, as if she wasn't honoring her late husband.

Evelyn watched her closely. She wasn't intruding into Poly's thoughts, but she knew Evelyn was trying to figure her out. Now faced with a damned invasion from the body snatching magicians, she'd never felt so close to Evelyn.

"We have a strong connection," her daughter said. "You can't see it, but can you feel it?"

"I feel it." Poly let out a sob and reached for her little girl.

Evelyn rushed into her arms and gave her a hug. "Everything is going to be better. I'll make sure of it."

"Thank you, but it's not your job to make it better."

Evelyn let go. "We still have a world to save, maybe many. Should we get to it?"

Poly nodded and followed her daughter through the tall steel door in the side of the building. Derek stood near the entrance and greeted Evelyn. They discussed the jailing of the three men, and Evelyn said she'd be there soon to inspect them, but she wanted to get Will set up first.

"Sorry, Mom, I'd love to give you a tour, but the enemy never sleeps." Evelyn gave Derek a few instructions, then led Poly through a series of passageways. They reached a small room with circular walls and ceiling. Julie, Lucas, and Will stood near the middle of the room.

"What is this place?" Julie asked tapping her leg. Poly saw the bulge from her broken Panavice and it probably killed her not having it at her disposal.

"This is where we see Marcus's plan through." Evelyn walked to the center of the room and pushed a few buttons on her Panavice. The floor shook and moved up, like a massive elevator. The metallic dome above them opened up, revealing the expanse of the structure above.

Poly gasped. It was so gargantuan, an airplane could fly inside. The platform they stood on continued to rise until it hit the halfway point and stopped. The noise echoed around the globe and she felt overwhelmed. *My daughter built this?* In a world where construction and technology had come to a near stop?

"It's beautiful, isn't it?" Evelyn said.

"Extremely," Poly said.

"Will," Evelyn looked to him, "I even gave you your very own captain's chair." She pressed her finger down on her screen. A metal chair rose up from the middle of the platform.

Julie and Lucas held onto Will and looked at the chair. "This whole place is an amplifier," Julie murmured to herself.

"Yes. He'll be able to connect to every person on the planet in here. Well, every person who has the nanobot Marcus planted during the Cough . . . The rest of us don't—"

"This is crazy. How can his brain handle that kind of input?" Julie said.

"I can handle it, Mom. Evelyn has trained me how."

"When?" Julie turned to look at him.

"Just now." At the sound of his parents' gasps, he continued, "We've been here for a long time. Evelyn's showed me what I can do to help save our world."

"You can go slow-mo like her?" Lucas asked.

"No, she has to help me into it. I can't do it on my own." He looked at the floor. "Yet."

Julie stepped in front of Will. "Evelyn, if you hurt my son—"

"If he isn't able to do this task, we will all die," Evelyn said.

Will pulled free from Julie and Lucas and walked to the chair. He took a seat and placed his arms on the steel hand rests, feet dangling in the air. To Poly, he looked like a baby; *this* was supposed to be the answer to the purge people's invasion?

"If he's going to do this—and I'm not saying he is—what are you going to do?" Julie asked.

"I believe this will summon their queen. Before that

happens, I need to get a particular piece of their magic, plus another trinket of hers. Once that's done, the queen and I will have a talk. She will see my side of the matter, or I will end her."

Poly didn't understand how these children were going to save everyone, no matter how capable they might be, and she saw the same look on Julie and Lucas's faces. Will wasn't even one year old yet.

"I see your doubt," Evelyn said. "I could go into great detail about how I managed to build this place, laying out the plan started by Marcus. Or how I have run the business of ZRB from the outside, ensuring a growing economy and stable society. I could also go into detail about how I reestablished most of Vanar's services and cut their recovery time by seventy percent, all while nursing my mom back to health."

"Hero parade," Lucas said.

"Yes, and I'd deserve one," Evelyn said. "I know it's hard to look at my tiny body and think of my accumulated knowledge as anything beyond pink ponies and coloring within the lines, but I assure you, this plan is our best option—our only option."

Guilt swept over Poly. She hadn't been there when her daughter needed her the most. Or maybe her daughter didn't need her at all. She appeared to be ruling over the worlds, doing things Poly had no idea about. How many worlds had she jumped to? Poly never felt so alone.

"I want a Panavice, and I want to see all the specs on this . . . machine," Julie said.

"Fine, but every second we waste could mean the death of a million souls." Evelyn walked over and handed her own Panavice to Julie, showing her how to get into the spec pages she wrote. "When you're ready, Will knows what to do," she said. Walking to the edge of the platform, she grunted as she pulled open a steel lid.

"Where're you going?" Poly said.

"I've got prisoners to check on. If this place falls, they could be the key to defeating these people."

"You're just going to leave Will to it?"

"Yeah," Evelyn said and stepped down the ladder. "We don't have much time for convincing. Do it or don't," her voice carried up through the open lid.

Poly turned to Julie. "I think she's right. This might be our best chance."

Julie let go of Will's hand and walked over to her. "What if she's wrong and this thing fries his brain? I mean, look at this place. How could she even know how to construct such a building?"

Poly fidgeted with her hands. She hated even saying his name. "Marcus designed much of it."

Julie raised an eyebrow as if to say, *exactly*. "We didn't sign up for this. We should have found another planet. Another world like this one, but without the dangers."

"Julie, this is our planet. Are we to just let everyone die? You and Lucas have seen what these things are going to do here. Don't you remember Hector's planet?"

"Of course I do. But aren't you sick of being in the middle? Don't you, just for once, want to be on the outside, ignorant of it all? I imagine most of the world is more concerned about getting power back on, so they can get to their Facebook page, or update Twitter."

"You want to be one of those people out there, oblivious? Don't you want to make a difference? After Joey died," her voice cracked, "I learned how fragile we are. It makes life that much more precious to me, and if I can save just one person, then I have to try. That person could be someone else's Joey."

Julie looked over her shoulder and Poly saw the tears in her eyes. "If I think for one second this thing is going to hurt Will, I'll stop it all. I don't care if the world burns for it."

"It won't." Poly didn't know that, but she stepped through the hatch and climbed down the ladder. She caught up to Evelyn in the hall and suspected she'd heard the entire conversation. Poly's gut told her Julie would make the right decision. She just hoped that didn't mean letting the world burn.

Evelyn didn't say much as Poly followed her through the various passageways, until they reached the cells.

Derek and five other men had guns drawn on three men in separate cells, handcuffed to the floor and sitting in their underwear.

"They say anything?" Evelyn asked.

"Not much, just said they wanted to speak with you."

Evelyn faced the clear wall between them and the inmates. "You, what's your name?" She pointed at the large man in the middle cell.

He pulled on the cuffs and the sound of clattering metal echoed around the room. "My name is Jeff, and I take it you are Evelyn?"

Poly looked at her daughter. How could these men possibly know her name?

"Yes, I'm Evelyn. I suppose you have a message for me?"

Jeff bent his neck and winced in pain. Poly eyed the man and she drew three of her throwing blades. He shook his head and then hopped off the floor a few inches. Each spasm made the chains clatter. After a few seconds, it got worse and he shook violently. Spit dribbled from his mouth.

"Help him," the twins yelled from the cell next to him.

"Don't even think about it," Evelyn said as Derek made a move to enter the cell.

She leaned closer to the partition, eyes squinted, as if trying to hear him speak. "He's doing something. Shoot him."

"I can't just shoot a man strapped to the ground. He's no threat," Derek said.

"He's going to take something," Evelyn said and grabbed at Derek's gun. "Shoot him."

Derek pulled his gun back from her hands and raised it at Jeff.

"I'm going to be sick," Jeff said and heaved.

"Mom, you should leave."

"I'm not leaving you."

"Then someone kill that man right now!" she screamed.

Poly jerked from her reaction and moved closer to the metal cage.

Jeff vomited over his chest and some of it got caught in his mouth.

"Stay back." Derek pushed Evelyn back and Poly followed, standing in front of her.

Jeff held a large piece of the vomit in his mouth. Poly realized it was a bag covering a golf-ball sized object. He used his teeth to tear into the bag and expose the round stone. He then set it on his tongue where it absorbed into his mouth.

Evelyn grabbed the Panavice off Derek's waist. "This is bad," she said, and slammed her finger on the screen. Four glass walls crashed around each of the imprisoned men.

"What happened?" Derek yelled.

"I told you. He took something."

Jeff yelled, and even through the thick glass, Poly heard the guttural scream. He pulled at the restraints, until they blew apart. He raised his freed arms up, with the broken cuffs dangling from his wrists. He stood and rushed toward the glass, striking it with his head.

"I don't understand," Derek said, keeping his gun trained

on Jeff. "Nothing should give a human that much strength. That glass is rated for fifty caliber."

"I told you to kill him, and now we've got a problem on our hands," Evelyn said.

Jeff crashed himself again into the glass. It cracked. Poly yelped and thought of the first time she'd seen a grinner slamming against Ferrell's gas station on Ryjack.

"If he breaks through, shoot him," Derek said to the men standing near him. "Evelyn, you need to leave."

Jeff punched a hole into the glass and pulled a big chunk of it out. He growled through the opening and ripped another big chunk of the reinforced glass down. He pushed through it and Poly swore the broken glass would have torn him to shreds, but he came out of the other side unscathed.

"Plug your ears," Derek said and Evelyn put her hand over her ears.

Gunfire erupted from Derek and his men. Poly threw a knife and struck Jeff's neck. It bounced off, the same as the barrage of bullets. He had a shield protecting him. Free from the glass box, Jeff rushed to the steel bars and grabbed them. The steel creaked under the strain, but held.

Derek raised his hands for a cease fire and the gunfire stopped. Poly's ears rang, as she eyed the twins; they too regurgitated.

Jeff screamed and bent back one of the steel bars. Not enough for him to get through, but in a few more seconds, he'd have a hole big enough.

Derek pulled out a square-looking gun and shot Jeff, sending high voltage into his body. Jeff shook and screamed again, yet bent another bar.

"The twins," Evelyn warned as one broke free from his restraints. "We need to fall back to the safety room."

Derek zapped Jeff again with little effect. "He's on something, but he's still just a man. We can stop him here. You take Poly."

The second twin broke free and walked to the edge of the glass.

"We don't have enough time now. That thing will run us all down before we get there." Evelyn slammed her eyes shut and kept her stiff arms at her side.

Poly watched the twins howl and slam their fists against the glass. They each created a hole large enough to get through. "Evelyn, we've got to go." She grabbed her daughter, but Evelyn kept her eyes shut. When Poly tried to move her, she couldn't. She might have weighed a thousand pounds.

Evelyn shook, with her eyes tightly closed. Her knuckles were white from her clenched fists, and she grinded her teeth. "No!" she screamed.

Jeff stopped moving and his whole body went limp, hanging between the bars. The twins had fallen as well, and lay still on the floor. Blood trailed from all their eyes, noses, and mouths.

Evelyn slumped to the ground. Poly dropped her dagger and held up Evelyn's head off the floor. Her limp body flopped around in her arms.

Evelyn opened her eyes and gazed at Poly. "Should have killed them to start with. I saw their plans, and once they see you, Hank, Julie, and Lucas, they'll want you as well."

"Evelyn, did you kill those men?" Poly asked with tears in her eyes. She remembered the first man she'd killed, and his face haunted her still. Each of her kills stuck with her like a bad dream she couldn't wake from. She never wanted her daughter to have to deal with something so awful.

"I had to. We waited too long from the start, and you all had a slim chance of survival. Besides, they would have found Will, Julie, and Lucas." Evelyn looked at the ceiling. "I'm not sure this place is safe. I may have underestimated these people."

Poly hugged her and wept into her shoulder. Evelyn's small hands patted her back.

Derek knelt next to Poly. "Let me take her to the infirmary," he said.

"I just needed to rest for a bit," Evelyn said and got to her feet. "That took a lot out of me, but now I know what I have to do. I saw it in Jeff's thoughts—the answer. There are others on her planet who are against her as well, her own daughter even. There are ways we can stop her if this operation fails. We need to have more than one chance at stopping them. Julie is smart, and Will knows what to do, so I need to do my part as well." Evelyn took a deep breath and locked eyes with Poly. "Mom, I'm sorry. I love you."

"No," Poly called out, but Evelyn was gone. She disappeared once more in her slow-mo, and could be on another planet by now.

Derek moved next to Poly and wrapped her up in his strong arms. Poly didn't resist. She needed a shoulder to cry on. She had a terrible feeling she was losing her daughter.

CHAPTER 7

KRIS STOOD BEFORE THE DOOR to the stone room and looked at the Panavice Evelyn had given them. Their child queen spoke of this great new place for them once they completed a task for her. She'd sent them coordinates, and taught them how to use the Alius stone, but Kris felt jittery looking at the real stone. He adjusted his life jacket and felt it irritating his neck. He wouldn't have worn it, if Evelyn hadn't insisted. They were all wearing one.

"She needs us. We must go," Naya said, putting a hand on his shoulder.

Kris nodded, pushing the Panavice into his pocket. "She needs us," he agreed. Raising his hand, he motioned for everyone to follow him forward. The steel door creaked as he opened it. He shoved it for the last couple feet and smelled the stale air seeping out from the domed room.

If any of them had known this stone was on their island the

entire time, everything would have been different. Tough thing, looking back, distorted with current knowledge. Leaving this world wasn't a problem. This world had grown past them, stepped over them; forgotten them in their haste to make the world great again.

Kris used his Panavice to light up the room. He'd watched Lucas use the stone enough to know the mechanics of it, and the rest of the tribe were well aware of it too, bouncing around the worlds as they evaded Marcus with the kids. This time felt much different, as the hushed group of mutants filled the dome.

"We're all in," Maggie called out from near the door.

Kris nodded and knelt next to the stone. Naya joined him, glancing around and rubbing her pant legs. He extended his hand and touched hers, calming her. She smiled and nodded her head.

He didn't need to look at the Panavice for reference, he and Evelyn had worked until he was able to do it with his eyes closed. He felt the sandpaper-like surface of the stone, then typed in the code. "Hold your breath, and remember what you need to do," he said as the stone hummed.

In a blink, the stone dome changed to a wall of dark water. Jasper blew out a great breath and kept the water from crushing them, yet the water still poured into the circle from the sides.

"Take a breath and swim hard!" Kris yelled out.

The water crashed against them from all sides. In the slosh, Naya slipped out of his grip. Water and bodies swirled around him. His life jacket pulled him along as much as anything else. Looking up, he spotted the gleaming surface. He pushed up with his hands and kicked with his feet, swimming hard.

A few other mutants were far ahead of him, breaching the surface. Reaching up, he felt the air with his hand first, then his head emerged. He took a deep breath of the alien air and looked around at the heads bobbing all around.

A wave rolled over them, sending him back into the water. He swam back up. "Get to the shore! Help everyone who needs it."

Talia screamed and flailed in the water. Kris took the young girl and lifted her above the surface. What had happened to her swimming partner? Thankfully, most of them were well versed in ocean swimming. Kris backstroked toward the shore, holding onto Talia until his feet could touch the sand.

Many of the tribe walked on the beach, but he searched the ocean for one person's face in particular, *his* swimming partner. "Naya?" he called out, looking around the tribe as they came ashore. "I'll be right back." He tore off his life jacket and looked out into the water. "Maggie, head count."

"Sixty-four."

Four missing. He trudged into the ocean, then jumped into the waves. "Naya!"

A body floated over the crest of a wave and he rushed to it. He turned it over and saw Banya's dead stare looking toward the sky. She must have been crushed against the ocean floor, or hit her head. He pulled her body to shore, handing her over to Jasper. Heading back out, a few more joined him in the search.

Despite the life jackets and knowing what was coming, they had three missing. In the next twenty minutes, they only recovered one more body. The other two were gone, swallowed by the sea. He knew of the danger, he knew of the risk, and it made it all the worse. He sobbed as a large wave crashed into him, sending him into a spiral under the water. He felt his shoulder hit the sandy bottom and watched the white water in the wave swirl by him. Thoughts of staying at the bottom nearly drowned him. Maybe he could just give up now and join them. The worlds had taken too much from him and his mutants.

Then he thought of Evelyn; she still needed him. His queen had a task for them to complete. Jumping off the bottom and breaching the surface, he took a deep breath. A big group was already exploring the edge of the jungle next to the shoreline. It wasn't in his people to ask about the dead. They moved on, and so would he.

He reached the shallows and dragged his feet in the sand. "Anyone figure out where we are?" he asked.

Maggie looked down the beach. "No trash."

No trash meant no people, or at least not developed yet. Back on Vanar, not a day went by when something didn't wash up on the shore. Things could be different this time. "Anyone see a structure or an aircraft?" Kris asked.

"Nothing yet. I sent a few into the jungle to scout ahead. Oh, and we were able to revive Banya."

Kris breathed a sigh of relief. "That's the best news I've heard in quite a while." If only he'd been stronger, he could have held onto Naya. *No, not now.* Not in front of his people. He pulled out his Panavice and swiped the water off to read the screen. Evelyn had sent him a note. He read it out loud.

"I hope you all made it through the jump. I'm not sure if I could ever forgive myself if anything happened because I asked for your help." Pain hit his gut when he thought about telling her of the deaths. He didn't want to upset her. "Assuming you are still willing to help me, you only need to walk east, down the beach a half mile. This is where you'll find the base of the vault."

Stuffing the Panavice back in his wet pocket, he looked over his tribe of people. This mission had already cost several lives, and he feared it could be just the start of their sacrifice. "We mourn the dead, *after* we help Evelyn." They grumbled in agreement, with tears in their eyes. He gritted his teeth and blew a strong breath through his nose. "Come on, we head east."

CHAPTER 8

"WHY *MY* HOUSE?" HARRIS ASKED.

"Do you have a better option?" Travis said.

"Yeah, your place."

"Too close to a populated area, in case something goes wrong."

Harris eyed Travis and thought he spotted hints of amusement in that grin, but no matter. He was right. This made for a better location. The house would be destroyed if the purge people came anyways. "Fine." He tugged on the large duffle bag. "But we start with Preston. We can check on the kids and find a way from there."

"Agreed."

Harris knelt next to the stone and typed in the code. Travis hovered over his shoulder and watched the code go in. "Still don't trust me?"

"No, and I never will," Travis said.

The room changed to the forest in Preston. "Trip?" Harris said, finding Trip and Hank facing a red-haired man.

"Harris," Gladius said from behind them. "Dad?" She came running toward Travis.

Harris, with one hand on his gun and the other on his bag, turned and saw Gretchen as well. "What's going on?"

"We're being invaded," Trip said and pointed to the sky. "This guy, Wes, was holding a portal open for them to flood us with the floating cubes."

"Great, more of you," Wes said and glanced at the stone. "They'll be here soon, and I wouldn't be surprised if they send detonation stones through first, to clear it out."

"Dad," Gladius said. "This guy has a way to their world. We can face the people who launched this attack."

This might be the break they were looking for. Harris squinted at the young man who called himself Wes. There was fear in his eyes, and he fidgeted, glancing at the Alius stone. "You can take us to the purge people world?" Harris asked.

"Dear God, is that what you people call us?" He raised his hands as Harris approached. "Yes, I can take you there, but we need to go now."

"I'll go alone," Harris said and lifted his bag to hang the strap over his shoulder.

"No way," Hank spoke up. "How many times has it gone bad when you used that stone? You need our help."

"Much as I'd like to see you go off into the great unknown, I agree with Hank," Travis said. "We have a better chance of succeeding if we're together."

Harris adjusted his bag and clenched his teeth. He swore Joey would be the last one to die on his watch. Now Hank wanted to go and risk his life again. With them going, he'd have to be more careful and make sure Wes didn't drop them into a trap. "Fine, we'll go. Show me the code."

"Whatever, but we need to go now." Wes explain the code and showed Harris the digits.

"Now show me another code," Harris said.

"What?"

"Another code. I know you know more than one code onto your planet."

"This is stupid. The first code I gave you would put us right next to my friends."

"Exactly why I want another code."

Wes glanced around the circle. "Fine, one more minute and we'll probably be dead anyways." He tapped a second code onto his arm.

Trip held onto Wes as he neared the stone and Harris knelt next to it.

"Get your shields on," Harris said and set his up.

"We don't have one," Gladius said. "The freaking invasion took them out."

"Here, take mine," Travis handed Gladius his Panavice.

"Thanks, Dad. Hank, if we stay close enough, we can share," Gladius hugged him around the waist.

"Hey, Gretchen and I are going to stay here to warn the rest of the family and make preparations," Trip said.

"If the cubes come, just blank out," Harris said. "It can't see you without your thoughts."

"Be careful, Dad," Hank said.

"Love you, son."

Gretchen and Trip stepped out of the circle and Harris eyed Travis. He didn't want to say it, but they didn't have a choice. Transporting what they were carrying was dangerous enough, and they couldn't let what they held get loose, or worse . . . be used against them. "Travis, we're going to have to get close enough to share my shield."

"I'd rather die."

"*Dad*," Gladius warned.

"Fine, but I'm not spooning you, and if you mess with me for one second, I'll stick you."

"I wouldn't expect anything less." Harris sighed and waited for Travis to get next to him. He typed in the code and then stood and put his arm around a repulsed Travis.

"Here we go," Hank said, holding onto Gladius.

Harris listened to the hum of the stone. Doing a quick turn, he found the place empty and parted from Travis. It was a dusty warehouse, but it looked to be empty.

"I hear something," Gladius whispered, still holding onto Hank.

Harris did too. They were somewhere populated, maybe a city. He couldn't make out anything through the window but the blue sky beyond.

"Yeah, we're in Miami. Do you guys have a Miami?" Wes asked.

"No," Harris said.

"Yes," Hank said. "We do."

Harris scanned the room again, holding tightly to his duffle bag. He stopped and watched Wes. The young man put his hands in his pockets and split his attention among the different people in the room.

"Show me your hands," Travis said and pointed his gun at Wes, while holding a knife in the other.

Wes yanked his hands from his pocket and held them up. "You guys have got to relax. I'm not the enemy here."

Harris walked closer to Wes. To his surprise, Wes didn't seem to have the same fear level as he did back in Preston.

Maybe all of his fear had been placed on what might have been coming out of the Alius stone. Harris eyed him, as if for the first time, and took in the young man as a soldier of some sort. He had no uniform, but he had that air about him. A confidence in his ability.

"Who are you, really?" Harris asked, and motioned for Travis to lower his gun.

"It doesn't matter who I am. What matters is, we want the same thing. We want to end these invasions of other worlds. We want to stop her before it's too late, and there is one person who can help us."

"Who wants to help us?" Harris asked.

"Our leader. She's been plotting for a while now, but we can't get close enough, the queen is always a step ahead."

"We know the feeling," Hank said.

"We should meet with her then."

Wes looked at the door and then the open window. "I don't know where she is."

Harris blew out a frustrated breath. "Then why mention her? This is turning into a waste of time."

"It's not that. She's in hiding. If we can get Evelyn to help, she could draw the queen right to us." Wes looked around and stepped toward the door. "We should leave. We won't be able to stop the queen if she finds us here."

"It's a one way stone," Travis said looking at the stone.

Harris lifted the bag. "Nothing can stop what's in this bag, I assure you of that."

"She'll stop it. She can stop anything, even time," Wes said.

"Gladius, what's the closest stone?"

"Five hundred miles to the north."

He cringed at the number.

"We should find a place to use it," Travis said, pointing at the bag.

Harris looked at Hank and Gladius. He knew if Travis was mentioning it with his daughter around, either he was playing a hand, or he felt the sacrifice of their lives was worth it to save the worlds. Too bad it wasn't going to come to that—if Harris had any say in the matter. "Wes, go to the door. We're leaving. Gladius, put your device shield on scramble. Maybe it will block us. Maybe she won't be able to see us."

"Done," Gladius said.

Harris did the same and pointed his gun at Wes's back.

"You guys can't show those guns out there. The cops will be on us in minutes. And if your little scramble trick works, she won't miss out on me getting arrested with a group of strange people."

"Do they know?" Harris said and motioned to the window.

"Who?"

"The people out there. The citizens. Do they know what you all do?"

Wes laughed. "The rubes? They don't have a clue what's going on around them. The ones with a gift, like me, are rare and hidden."

"Most of this planet doesn't have a clue about the queen and her invasions?" Harris asked.

"No, and if they do, their memories are corrected so they don't. This has been going on for a long time. You might even have people like us on your own planet and not even know it. We are very good at that."

Harris looked to Travis, who had the same distraught look. Killing the innocent wasn't something Harris wanted any more of. Let alone a whole planet of people who were ignorant of what one of theirs had constructed. His bag just got a lot more complicated.

It was interesting she hadn't touched her own planet. That was probably why she created the Alius stones; she had to get the people off her planet. He hefted the bag and wondered what to do with it now. Plans had to change, as they always seemed to do.

"Open the door." Harris pointed to the door behind Wes.

Wes shrugged and pulled open the creaky steel door. Bright sunlight filtered into the dim room. Harris covered his eyes from the blinding light. It was too bright for the sun. He raised his gun when something struck him in the face. He growled and tried to lunge toward the light, but he couldn't move. Frozen in place, only able to move his eyes, he gazed at Travis, Hank, and Gladius, all frozen in place. Their eyes moved and he saw the strain in them. What was this magic?

"For Christ's sake, I thought you guys were some of her goons, or even the queen herself. That sun stone about gave me a heart attack," Wes said as he walked behind a young girl with a long braid of black hair running over her chest. She sneered at them and tugged on her braid. "You didn't have to freeze stone them. They want to stop the queen, same as us."

"Stupid of you to bring them here," the girl with the braid said.

"They tricked me and wouldn't take the first stone location."

Harris struggled to get control of his body. Whatever they did to him, it'd paralyzed him like a statue.

"Hold on. Do they know the little one?" Braid girl's face whipped around to face Wes.

"Her name is Evelyn," Wes said.

"You guys okay?" a voice called from outside.

"Yeah," Wes said.

Braid girl ignored the outside voice and moved close to Wes. "Are you telling me that out of the billions of people on that planet, you ran into the ones who know her?"

"Yes, and they know how to use the world stones. I think those two," he pointed at Harris and Travis, "are from a different planet than those two," Wes said, gesturing to Hank and Gladius.

"Holy shit." She gazed at Harris with wide eyes. "This is bad. If she finds them here, she will get the information out of them. We need to jump out of here, right now."

"They're under paralysis. You think it's safe?"

"Come on." She rolled her eyes. "David, get in here. We're going to jump."

Another young man came into the room holding a small stone in his gloved hand and keeping a keen eye on Harris and his friends.

Harris had never felt so helpless in all his many years. And the fact that a small group of kids had rendered him useless sent him to the boiling point. He continued to fight for the use of his body, but it didn't respond to any of his commands.

How could these kids overpower them so easily? What kind of tech did they have? They didn't seem exceptionally smart, but their cavalier attitudes disturbed Harris. And what did *jump* mean? The Alius stone was a one-way.

"I'll get the couple over here," David said and brandished a purple stone in his hand.

Wes walked over to Travis. "Kylie, you get the grumpy looking one, okay?"

"Oh, what, you don't want me near that hottie?" She pointed to Travis.

"That's not what I—"

"I'm joking, let's just get out of here before she shows."

"Oh," Wes said and pointed at Harris, "they have some

kind of tablet that shields them. This one said it might even block them from her."

"Really? A high tech race . . . Nice," Kylie said.

Harris moved his bottom lip and felt his finger twitch.

"And I think he's got a nuke in that bag, so be careful."

Kylie laughed. "Usually one would lead with *a nuke's in the bag*, but it's an afterthought for you."

"They're ready," David said, holding Hank and Gladius's hand in his.

"Fine," Kylie took hold of Harris's hand. She looked him in the eyes. "What you think you know is about to change. You ready for this?" She pulled a small purple stone from her pocket and pushed it into Harris's hand and squeezed her own over it.

Harris fell through the floor. He kept his eyes open and spotted Kylie in front of him. The room had turned into a swirling storm of liquid, just out of his reach. The noises roared around him and he would have sworn a powerful wind spun around him, yet he didn't feel it—just an odd stillness and the motion of falling.

The ground under his feet firmed and they were in a forest, not unlike that of Preston. Tall oaks and bushes filled the landscape. Kylie took a step back and her feet crunched over dead leaves. How did he get here without an Alius stone? Did these people find a way to travel using those small purple stones?

Wes and Travis popped into existence next to him, and on the other side, Hank, Gladius and David appeared.

Harris's mind reeled from the knowledge these people had. Not only could they create the Alius stones, they also had the ability to portal without one.

"Okay, we're going to unfreeze you, so don't try anything stupid," Kylie said and held another stone in her hand.

"Remember, we want the same thing here."

"Yeah, sorry for the freezing stones," Wes said.

Harris's finger twitched and he felt some warmth in his muscles as they came back under his control. He maintained his frozen state, yet a growing confidence made him measure up each of the three kids who had sacked him with such ease. They had these strange stones, but he didn't see any guns on them. If he avoided their stones, it may be enough.

Kylie moved closer with the stone and Harris timed his attack in six steps. She reached out and he grabbed her wrist. She yelped and dropped the stone. He spun her around to Wes, just as a stone struck her in the chest and bounced to the ground. Harris lifted Kylie and ran at Wes, who raised his hands and shielded himself as a child might from an abusive parent.

He crashed into Wes, then spun around with the two of them subdued and on the ground. He expected David to be the difficult one of the group, but as he turned to face him, Gladius had him on the ground with a knee in his back and a blade pointed at his neck.

"Don't hurt him," Kylie said. "We were going to unfreeze you. You didn't have to attack us like that."

"None of you move," Harris said, as he put a foot on Wes's back.

Kylie flinched. "This is stupid. We want to stop her, just like you."

"Who are you kids?" Harris said.

"Don't tell them anything," David said. "They're probably working for her. If we stop talking, maybe only we will get punished. The rest can keep on."

Harris sighed and put his gun back in its holster. He lifted his foot off Wes's back and helped him and Kylie onto their feet. They looked confused and patted the leaves and dirt from their clothes, while giving Harris some distance. "If you're on our side, you're going to need to show us something to prove it. We need some evidence of your true intent."

Kylie looked at David, then back to Harris. "Our leader will know what to do."

"Who, the queen?" Gladius asked.

"No, the person running our group of rebels. If anyone can show you how much we are committed to ending the queen, it's her." Kylie pointed to the woman standing on the porch of the cabin.

"I suggest you take your hands off my idiotic friends," the woman on the porch said, glaring at Gladius. She didn't appear to be much older than the rest of the kids, maybe early twenties. She had a way about her though, almost like Gladius—a confident, mischievous smile, mixed with a lot of wild in the eyes.

"And who are you?" Harris asked, putting his hand on his holstered gun.

She laughed and took a step down off the porch. "What did you do to convince them to take you here?"

"They know the little one," Wes spoke up. "Her name is Evelyn."

"What?" she asked with a furrowed brow. "Where is she?" When no one answered, she took a step back and stuck her gloved hand into her pocket. "We have ways of getting information from you."

Harris marked his shots. First, this woman on the porch. She seemed the most dangerous, and if her falling didn't put the rest in line, then David, Wes, Kylie—in that order—but Hank would be his primary save target. He couldn't have another of the kids on his conscience. Travis would be equally willing to save Gladius. "It doesn't have to be like this," Harris said, hoping that for once a situation involving him wouldn't end in people dying.

Not long ago, he would have killed each of these purge people without thought. Thoughts got in the way, but he needed a change.

Travis glanced at him, and the unspoken words of two soldiers were passed. Harris sighed and gazed up at the young woman, with her cocky smile and little stone rolling around her fingertips.

Harris drew his gun out so quickly, the young woman didn't have a chance to even blink. Then, the gun was gone. Travis's as well. They exchanged looks. Did he grossly underestimate these purge people's capabilities once again?

Looking forward, he saw the very reason for his weapon's sudden disappearance. The little girl, wise beyond all her years, stood between him and the young woman on the porch. He hadn't seen Evelyn in some time. She'd aged. Not so much in the visual sense, but in her stiff stance, her defiant look, and the way her eyes locked onto him, scolding him, as if *he* were the child.

"I can't have you killing our best chance at stopping the invasion," Evelyn said.

CHAPTER 9

THIS IS CRAZY. **LUCAS PACED** near his son, who was sitting in the chair and looking up into the enormous dome above. "Come on, let's get him out of here. Evelyn can't be trusted. We have no idea what this thing is going to do when it's turned on."

"Quiet," Julie said as she continued to scan through Evelyn's Panavice. "I think this machine might be legit." She looked up at Lucas. "It might actually work."

"He's our *son*," Lucas said and pointed at Will. Julie ignored him and continued to scan pages. Lucas grunted and picked up Will from the chair. "If Hector made it in that world, so can we. Anything is better than hooking him up to something Evelyn and Marcus created."

"And what, screw the rest of the world?" Julie asked.

"We have to protect our own, Julie. Haven't you seen what happens when we push fate? Where's Samantha? Where's

Joey?" His voice cracked as he mentioned his best friend's name. Pulling open the hatch, Julie yelled at him.

"Stop, Lucas."

He stopped with one foot on the ladder.

"Daddy, it's okay. I want to do this," Will said. "Evelyn and I talked about this. I'm prepared."

Lucas couldn't look his son in the face. All he wanted to do was take him away from all of this. He hated himself for letting it get this far.

"Lucas, without Will to blank the minds on Earth, then people will die. Not just a few, but all of them. We are talking about *billions* of lives. If we have even a chance of this working, then I think it's worth it."

"So you're willing to risk his life for the rest of theirs?"

"Yes. If we don't do this, we all die."

"No, we know something the rest of this world doesn't. There's a way off this sinking ship."

"Where? Vanar is doomed as well. That leaves only Ryjack or Arrack."

"You're smart, Julie. There are a million worlds. With our shields, we can explore until we find one."

"And then what? Wait for the purge people to come to that one too, living in fear, living with the knowledge we let our friends, our parents, our world, meet their death. I can't live with that, and I know you can't either."

Lucas stood from the hatch and looked at his son, who seemed to be soaking in the conversation. Julie was right, of course. He could never live with abandoning his friends. And what about their parents?

"I'm ready for this, Dad," Will said. "I don't want all those people to die because we were too scared to try."

Lucas laughed a little. "You're too smart for your own good, you know that?"

"You can never be too smart." Will smiled. "Besides, Evelyn has a plan. If she can complete it before the purge people launch their reclamation phase, then maybe I won't even have to control the minds of the world."

"Fine, but if I see anything wrong, I'm pulling the plug on this."

The floor vibrated and a pounding sound echoed through the massive chamber. They looked down as another strike shook through the floor.

Julie's Panavice dinged and she read the screen out loud. "Text from Evelyn. Wait there and don't turn on the machine until the last minute. I may be gone for a while."

Gunfire erupted from below. Soft sounds of cracks and thuds sounded. Lucas winced at the noises and gazed from the door on the floor, then back to Will and Julie.

"Don't worry, Evelyn is handling them," Will said.

"You should check it out," Julie said and called Will over to her.

Lucas nodded and grabbed his bow off the floor, next to the ladder. "I'll be right back. Close this door and lock it."

He closed the hatch over him and waited to hear the lock before descending down the ladder. He jumped off the last few steps of the steel rung and darted toward the gunfire. A few steps and the last vibration ended. Then silence. No bangs, no gunfire.

As he got closer, he heard voices. Getting past the last corner, he spotted Poly. "What's going on?" He saw the bodies in the cells nearby. One of them hung between bent bars, with blood dripping from his eyes.

"She's gone," Poly cried. "I think she's going after the queen."

"She texted, saying Will should carry out the mission."

Lucas looked at the cells.

"Are those the guys you captured outside?"

"Yes, but they took some kind of drug and become crazed, with unbelievable strength. If Evelyn hadn't stopped them . . . ." Poly looked at the men and held her hand over her mouth.

"Sir, we have crafts incoming, a lot of them," a uniformed soldier said to Derek, holding up a Panavice.

"Set defenses up and let's make sure these people don't get anywhere near here."

"Aye." The man hurried off and Derek looked back to Poly.

"There's a large group heading here. Air defense will take them down. And if any make it to land, we'll have plenty of surprises to slow them down."

Lucas's heartbeat picked up as he took in the information. People were coming to attack them, to stop what his son was about to do, no doubt.

"Lucas, right?" Derek said.

"Yes."

"Think you can man the sound cannons?"

"Where are they?"

"When they get close, you push this button." Derek handed him a Panavice and showed him. "Think you can handle that?"

"Yeah."

"Good, because if these people get into the dome, we won't have much of a chance of stopping them. Evelyn planned on an attack, but little goes as planned." Derek turned and ran down the hall.

Lucas held the Panavice in his hands and stared at the screen displaying the desert around the dome. It looked more like a picture until he spotted movement in the sky. Little black boxes he knew all too well, floated around in the sky. A swarm of them, hundreds.

Gunfire sounded, then missiles streaked across the sky. The bullets and missiles struck the cubes, sending a rainstorm of debris falling to the earth. But the defenses couldn't keep up. More cubes landed, getting through the assault—over a hundred of them on the ground now.

Lucas did the math, and if those cubes held just one person each, they'd still be greatly outnumbered. He wished he had his friend by his side with double guns and slow motion powers. Harris and Hank came to mind as well. Where were they?

"Come on, Derek told me of a com center just over here." Poly pulled at him. "We can monitor the outside better from there."

Lucas adjusted Prudence on his side and wondered how useful his skill in bows would be against such people.

"We can do this, Lucas. Remember Ryjack? You killed hundreds of grinners. What's a bunch of trespassers going to have on us?" Poly lead the way out of the cell area and into a small room filled with large screens displaying the entire surrounding area.

"What happened back there?" Lucas asked.

"You'll think I'm crazy, but Evelyn killed them. She willed it with her mind. If she hadn't done it, those monsters would have torn through all of us."

He didn't think she was crazy. At the fair, he thought he'd felt prying fingers in his mind. But they didn't have Evelyn by their sides now. "If those three came close to killing us all, what chance do we have against an army of them?"

Dust stirred on the screen as more of the cubes landed in a wide berth on one side of the dome. Lucas leaned in closer. The wind pushed the dust away and revealed a large group of people headed toward them.

"Arrogant," Poly said. "They are grouped up like we couldn't hurt them if we wanted to." Her mouth crunched up to one corner as she got closer to the screen.

Lucas stared at the side of her head and realized he had not been alone with Poly in a long time. He thought of the first time Joey started looking at her in a different way. Joey might not have admitted it, but at their eighteenth birthday party he'd noticed the difference. He spotted a spark in his eyes as he gazed upon Poly, even if he said he had a thing for Samantha at the time.

He choked up at the thought of his friend. "You know, I wish we were there more for you after Joey. . . ."

She turned away from the screen. "You were there. Believe me. When I finally had my thoughts together, I used my memory of you and Julie, all of you, to get me through the darkest days." Tears built up in her eyes. "But now Evelyn is gone again. I don't even know what she's doing. Does Will do that too? Does he just leave you?"

"He's distant sometimes, but he hasn't left us, as far as I know. He'll outgrow us quickly, though, and I'm terrified of that day. I can't imagine doing this without Julie." He regretted saying it the second it left his lips.

"You're lucky. I feel like Evelyn doesn't even need me now. In fact, I think she feels like I am a weight on her shoulders."

"No, I don't believe that. She loves you, we all love you," Lucas said and wrapped his arms around her in a big hug. "And in a little bit, we can see how well Evelyn loves us with these defenses," he joked.

"Look, one of them is waving." Poly pulled away and pointed to the screen.

An older man walked ahead of the group. He looked thin, and maybe Asian, as he approached with both hands up. His mouth moved, but they couldn't hear the words.

"What do we do?" Lucas asked.

Derek rushed into the room. "They want to talk."

"With who?" Poly asked.

"You, he's calling you out by name."

"How the hell does he know my name?"

"He's saying Evelyn sent him."

CHAPTER 10

WIND BLEW ACROSS THE DESERT floor, tousling Poly's hair as she stared at the man waiting for her a hundred yards away.

"You sure you want to do this?" Derek asked. "Evelyn has many defenses set up to take care of these people."

"Yeah, I do. Even if I can stall them for a while, it could give Evelyn the chance she needs to find a way to stop this invasion."

Derek glanced back at the door and then at her. She hadn't made full eye contact with him until that moment. He had a toughness to him, much like Harris, but a softness hid behind the eyes. They reminded her of Joey.

She cleared her throat. "I'm ready."

"Fine," Derek said. "You know, you remind me a lot of Samantha."

Poly battled the small rush of anger and sadness that flowed through her veins, but smiled anyways. "Just make sure you have my back."

"I'll be right next to you."

The door opened and Poly swung around to see Lucas leaning out. "I'm going with you. You can't be alone with this guy." He gestured toward Derek.

"No, you need to go back to Julie and Will. If this goes bad, you may be our last stand."

"Okay, but if anything happens to her, Derek, I'll hold you accountable," Lucas said.

"I'll let you skewer me personally."

"Lucas, tell Julie how much I love her. I'm so sorry about Evelyn. I know she meant well, but it all came out wrong."

"I will," Lucas said. "Are you sure about going out there? That sounded almost like a goodbye."

"I've missed a few goodbyes already. I won't miss another."

Lucas nodded, then left down the passageway and out of sight.

"Ready?" Derek asked with his hand on the door.

She motioned for him to get on with it.

Blood pumped through her veins, and she took a deep breath of the dry, dusty air to calm her nerves. She'd spent too many hours with Travis to not know this man was about to demand something she could never give.

Getting within ten feet of the man, she studied his worn face with a scraggly goatee and beard. He looked frail, yet the steel in his eyes told of the many days left in his mind.

"That's close enough," Derek whispered.

"Are you the mother?" the man said in a raspy voice, laden with an Asian accent.

"I have a daughter."

He laughed. "You are the mother of the little one. I have a proposition directly from our queen regarding your daughter, and another boy much like her. She will not attack a single person on this world, and never return again, in exchange for the two children."

"No," Poly said.

"We are talking about a few billion lives in exchange for two. She has never made such an offer."

"Tell her to screw herself."

He laughed again, and looked over his shoulder at the small army they'd gathered. "We are not like anything you've ever encountered. We've face worlds so far advanced from your own, you look like cavemen in comparison. Why do you think we can't just do both, take your child and this entire world?"

"If you could, it would be done already. Your queen fears my daughter, she fears what she is capable of. I'll give you one chance to pack up and leave here. Never come back to this world and maybe I can convince my daughter to not pursue your queen any longer."

He moved his gloved hand in one quick motion, until his fingers were holding a stone. "You know what this is, don't you? I can see it in your eyes. You've met the twins then?" He smirked. "This is a stone made by our beloved queen herself. It has the power to destroy all of you."

"Go ahead." Poly was so sick of people coming into her life and trying to push her one way or another. After losing Joey, and now feeling a loss between her and Evelyn, she didn't care what this purge person did or thought.

He chuckled and stowed the stone back in his pocket. "You're making a mistake, young lady. She wants what you have and nothing will stop her. I ask you one last time to take this offer. Give us your daughter and the other one like her."

"My offer stands. It is your decision, whether you want to

live through this day or not," Poly said.

The man's smile faded as he threw something at Poly. Derek jumped in front of her and caught the stone, inches before striking Poly's face. Derek groaned, but turned and fired on the man as he reeled back with another stone. Bullet holes peppered the man's body, and he fell to the ground. The stone hit the ground next to him, cracking open like an egg. A green cloud lifted from the broken stone and widened toward her and Derek.

Derek fell to one knee in front of her, clasping his arm. "Go, run." He pushed Poly toward the door.

She pulled Derek to his feet and ran with him, more carrying him than anything else. She yanked the door open and pulled Derek inside, then slammed the door shut and locked it. She kneeled next to him. Sweat beaded on his pale face and he clutched his arm.

Poly gazed at his blackening hand and shook her head. "What do I do?" She thought of one of Vanar's healing machines, but they were hours away from a stone.

"Cut off my arm, it's traveling fast." Derek squeezed his arm. He lifted his head long enough to look at it before falling hard back to the floor. "Cut it off!"

Poly couldn't breathe as she pulled out her dagger from her sheath at her waist. She looked at the red dragon embroidered on the handle—another homage to Compry. The blackness crawled past his wrist and she pulled her knife back, shaking her head. "I can't do this, Derek. I'm sorry."

"You have to. Use your sword."

My sword. She closed her eyes and reached back, feeling for it. She hadn't used it in a long time. It reminded her too much of Joey, and after wearing it for so long, it felt a part of her. Pulling it out, she listened to the sound of it sliding through the sheath. This could cut Derek's body in half.

"I'm going to raise my arm, then let it go. Cut it off just above the elbow," Derek said. "I have a vile Evelyn gave me, I'll smear it on afterward to stop the bleeding."

Poly got to her knees and looked at his raised arm, making her spot of impact just above his elbow. *This is insane.* "On three. One, two, three." She swung hard; it gave only the slightest resistance as it cut clean through his bone. The arm, black and shriveled, fell to the ground.

Derek shouted, but shoved a handful of white goo onto his stub. The bleeding stopped and he fell backward onto the floor, thumping his head.

Breathing quickly, Poly stayed on her knees, staring at a motionless Derek. She couldn't believe what she'd just done. Shaking off the blood, she sheathed it.

Footsteps pounded toward her and several men slid onto the floor next to Derek. "What happened? They cut his arm off?"

"The poison, it would have killed him," Poly said. "I—I had to. . . ."

The two men picked up Derek and carried him off. The distant footsteps dissipated and the entry fell silent.

Poly stood back from the wall and avoided the dead hand on the floor. She had an army to repel and the most knowledgeable man in the building just had his arm cut off. Pulling out her Panavice, she texted Julie. If they found a way to get through Sanct alive, they'd find a way to stave off these stone-throwing scumbags.

Someone pounded against the steel door, then a sound boomed around the small entry.

She turned and ran toward the monitoring room. She texted Julie again and glanced back to see steel doors sliding shut and locking.

"Thank you, Julie." She ran, making her way down a series of hallways.

Julie ran out of a doorway and stopped in front of her. "You okay?" she asked.

"Yeah, thanks for coming. Let's get to the monitoring room," Poly said, and they darted into the room. Half of the screens showed white. "They broke?"

"No, they used some kind of smoke bomb and fogged out half the dome. Good thing I know Evelyn's coding. I spotted most of her defense mechanisms in the program. Lucas told me about a weapon Derek wanted him to use. Watch this." Julie pushed on the screen and the ground rumbled, monitors moving around on the walls. Some of the fog left one of the screens and Poly thought she saw objects flying around in the mist. Maybe even body parts.

"You're killing them?" Poly asked.

Julie pressed another button on her screen and a high pitched sound emitted from around the building. "Sound waves, concentrated."

"Just scaring them off?"

Julie laughed. "You think they can live through a three hundred decibel, concentrated sound wave?"

The squeal from the sound rang in her ears and she put a hand on her stomach.

"Don't worry, it's directed at them, we're just getting some reflection," Julie explained. "Next, we have some sensor guns." She pushed another button on the screen.

From the clatter of automatic gunfire and the deeper thud of artillery fire, Poly didn't think a cockroach would be left out there. She put her hands over her ears and gazed at the monitor, tensing her muscles.

More of the mist cleared and the dirt landscape appeared. Poly stared at the screen in disbelief, as a group of people huddled around each other, with a clear dome protecting them. Not all were lucky though, many were either dead, or holding their heads in agony.

"They have some kind of shield," Poly said.

"They can't stay in there forever. I'm going to save the bullets." Julie pressed her finger on the screen and the gunfire ceased.

"What do we do now?" Poly looked back at the door, hoping no one had breached it yet.

"They're moving, look." Julie pointed at the screen.

Poly watched the group move as a unit, closer to the building. "Do something," she said.

Julie scanned through her Panavice, finally deciding on something. Pushing a button, she looked at the screens. "I energized the outside walls. They get within five feet and they'll get zapped with a million volts."

The group stopped fifty feet back from the building. All of their hands rose in unison and they faced the sky, throwing stones toward the top of the structure. Poly, having a terrible feeling of what those stones were about to bring, stepped back from the monitor as her body got a fresh jolt of adrenaline.

A couple of the screens showed the stones arching up to the belly of the building. The first stone struck and melted through. Then the rest hit, creating a huge hole in the steel cladding. Poly knew what the stones were going to do. "We've got to get out of here." She looked at the back door of the room. She walked to it and looked across the hall. An explosion rocked the building and she stumbled into the hall. "Please tell me Evelyn planned for an escape?"

"I don't know, there's nothing on here but—" Julie got cut off by another large explosion. "They're in the building. Dammit." Julie scanned through the pages on her screen and then she brightened. "There's an escape room. I'm texting coordinates to Will and Lucas." She jogged out of the room and down a passageway, away from another explosion.

"This was supposed to be our last chance to save the world," Poly yelled at Julie's back, as she ran to keep up.

"I guess we better find a new way to save the world," Julie answered. "Because this place is gone." She slowed down at a collapsed section of the hall.

Stark sunlight poured into the building from a gaping hole coming from the ceiling. Liquid dripped onto the floor and hissed. Julie made a right turn and jogged away from the dissolving section of the building.

They made it down several flights of stairs, then ran up to Lucas and Will, who were standing in a steel room. Four other men joined them, and Derek leaned against a wall with his arm bandaged. His pale face regarded Poly as he swayed.

"Derek," Julie said. "You know the way out. What do we do?"

He sparked awake at her strong voice. "They've breached?" He looked around the room and then at the floor. "This was the last chance for all of us. I've failed Evelyn."

"Dude," Lucas snapped. "Save the pity party for after we get out of this. Now get us the hell out of here."

"This is labeled as the last resort room, this has to be it," Julie said, pointing at her Panavice screen.

Derek kicked off the wall and pointed at a small panel. "You're right, this is it. I'd hope to never need this room, but bless her mind for thinking of it." Another explosion rocked the room and he fell to one knee. He sprung back up and used his functional hand to slap open the metal door and reveal a screen. "I need Will," he said. "It will only respond to him or Evelyn."

"Why?" Julie asked.

"That's the way she set it up."

Will walked to Derek and looked up at the screen.

"Just put your hand on the screen and the computer will do the rest," Derek explained.

Will raised his hand and almost put it on the screen before lowering it. He looked back at Poly, then the rest of them in a quick glance. "If I do this, that's it," Will said. "We lose everything. Maybe we should fight our way through this?"

Julie moved closer to Will and held his hand. "This isn't about win or lose, this is about surviving." She took his hand and slapped it against the screen.

The room hummed and vibrated under their feet. The steel doors slammed shut.

"What's going on?" Poly asked.

"I think we're about to go for a ride."

CHAPTER 11

EVELYN WALKED AROUND HARRIS AND gazed at the woman standing on the porch. She was frozen in time, but her embers still flowed, even more than the rest. It must be an indication of how strong they were, but in what?

It hadn't taken her too long to find her friends. Their Panavices, designed by her, kept a signal only she could trace. What she found more unusual was the company they were keeping.

Evelyn took Harris's gun out of his hand, then Travis's as well. She hated disarming such men; they'd surely see it as an emasculation, and further their distrust of her. But she couldn't let them kill these purge people. Not *these* ones anyhow; not yet.

She released time and chose the spot between the two warriors. Harris took half a second to assess the new situation, Travis a hair behind him. "I can't have you killing our best chance at stopping the invasion."

"You're the one?" The braid girl asked.

"Yes, and I don't have much time. Every second I spend here, means Earth is that much closer to getting taken."

"Evelyn?" The woman on the porch said, lowering her stone. Her mouth hung open and she tilted her head.

"Not expecting such a little girl?" She'd become tired of her form and the instant lack of respect it granted.

"No, it's not that. I just wondered if you were real. We've heard so many stories, but never had any proof. After a while, you stop believing."

Evelyn knew how to handle this type of person. "What's your name?"

"Jackie."

Good, already giving honest answers. "Why don't we go inside and discuss the end of the queen?" She looked to Harris and then to Gladius and Hank. At first, it surprised her to see them all in the purge world. Most curious indeed. If she hadn't showed up, what would have been their end game? Kill these purge people, maybe torture the girl with the braid until she squealed like a pig?

"Sure," Jackie said and motioned to her friends. She stepped further onto the porch and looked back, biting her lip.

This Jackie person might be more difficult than Evelyn first thought. Her thoughts bounced around, with a constant trail of sarcasm, as if she argued with herself as much as anything else.

"What are you doing here?" Harris asked.

Evelyn hadn't had too much interaction with Harris, but he had one of the strongest minds of anyone she'd come across. "Saving the world," she said. "The better question is, what's in that bag?" She glanced down at Harris's bag and then to Travis, who had yet to make eye contact with her.

"You know," Travis whispered.

Evelyn had suspicions, but if they brought that thing to this planet, then they had a lot more on their mind than simply killing the queen.

She walked with Harris and led the group up the stairs. They entered the open door of the cabin. "Nice place."

The main room looked like a log cabin. A large main room with an oversized fireplace, rustic furniture, and a large table with carved edges and timber chairs. A barrel sat in the middle of the room, filled to the top with water and a single stone floating in the middle.

Jackie leaned against an old oak table with her arms crossed. "It's a shit hole, but we keep these safe houses all around the world. We found a few stones to protect us from the queen. They can't detect us in these places, yet we still need to be cautious."

"Just give us her location and we'll go there now," Harris said.

Evelyn frowned at his abrupt demands. As smart as the man appeared, he didn't know people as well as she did.

"Evelyn knows. She was there, not long ago."

"Yes," she said, trying to understand the purpose of the barrel of water. "I have already engaged in the queen's compound. It is unlikely I would be able to use the same entrance point. The queen isn't foolish. She'll have closed off that entrance by now."

"Just show us on the map," Harris said and pulled out his Panavice.

"I didn't log it. I—I had trouble there."

"Trouble?"

"She was able to do the things I can do." A flash of the queen's control over her made her wince. When they met again, things would be different. She would be prepared. She saw into the mind of the woman and knew her secrets. Soon, Evelyn would have the one thing she held most precious. "If we are to beat her, then we need to get closer to her without her knowing it. Her daughter has been mentioned. Who is she?"

"She's my best friend." Jackie's lips thinned. "And she's been missing for a long time, her and her man."

"Is she alive?"

"Yes."

"Where is she?"

"The queen sent her somewhere, maybe another world. I think she did it because she didn't want her to see what was coming. I believe her daughter is the only person in the world who might be able to get the queen to lower her guard. And for that reason alone, she's hiding her from us."

"Maybe she's hiding from you," Evelyn said, then regretted it. People had a way of perceiving a valid argument as an attack.

Jackie pushed off the table and took a step closer to her. "If she could get back here, she would. She's one of the most honest, decent people I've ever met. If she saw how her creation was being used, I'm not sure any of us, including her mother, could stop her."

"What do you mean? What did the daughter create?" Harris asked.

"She's the one." Jackie stopped and turned to face the barrel of water. The water shook in it, and ripples rolled out from the stone. Evelyn sensed a change in her demeanor. Her whimsy switched to hyper focus. "They're here," she whispered.

The stone in the barrel floated to one side and butted against the wood. It pushed over the top and bounced along the floor, toward the door.

"Everyone, jump. They've found us." Jackie turned to Harris.

"Was it you?"

"No."

Jackie leapt next to Evelyn. "We need to go."

"I don't need any help."

"I need to show you the next jump location, and how I think we can get the daughter back," Jackie said, then faced the front door. "Jump location four," she screamed. "Everyone pair up."

Evelyn thought of slowing down time to assess this threat, but she didn't want to run into the queen just yet, and Jackie intrigued her. She'd let the event play out at normal speed.

Jackie grabbed her and clasped a stone between their hands. Evelyn tried to pry her hand free, but the world fell out from under her feet. The falling sensation, mixed with the swirling world, left her breathless. What was this technology? Could these people travel around their world with just the use of these stones?

The idea made her sick with excitement. Traveling took up most of her time; running from one Alius stone to the next. To have the ability to leap across great distances with the use of a stone . . . it would change her world entirely.

The ground firmed under her feet and Jackie held tight to her hand, keeping her from falling.

Evelyn had jumped a thousand times using the Alius stones—this was different. The Alius stones were more of a light switch, even in slowed time; you were in one place, then another.

Wide eyed, she took in her surroundings, and for the first time in a long time, felt an amazement about the world. "You have to tell me how these stones—"

A gloved hand slapped an object on her arm. "Sorry, I need you in order to get my friend back," Jackie said with a sympathetic look.

Evelyn pulled away and felt the dull pain entering her hand.

On instinct, she went into slow motion. Jackie stood there, frozen and gazing at her. Evelyn wished she could enter people's mind in that state, but they came across as blanks. She wanted to ravage Jackie's mind and find out why she just slapped this thing on her hand, and what it did.

Evelyn moved and her legs responded with great difficulty, sending her heart racing. What had this woman used on her, and where was the rest of her group? Had this been a trap? Evelyn gave it only a twenty percent chance Jackie and her friends were working with the queen. How could she have miscalculated so badly?

The first step felt like lead had encased her leg. She grunted in pain and even in the tiniest of time that passed, she felt the poison of whatever Jackie struck her with work into her, constricting each of her muscles and pulling on her mind to stop.

Looking back, she spotted Jackie, still frozen in her time. She needed much greater distance. An Alius stone couldn't be too far away. She trudged through the forest and called out in pain as her left leg locked up entirely. Supporting herself with her right side, she pulled out her Panavice and located the nearest stone.

She gazed at her location, northern China. She knew the language and could probably get around with some planning, but a handicapped little white girl roaming the street of rural China would stand out. If she got that far.

Gripping the Panavice with her right hand, she pushed on. The next five minutes were as if someone was shoveling sand onto her back, while another person injected a new body part with a paralyzing poison each passing minute. Everything in her body screamed for her to stop. Half her body now felt numb and dead. Her arms dangled to the side and she had to swing her leg around to get a step forward.

"Come on, Evelyn. Don't be a damned quitter." Forty more miles and she'd get to the jump point.

Her face became numb and drool dripped from her open mouth. Breathing became ragged, as her chest wouldn't allow deep breaths. Even her eyes blurred, and the dull hum of the world diminished to almost nothing. She cried out, but it sounded more like a groan. Her body gave up on her. She landed on the grassy bank, next to a small stream. Her legs wouldn't move and her left arm had long ago lost its usefulness. Her right shoulder had some muscle left in it, and her neck.

If she lived, she'd find a way for this whole planet to pay.

She pulled her Panavice up to her face and used her nose to flip through the screen as drool ran down her mouth and froze in the air as it dripped from her.

Jackie would be far enough away now, she doubted they'd ever find her body. She had to send Harris, Travis, and Gladius one last note. The fate of the world might depend on one of them getting the message.

If she passed out, would time continue on? Would the world snap back and leave her there, or would she be suspended forever, with seconds ticking by like years, and her body perpetually frozen in slow motion? A thousand years may pass for her while it took them days to find her.

She shut her eyes and struggled to get her heavy lids back open. She thanked the heavens her neck still had a hint of feeling and responded to her commands. She texted them, using her nose. Hopefully, they would be able to follow the message and find her body.

If they all failed, the purge people and the queen would take Earth, Vanar, and continue their rapture of the worlds. If she failed, the mutants would die. If she failed, none of the wrongs she set out to right would happen. The balance of the worlds would shift.

She wished she had the strength to tell her mom she loved her, but her neck finally gave in and her face rested on the Panavice, unable to move. She closed her eyes and heard the sounds of the world come alive. Then blackness, as whatever Jackie struck her with took hold.

CHAPTER 12

A TALL DOOR WITH SYMBOLS etched around the perimeter stood in front of Kris. He rubbed his chin and tried to find any meaning to the symbols, but failed. It hadn't taken them long to find the door, as it stuck into the bottom of a rocky hillside. It didn't have any right to be there, and it seemed odd for anyone to put such a door in the middle of nowhere.

"It's probably a riddle, written in some crazy language from this planet," Maggie said.

"I don't know, I've seen this somewhere." He pointed at the bird at the top of the door.

"Just let me melt it," Maggie said and held up her glowing red hands.

"No, Evelyn said there would be traps. Something very valuable is inside and we must be cautious. I'm not losing any more people today."

Maybe they didn't even need to open this door. Maybe it didn't matter what treasure Evelyn needed inside. They had the real treasure of this new planet; a fresh start, to be their own people. Away from the world that treated them like freaks and second rate citizens based solely on their genetics.

This was their promised home. He pressed his lips together and looked at the ground, angry at his selfish thoughts. Evelyn had given this gift to them, the least they could do was help her.

"Get your dad," Kris finally said to Maggie.

Her eyes lit up and she grinned. It didn't take her long to find her oversized dad. A man who could single handedly pull down a tree and carry it back to camp. The big man walked up to Kris, with his fiery redhead of a daughter skipping along next to him.

"Char," Kris addressed the big man. "I want you to watch this." He showed him the smooth rock in his hand, then faced the door. He loosened his shoulder, and spun his arm. It spun so fast, it became a blur, yet he still felt the motion and had control. He released the rock and it cleared the thirty feet to the door in a fraction of a second. The door shot out an electrical bolt and destroyed the rock midair. Nothing but pebbles pelted the door.

Char's eyes narrowed. "Need a bigger rock."

Kris laughed at the simplicity of it. But he was right. "You think you could put one through that door, from this distance?"

"Just get me a rock worth a damn and I'll blow the hinges right off that tin can."

Kris smiled and looked back at the terrain. A rock outcropping sprung out of the forest. After searching for a while, they found a rock that made Char and Kris happy.

They made it back to the same spot, with Char carrying a

boulder that would have crushed any normal man by the sheer weight. Char waved to the rest of the tribe and a group gathered around to watch the spectacle. Kris wasn't exactly sure what to expect, so he urged people to stay away from the door.

Getting the tribe settled behind Char, Kris nodded to the big man. "Give it a good throw."

Char reached back with both hands, as if throwing in a ball at a soccer game. He ran forward a few steps, and threw the large rock with a roar. The rock struck the door, dead center, and a bolt of electricity danced around it, zapping it. The rock fell to the ground below the door.

Kris hadn't expected the rock to penetrate the door, but it solved another mystery. He leaned forward and saw the dent. "We need an even bigger rock."

A longer search led to a boulder ten times as big as the first rock Char threw.

Kris looked up at the big man holding onto the rock like a bundle of laundry. He cupped the sides of his mouth and yelled, "Throw it."

Char heaved the rock into the air, and out toward the door, hitting it hard enough to make the ground shake. It blew open the door; the blackness beyond appeared.

"Yes, Dad! You did it," Maggie yelled out.

"Stay back, we don't know what's next," Kris said. He tossed a rock and it sailed past the doorway. No electrical current. He edged closer to the opening, keeping a hand up for protection. Nearing the door, he braced himself for a shock. Nothing. He stepped over the fallen door.

The features of the dark room came to as he entered and stepped out of the light. He wasn't exactly sure what to expect, but nothing as plain as the next room. Simply another room with a door, much like the first, stuffed into the stone wall. But it wasn't exactly the same door. The markings were different.

"What's past these doors?" Maggie said and Kris jumped at her voice.

"A treasure important to Evelyn."

"How do we open this one? I don't even think a boulder big enough to break it could fit in here."

"No, I suspect this door is going to be tougher. Look at the steel jamb, twice as thick," Kris said and squinted at the door. "Stay back." He put a hand on Maggie's shoulder.

"I could melt it."

"No."

"Think I should try and break this one down?" Char asked from the broken doorway.

"Let's be patient." Kris picked up a few pebbles from the dirt floor and threw them.

The pebbles hit the door, and the unexpected happened. They didn't fall to the ground, nor cause an electrical charge. They disappeared. He picked up a handful more and tossed them again—same result. The door seemed to absorb the material.

"Get a bigger rock," Kris said and Char brought him a hefty rock.

He heaved the rock and it struck the door. Small ripples formed on the surface, then the rock sank into the door like falling into honey.

"You think it melts into the other side of the door?" Maggie asked.

"Good question. I have no idea."

In a few minutes, they gathered some jungle rope and attached it to a rock. Kris swirled his arm a few rotations and sent the rope and rock into the door. He held onto the rope and felt the tug as the door pulled it in. The rope tightened and slid through his hands. He tried to keep his grip, but it pulled harder.

"Char, grab the rope," Kris said.

Both men formed a tug-of-war line, but they might as well have been wearing skates because the rope pulled them across the floor toward the door. Halfway across the room, Kris let go and Char followed. It fed into the door at the same pace, until the end of it disappeared.

"You hear that?" Kris said, turning his ear toward the door. "I thought I heard a clunk. Get Lupe, please." He said it, but she didn't need to be summoned. The woman heard everything, yet kept a tight lip. He always admired her for that.

Seconds later, Lupe came through the door, looking around as she adjusted to the darkness.

"Lupe, I need you to listen to this." Kris tossed a stone at the door.

"Listen for what?" Lupe said.

"Wait for it." The rock disappeared and Kris raised a hand for silence. The distinct sound of a rock striking more rocks came through.

"It fell for a few seconds. The air is thicker in there and the rocky bottom is solid rock. I heard it bounce several times," Lupe said. "I hear something else as well. A humming sound. Very faint." She leaned closer to the door.

"Stay back from the door." Kris grabbed her and pulled her back. "We don't know what that thing is capable of."

"It fell for a few feet, but landed on a solid bottom."

"This is stupid," Maggie said and her hands ignited. She slammed her hands against the door and then fell through.

"Maggie, no!" Char said and charged at the door.

"*Wait,*" Kris called out, but the big man plowed into him,

sending them both into the door.

The door moved over his head. He closed his eyes and mouth as it moved over his face. He felt the door free him and he turned to the blackness of the next room and fell. He wasn't sure how far, but definitely more than a few feet. He grabbed at the darkness, as if it had matter, and slammed against a pile of rocks. He felt his left arm break from the impact and then his knee hit another rock and jammed his leg. He cried out in pain.

Kris would need medical attention. He felt around the break; the bone hadn't gone through the skin. His knee hurt, but he thought he could stand on it. The blackness around him took on a life of its own, and he thought he heard things.

"Hello?" he called.

"Bit more than a few feet, Lupe," Maggie yelled. "You okay, Dad?"

"Yeah, this hard floor broke my fall," Char said.

"Sorry, guys, guess I got impatient up there. I really thought I could just melt these doors."

A red glow lit up the chamber and Kris held his hand over his eyes as Maggie held onto glowing red rocks. "Where the hell are we?" she said, looking up.

Kris for the first time got to see what they were in, and looking up, he almost preferred the darkness. Above them, ran a four-sided shoot, with smooth as glass walls, gleaming in the red light. The doors above them, one on each side, sat a good fifty feet above.

"We are not going to die in here, Maggie." Kris said.

"I never said we were."

CHAPTER 13

"WHERE'S EVELYN?" GLADIUS ASKED, LOOKING around the massive white building.

"I . . . she should be here," Kylie said and pulled on her braid.

Harris held out his gun and pointed it at Kylie. "Where is she?"

"I don't know, Jackie portaled with her."

"She took her to the queen, I bet. She's going to try and exchange the little one for the daughter," Wes said.

"Shut up. She wouldn't do that, Wes," Kylie said.

"And you did nothing to stop it," Gladius said. It wasn't as if she liked the little weird girl, but she was probably their only chance to stop these people. If *she* got bamboozled by that vile Jackie girl, then it probably meant the end.

"Tell us where she is," Harris said, keeping his gun trained on Kylie.

"She could be anywhere. I don't know," Kylie said.

Gladius wanted to yank the girl's braid and chop it off. They all knew, they had to. If Harris wouldn't do what needed to be done, she would. She stepped closer to Kylie, with knife in hand.

Hank grabbed her shoulder. "These aren't the bad guys."

She closed her eyes to conceal the eye roll. Hank and his damned do-goodiness. Vanar would take these people and flush them out. Each one of them had seen some stuff, she knew that much from looking at them. They all had an arrogance about them. Probably because she couldn't do the things they could with their little stones.

"Where are we?" Travis asked.

Gladius hadn't given it a good look yet; as she gazed at the high ceiling and the broken glass wall, it felt as if it had been somewhere important at one point. Now, the weeds grew in from the broken walls, and scorch marks marred the perfect white walls. A dry creek ran through the middle of it with ornate white bridges crossing it. The whole place gave Gladius the creeps.

"This was a place of learning. Before the war," Kylie said. "You know, Jackie isn't a bad person. She just wants her friend back."

Gladius scoffed. "And you think we're going to be okay with her using our friend to get that done?"

"No," Kylie said. "Listen, you don't get it. The *queen*, as you call her, is the ruler here. She's going to find out we helped you and then we're all dead, or at the very least, stuffed away somewhere. And whatever is in that bag, isn't going to change a damned thing. She'll read your mind and stop time if she has to. She'll stop you. That is why Evelyn was so important, she got through all the defenses. She made it to the queen and faced her. She is the only one who had a chance to stop her, and now Jackie took that away from us, and you."

Gladius felt a vibration in her pocket and pulled out her Panavice, at the same time as Travis and Harris. She gawked at the message from Evelyn.

Help.

Harris eyed her, then Travis, as each of them read it.

"What are you all looking at?" David asked.

"Our friend needs us," Travis said. "I'm getting to the next stone."

Jackie popped into existence near David. "Where is she?" she said with rage.

"*You* took her," Gladius said.

"She escaped and I know you all can track each other with those tablets, so just tell me. Where is she?"

"We'd never give up one of our friends."

"This is impossible. I used a suspended stone on her, and she blinked away. I can't find her. So, if you don't want her stuck in suspended animation for the rest of your lives, I suggest you give me her location."

Jackie produced several stones and kept them between her fingertips, like a magician might with a stack of cards. Gladius watched her slide into an attack stance and had to give the woman credit. She had balls to confront them, or maybe it was pure arrogance.

"Don't do this," Kylie said. "We'll find another way. We aren't like this."

"Shut it, Kylie," Jackie said.

Gladius raised an eyebrow at Jackie's tone, bordering on manic. She knew crazy and how dangerous it could be.

"Jackie, maybe we can find a middle ground here. After all, I think we both are after the same thing," Travis said.

"What are you, some politician? You have no idea what's

going on here, none of you do."

"Help us understand then," Travis said.

Gladius hated when her dad did this diplomatic crap. She wanted to throw a blade right between Jackie's eyes and end it.

"You're just a rube, all of you are. The only one who had potential is Evelyn, and I want her back. I don't want to hurt you, but I'll do what I have to do," Jackie said.

"You aren't going to hurt us," Travis said and motioned for them to lower their weapons.

Gladius grimaced and lowered her blade.

"I just want my friend back, okay? And Evelyn was my ticket to her."

Travis walked closer to Jackie. "I know what it's like to lose someone close to you, and I'd do anything to get them back as well. But you're fighting the wrong people. We can help you. Do you think Evelyn is going to be so careless next time she sees you? If she chooses, she will end all of you, before any of you know what happened. But there is a way out of this, a way where we all win. You help us get to our friend, and we'll ask her to help you."

Jackie lowered her hand. "You think she would help us after what I just did to her?"

"If the cause is noble, she would."

Jackie shook her head and looked at the ground. "I just tried to trade her away. What makes you think she'd help me now?"

"Because she's a child. Even with all that power, she's only amassed experiences for not much more than a year. She hasn't been beaten down with distrust and hate like the rest of us. She still finds good in people, for now."

Gladius resisted a smirk. Her few encounters with Evelyn didn't seem like they were dealing with a naïve child, but a mastermind and manipulator. Her dad was good.

"Fine, but I'm going with you. She's going to need a reverse stone." Jackie held a stone out.

"Okay. It's just me and you," Travis said.

"You can't trust her, Dad. She's already proven that," Gladius said.

"I can handle this, Gladius."

Jackie sneered at her and stuffed the stone in her pocket. "He's your *dad*?" She swung her attention to Travis. "What, were you getting busy at ten years old?"

Travis squared his shoulders and spoke in an authoritative voice. "The deal is, Jackie, I want the rest of your friends to help my team in stopping the invasion."

She laughed. "You think it's stoppable? The reclamation has been fine-tuned, to where the best you can hope for is to slow it down. Everything she has created is a damned model of efficiency."

"We have something that can end it, we believe," Travis said.

"You going to use your bomb?" she asked, pointing to Harris. "Whatever. You guys help them out," Jackie said to Kylie, Wes, and David.

"We'll do what it takes to stop this."

"God, I hope so. I'm so tired," Jackie said and looked at the ceiling. Gladius thought she spotted tears welling in her eyes. "All of this fighting and running . . . That little girl gave me some hope, hope there could be an end to all of this. I'm sorry I tried to use her."

"If you hurt her. . . ." Gladius warned.

"She should be okay, we just have to find her," Jackie said. "Just me and you?" She looked to Travis.

"Yes."

Jackie faced David, then Wes. "Show them the production center. If we ever had the means to take out one camp, that'd be the one."

"Thank you," Travis said.

"I don't want you going alone with her," Gladius said.

"Don't worry, I'll be fine. I'll get Evelyn and be right back."

Gladius's lips thinned and she felt Hank's hand on her shoulder. She knew her dad could usually handle himself, but he had a soft spot for the female species, and she hoped this black widow wasn't spinning a web to trap him in. These purge people had strange powers; who knew how far they went.

She watched her dad walk off with Jackie in close conversation, before they disappeared using one of those portal stone things. Gladius huffed at his quick departure, without so much as a goodbye.

Gladius turned to face Kylie, who seemed stunned by Jackie's quick appearance and disappearance. "So, take us to this place she mentioned."

Kylie tugged on her braid. "But it's on a planet where the dead walk and no one would ever go there."

"Don't even say it," Hank said.

"You know the planet?"

"Are you talking about Ryjack?" Gladius said. She'd heard of it from Hank, but he refused to show her these abominations of humankind.

"Yes. Isn't that the most peculiar name for an Earth?" Kylie said.

"So you're saying the most damage we can cause to this invasion is to stop this base of operations on Ryjack?" Harris asked.

"Besides getting rid of the queen herself, yes. She keeps her production center off of this earth, *to keep it clean*, as she says."

"Okay, when can we leave?" Harris said.

"Now, I guess." Kylie shrugged.

They paired up once again, with Gladius sticking close to Hank. She demanded to be transported with him. Once again, Gladius felt the portal stone soak into her. The world swirled around and the sensation of falling lasted until their feet firmed.

"World portal's right over here," Kylie said and let go of their hands.

Gladius spotted the Alius stone, learning that their purple stone could only travel within the world they were in. That's why they still had to use the Alius stones. She walked with Hank, keeping an eye on the surrounding forest. Something didn't feel right, almost as if someone was watching. She gripped a knife and spotted Harris tapping his gun.

"You guys ready?" Wes said kneeling next to the stone.

"Hold on," Harris said. "Somethings coming."

"We've got to go," Wes said and put his hand on the stone.

Harris had his gun out in a split second. "You put your other hand on that stone, and I'll blow it off."

"Wes, get us out of here," Kylie said. "A freaking drone's coming. Harris, if you don't let him put in the code, we're all dead."

A buzzing sound grew and Gladius looked up into the sky, past the tree canopy. A black cube, much smaller than the ones on Earth, hovered above.

"Crap, it's spotted us. She'll be here any second," Wes said. "I'm putting in the code."

Harris looked to the sky and nodded.

The stone hummed and a gust of wind blew by them. A woman appeared in the forest. She stared at Gladius and she felt pressure in her mind. Gladius screamed and grabbed at the sides of her head, begging for it to end. So many memories flooded through her.

She kept screaming and felt Hank grabbing her and shaking her. "You've got to stop screaming," he said. "They're going to hear you."

Gladius opened her eyes and lowered her hands. Another forest, in another world.

"Too late, here they come," Kylie said, holding multiple stones in her hand. A group of grinners stumbled toward them.

Gladius fumbled for her knives and got three blades in her hand. The sickening groan and the foul, black mouths made her want to throw up.

Kylie threw a stone and it hit the chest of the first grinner nearing the circle. It bounced off its chest and cracked open like an egg. A cloud formed around the group of grinners and each one fell to the ground in a heap of ashes.

"What the . . .?" Gladius had the horrible realization these people could have easily killed every one of them, at any given time.

"Jackie invented that one," Kylie said and smiled.

"How do you make them? I want one," Gladius said looking down at her knives. She touched the sides of her head. "Who was that woman back there? She got into my head."

"That was her, the queen," David said in disgust. "And now she knows we're with you."

"Guess that means I just lost my corporate job," Wes said. "And I was *this* close to a promotion." He pinched his fingers close together.

"Shut up," Kylie said. "Did she find out where we were going?"

"I don't think so. She was just pulling out my history—who I am. I think she wanted to hurt me."

"She only wants one thing," Kylie said.

Bushes rustled in the forest and more grinners appeared.

"How far to the base from here?" Harris asked.

"Not far, when you have a portal stone," Kylie said and held up a purple stone. "You ready?"

They portaled and freezing air hit Gladius like a slap on the face. Wind blew past her, and a humming sound roared all around them. Kylie rushed and huddled up with Wes and David. Hank held her, and Gladius cursed for trusting these people once again. In the darkness, she still spotted them, they looked like they were going to jump. They were going to leave them there and let them freeze to death.

The cold seeped into her throat and body with each breath. Her thin shirt and pants clung to her body. She outstretched her fingers and wanted to throw her blade into the heart of Kylie. She could probably take her dead body and get a few minutes of warmth.

Then a glow appeared around the three of them. It dangled in the air and grew. Soon, Gladius backed away from its brilliance. She'd never seen such a terrifying and beautiful object in all her time. She was sure the glow was going to kill her. Kylie, Wes, and David approached. She didn't think she could do anything to stop them.

CHAPTER 14

FAR FROM THE DOME AND the collapsed dreams of humanity's hope, Poly leaned her head against the SUV's window. If she watched long enough, she'd spot a black cube flying across the sky.

Lucas drove down the dirt road, with Julie and Will in the front. Derek sat next to Poly in the back. She glanced at his bandaged stump. She didn't think she'd ever get over cutting his arm off.

At least they didn't have to walk. Evelyn had planned out a few cars in case of this very escape. Poly was proud of her little girl, but she hadn't heard from her, and had no idea where she was. The worry of it wrenched at her gut, and made her silently gaze at the passing desert.

"We should warn people," Julie said. "If there is a way we can even save one city, we have to try."

"How long until these things start grabbing us?" Lucas asked.

"Evelyn told me of their progression," Derek spoke up. "They set up their reclaiming towers first, then they start the snatch and grab."

Poly felt her Panavice vibrate in her pocket. She yanked it out and hoped to see Evelyn's number, but the ID wasn't familiar. She pressed the button and heard a familiar voice through the speaker.

"I don't know if it's working," Trip said, then a clatter of noise, as if he'd dropped it.

"You're doing it wrong. There's a connect button," Gretchen said.

"I hear you," Poly said.

"You hear that?" Trip asked.

"Hear what?" Samantha's mom replied. "Did you call her?"

"I don't know. It says ping, connect, nudge, and some other crap I don't know how to pronounce," Trip said.

"Here, give it to me."

"No, let me just look at it again. I think I found her."

"Guys?" Poly said.

"Just hit the connect button."

"I did, I think it's ringing."

"Trip, can you hear me?"

"Hey, Poly, how did you know it was me?"

"Caller ID. You guys seen Evelyn?" Poly asked.

"No, but the lot of you just went to the purge people's world."

"Hank and Gladius?"

"Yep, with Travis and Harris. We caught one of them bastards at the portal stone. Where you guys at, out saving the world I assume?"

"We failed."

A pause. "Yeah, we've been hearing them on the hammy.

Every major city seems to have one of them towers now."

Julie looked over her shoulder. "He has a ham radio?"

"Sure do. Knew something like this would eventually happen. These portal stones are like keeping the front door open with a welcome mat; anybody can come on in and take your stuff."

"What's your broadcast power?" Julie asked.

"One and a half kilowatts. Though, I don't have the license for that much juice. But being what things are these days—"

"Trip, we're coming to you," Julie said.

"Good, I've got supplies and guns. We can take it to these bastards," he said.

"We can't do much, but maybe we can save a few."

"POLY," TRIP YELLED AND JOGGED up to her as she exited the vehicle.

She couldn't help but smile as he wrapped her up in a big hug and shook her. "Hey, Trip. Good to see you guys."

"Where's Evelyn?"

"I don't know." Her stomach plunged.

He frowned and set her back on the ground. "We'll get through this. If we can take out Marcus, we can handle some flying blocks."

"I think Julie has a plan."

She did and they all went into Trip's strange, caged room and discussed the idea.

"Let me get this right," Trip said, pointing at his wall of ham radio equipment. "You can hook up your boy to my radio, and transmit a signal to be picked up by these things Marcus implanted into the world's population?"

"Yeah, basically," Julie said with her hands on her hips.

"I'm not some hundred kilowatt broadcasting tower here, we aren't talking about reaching the whole world, or even the whole nation."

"I know, but if this can reach anyone, we have to try," Julie said.

Poly looked at her Panavice, trying to force a text from Evelyn.

"Great, let's do it," Trip said and went to turning dials and flipping switches. "What's the frequency?"

"My Panavice will take over the controls," Julie said. "It's not a normal kind of radio frequency. I went through Evelyn's notes on the structure she built, and I think we can achieve something similar here."

The house rumbled and they all looked to the ceiling.

"Another one of those buggers. A guy in Tallahassee and another in Minnesota said they saw them spawn a tower, sucking in everything around in a matter of minutes."

Poly knew the towers well. She shook her head at the thought of Hector. What a crap deal he got. They freed him from one hell, only for him to experience it all over again.

Julie spent the next ten minutes setting up Trip's equipment, and attaching several electrical leads from her Panavice to Will's head. Lucas paced nearby and didn't look happy.

"You sure about this?" he asked.

"No, but what choice do we have?"

Lucas tossed up his arms and then pointed in the direction of the Alius stone. "We have a freaking ticket out of this place."

"Would you stop talking about that?" Julie said.

"Fine, but if this doesn't work. We're gone."

Julie made eyes at Poly, then grunted and got back to work. She set up the last lead on Will's head as he swiveled on Trip's office chair, smiling.

"Don't worry. I'll save them," Will said.

"You know what to do, right?" Julie asked.

"Yes."

The radio crackled and a panicked voice came across. "Something's happening. Green lights are glowing on the tower and the cubes are flooding out. You there, Trip?"

"Got a low wattage for a backup," Trip explained, as he rushed to the radio on the other side of the room. "Yeah, buddy, I got you. What's going on?"

"They're pulling people into those cubes. Their sucking them in. Hundreds of them!"

"Now," Julie said, and Will nodded. He closed his eyes and Julie pressed a button on her Panavice.

Will sucked in a deep breath and his eyes went wide. Lucas ran to him, but he held up a hand, telling him to stop. "So many. . . ."

"Buddy, you there?" Trip said.

"I reached him," Will said. "I'm . . ." he paused for a few seconds, "connecting with them."

The house shook again, but this time, it didn't stop. Poly looked at the ceiling and then to Julie.

"Those things read our thoughts, we have to run away from Will. They'll tear this house apart. Go!" Julie yelled.

Poly ran out the door, across the family room, and into the front yard. She spotted the cube, hovering high above the house.

"Lay on the ground and blank out. Think of nothing," Julie instructed, before falling to the ground. A glazed looked came over her eyes.

Lucas did the same and Gretchen followed suit.

Poly laid down, but all she thought of was Evelyn. She slammed her eyes shut. *Blank. Blank out. Come on.* The ground below her fell away, and for a brief second, she thought she'd entered a state of total disconnect; then she opened her eyes and realized she'd floated a few feet above the ground. Rotating, she faced the black cube pulling her in.

The soft humming sound, along with the wind blowing through the trees, made a peaceful setting. Before Joey's death, she might have screamed and fought to get away. But what was the point? The thing had her.

"Like hell," Trip bellowed.

She turned and saw him standing on the porch, holding a shoulder-mounted rocket launcher. He fired and the missile shot toward the cube. She watched it fly by and strike the cube in the sky. The thin shell shattered, falling to the earth in pieces. She struck the dirt driveway hard.

Julie jumped up and ran to her. "You okay?"

"Where the hell did you get that bazooka?" Lucas asked Trip.

He laughed. "When the world collapses from a deadly contagion, things go unnoticed from certain stockpiles."

"You crafty dog. What else you got stored up in there?" Lucas pointed to the house.

Julie leaned closer to Poly and examined her body.

"I'm fine," Poly assured.

"I don't think we're safe here," Julie said as another chunk hit the ground.

Poly saw three cubes descending upon them, and had to agree.

CHAPTER 15

TRAVIS WALKED BEHIND JACKIE. THE woman had to have known of the sword at his side, the gun on his other side, and even the various blades around his body. Yet, Jackie walked with such confidence that Travis suspected the woman either had no fear, or was foolish—both dangerous attributes. He'd ride the middle until he found out. "So, have you asked the queen where your best friend is?"

"You think she'll just turn her over to me?" Jackie laughed. "The only thing I ever got from her was that she was keeping them safe until the next phase of existence."

"What does that mean?"

Jackie sighed. "I don't feel like explaining our entire history. Why don't you just keep leading me toward her?"

Travis looked down at the screen and pointed ahead. Evelyn hadn't moved since he first got the message. As much as she bothered Travis, she felt like another daughter to him. If this Jackie girl hurt Evelyn in any kind of permanent way. . . .

"How much further?" Jackie asked.

"Just keep walking."

"Are you going to tell me who that girl back there *really* was? A sister?"

"She is my daughter," Travis said.

"Oh come on, you're like the same age as her."

"Not quite. I'm over four hundred years old."

Jackie stopped and turned around. "Shut your mouth."

Travis enjoyed shocking her, but he wouldn't go into details. "How long's your friend been missing?"

Jackie turned around and started walking again. "A few years now. There's a chance her mom killed her and is lying to me, but I just have this gut feeling she's out there, waiting for me to find her. You ever get that feeling?"

"Yes."

They walked next to a running creak, stomping down a path through the tall grass.

"What makes this girl so special?" Jackie asked. "I mean, how is she the way she is? Did she . . . take something, or use something?"

Travis frowned. He disliked people not getting to the point. "She has two amazing parents. She was born the way she is. Is there any other way?" He knew Vanar far exceeded Jackie's world in technology, but they had these stones.

"In this world, there's always another way."

Travis watched her as she walked. She had some grace when she let some of her walls down. He liked a woman with walls; fun to climb them. But this woman seemed to have more barriers in place than most. She would grab at the stone sack on her hip when she caught herself relaxing, tensing up and looking around in a rush.

"Those stones are a very interesting tech. You guys make them yourself?"

"They are our curse."

"Can anyone use them?"

"Perhaps, but making them is the tough part. Rubes like you could mix up ingredients until the end of time and never make what we can."

"And you used one of these stones on Evelyn?"

"Yeah, just a paralysis stone. She'll be fine."

Travis stared at the screen. Evelyn's location sat about a hundred feet behind them. He even spotted some fallen grass and a rock outcropping she'd probably hid in. "That's far enough," he said.

Jackie scanned the surrounding area. "I don't see her."

This is the part he was dreading. "Why don't you tell me your end game?"

Jackie's eyes narrowed. "Is she even out here?"

"She is, but I can't just let you near her again. You tried to trade her off already. As you said, it sucks to lose someone close." Travis clicked his shield on.

"I told you, I don't want to hurt her."

"No, you just want to trade her to someone who *will* hurt her."

"I don't know what the queen wants with her."

"Yes, you do."

"This is stupid. Let's just get to Evelyn. She needs this stone." Jackie held a milky stone up.

Travis studied the stone in her hand. He'd figured there'd be something to counteract the effects of whatever this woman did to Evelyn. "You know as well as I do, Evelyn is probably the only person in the worlds who can stop your queen.”

“She's not my queen,” Jackie said with gritted teeth.

“What if I told you, Evelyn is in the process of procuring exactly what you are looking for?”

Jackie's eyes went wide. “What do you mean?”

“She is getting the very thing you want.”

“I don't believe you. How would she even know?”

“You very nearly ended the one person who can finish the job. Evelyn was in the queen's mind. She knows things, she's seen things.”

Jackie paced near the water.

Travis spun around when he heard a noise, and saw Evelyn stumble into the creek. She staggered forward and Travis brought out his gun and pointed it at Jackie. “What's wrong with her?” he asked, splitting his attention between Jackie and Evelyn.

Jackie sputtered. “I—it's impossible. She should be unconscious. In a coma. No one can get out of that stone.”

“She's not just anyone.”

Evelyn took another step, glaring at Jackie before her eyes rolled back and she fell face first into the water.

Travis ran to Evelyn and pulled her from the creek. She felt cold and stiff, and briefly, he thought she'd died. He brushed back her wet hair. “Evelyn?” He gave her a light shake and touched her cheek. “Evelyn, you there?” She didn't respond and he adjusted her limp body in his arms.

“Here,” Jackie walked up and held out a green stone with white streaks. “This should help her.”

“This is different than the first one you showed me.”

She sighed. “Noticed that, eh? I changed my mind. If there is a chance she can help, I have to take it.”

Travis nodded. “You know what I'll have to do if you hurt her?”

"You could try." Jackie rolled her eyes. She placed the stone on Evelyn's hand and it dissolved into her skin.

Evelyn moved; small motions with her limbs at first, and then she lunged out of Travis's arms, knocking down Jackie.

Seeing her well, sent Travis into elation. He had his doubts about Jackie, but he knew in the end, she'd have to choose her path.

"How could you use such a stone on me?" Evelyn asked, grabbing at Jackie's throat. "That was an *eternity* for someone like me."

"I'm sorry." Jackie pushed her arms away and backed up.

Travis watched Evelyn disappear right in front of him. He wasn't sure where she went, until Jackie screamed and fell to the ground.

Evelyn appeared, standing behind her, fist clenched and breathing hard. "I trusted her and she did that to me. Touched me with her stupid stone."

"What did you do to her?" Travis rushed to Jackie's lifeless body.

"I put it in her mind that she needed to lay down and not move. I want her to feel what she did to me, only it would take years for her to feel the way I did."

Travis put his ear next to Jackie's mouth and felt a faint breath blowing. Her eyes remained open and unblinking. He set her on the thick grass and looked over to Evelyn. She glared at Jackie. "I don't agree with what she did to you, I don't. But we can't just retaliate against people. She wasn't attacking you. You weren't in danger."

"She's strong, Travis. I don't think you realize it, but she could have hurt us both. She already tried to hurt me once. Why would I take a chance on her?"

"I believe she was going to help us."

"I could have killed her like nothing, if I wanted." Evelyn

snapped her fingers. "Nothing more than stepping on an ant. But I didn't do it because of you, Travis. I knew you'd disapprove."

"People can make mistakes, then learn from those mistakes."

"And do you feel Harris has learned from his mistakes?" Evelyn asked.

It stung, and Travis winced at the reminder of his history with the man. "That's different. Harris hurt my family, time and time again."

"Starting with Maya?"

Travis stood and from that height, Evelyn looked like one of his little girls—Compry maybe—but her eyes held so much intelligence, the little girl persona felt like a lie. "Yes, it started with Maya, and ended with Compry. Your mom is the only reason Harris is still alive today."

"Oh yes, the famous duel. The one I know of through tales told by the Six. Yet almost nothing remains of your past when I dig. Harris's virus wiped everything off the servers."

"You could ask me."

"People tend to embellish, manipulate, project, and outright lie when it comes to telling of their past. Their minds are polluted with partial truths and self-delusions. I find if I gather enough information from many points of view, I can come to a general consensus of truth. I haven't asked you because I don't want a slanted story."

"You speak as if you're not human yourself. Stories people tell are just that, stories. If you want to hear my side of the story, you only have to ask."

Evelyn stretched out her fingers and looked down at Jackie laying in the grass. "Another time, perhaps."

Jackie hadn't moved and Travis wondered what they should do with her body. He looked around and in the distance, he saw a car driving down the road. They weren't too far from civilization, but who knew where the nearest Alius stone was.

"She probably has more of those portal stones," Evelyn said and pulled Jackie's sack from her waist. She opened the bag and looked at its contents. "I see a purple one." She took Jackie's glove off and put it on her own hand. Then she pulled the purple stone from the sack and held it up in the sky.

"You think it's safe to use that thing?" Travis asked.

"One way to find out, put your hand next to Jackie's."

Travis didn't like it, but he kneeled and placed his hand next to hers.

Evelyn did the same with her bare hand. "Here we go."

CHAPTER 16

COLDNESS SEEPED INTO HIS FINGERS, and with each breath, Harris felt a pain shoot through his lungs. An orange light came from the three purge people gathered in a tight circle. The light came from a small orb, dangling from a string that Kylie held. The purge trio opened their circle and motioned for the other three to come over.

Harris felt the warmth from the orb, like an inviting embrace. He staggered toward the group, with Hank and Gladius following close behind. Each step brought more warmth, and its glow warmed him from the inside as well. He felt as if some of the miles and centuries of weight that'd piled on him through his life were lifted off.

What is this magic?

He slapped his face and the pain sent some of the warm fuzziness away, renewing the weight slumped on his shoulders.

He pictured his first wife, and then flashes appeared of her being killed in the basement of MM's bunker. He should have never brought her there, but she knew the systems better than anyone in the world. Without her, they would have never gotten past the first door.

The orb moved and he moved with it. They all were guided by its glow. It swayed with Kylie as she walked. The purge people spoke, but the wind and cold just outside of the orbs power, threatened to overtake them. He just needed to stick close. It felt good to look at it. He wanted to get lost in its softness and heat.

He slapped his face again.

They walked past trees with frost for leaves, and the wind pushed against them, sending chunks of ice to pelt their skin. The thick trees thinned out to nothing, and they crossed a frozen field. The orb beckoned them to continue and Harris gazed at it more than anything.

Before too long, Kylie stepped onto a wooden porch of a house and opened the front door. She entered the house, and Harris lost sight of the stone. He blinked and shook his head.

"Gladius, Hank, you guys all right?"

They didn't answer, and walked into the house.

"They'll be fine. That stone just has an effect on people. That's why we use it in three's," David said. "Come in and we can plan our attack."

Harris nodded, gun in hand.

The house wasn't more than a hunter's shack. The main room had a small pot belly stove with a skillet on top. The only door in the room led to a bathroom, he suspected. The six people made for a cramped space, and the orange glow from the stone heated the whole room. He averted his eyes from the light.

"Just don't look at it for too long. It . . . makes you feel things," Kylie said and covered the stone.

Hank and Gladius took a step back, then hugged each other. Harris looked away from the affection and stared out into the darkness beyond.

"We're in Siberia," Kylie explained. "Those dead things won't make it in the cold, and the queen thought this planet held potential not to be found by travelers."

"Travelers?"

"Sure, people who use the portal stones."

"You've met others?"

"I haven't, but the queen alluded to it. She said there would be people who'd pop in and out of worlds, looking for something, but she wasn't sure what. That's why she liked this planet. On the surface, it appeared ruined. No one would look in Siberia on a dead planet."

"You didn't create these Alius stones, did you?" Harris said.

"The travel stones? No, but the queen found them shortly after her," Kylie cleared her throat, "transformation."

Harris turned away from the window to face Kylie, and set his bag on the floor. "The queen saw us, right before we jumped. She might follow us here."

"If she had, you'd be dead already."

"If she is this god-like person, why hasn't she killed you yet? Why are you spared?" Harris asked.

Kylie looked to David and Wes. "We don't know exactly. Maybe it's because we were friends with her daughter. But I think she wants to keep us around, like cattle—a last resort to finish her final transformation."

These people showed a power he didn't know possible. It made him think of Hank and the rest of the Six. When they'd first met Harris, he'd come to them as a magician of sorts. He'd impressed them with Vanar tech and wowed them with simple tricks they didn't understand. Was he like them now?

When Harris didn't speak, Gladius stepped forward. "You help us bring an end to this invasion, and we'll help you bring an end to the queen."

"How can you help us?" Kylie asked.

"Please, we have tech way more advanced than you," Gladius said. "There will be a time, soon, where Evelyn comes after the queen. And believe me, she will end her reign."

"You don't know what you're talking about, but I want to believe you," Kylie said, as David huffed.

"You brought us here to put a pinch on the invasion," Harris said. "I take it this production facility is close?"

"Yes, very."

"And how do we get there?"

"We'll have to walk."

"Then what are we waiting on? You just get me close and I can set this up."

"What's in the bag?" Kylie asked.

"The end of whatever is here. But once I set this, we won't have long to leave." Harris went back to the window and watched the wind stir up the snow. He squinted at a motion outside. He could have sworn a man had walked by. "Who knows we're here?" He pulled out a gun and hoped his cold fingers worked well enough.

"No one," Kylie answered.

"I just saw something moving out there."

"Probably just a tree."

"If Harris said he saw something, he saw something," Gladius said. She took out her dagger, and Hank grabbed the iron poker leaning against the pot belly stove.

Harris backed away from the window and turned sideways, to give him a line of sight from the front door to the window.

A knock at the front door made Kylie jump and grab at her chest.

"Who the hell is that?" Wes asked. "They find us?"

"No way. Impossible," Kylie said.

Another knock.

"Open the door," Harris said and held his gun out.

Kylie walked to the door and turned the handle. The wind blew the door open and snow swirled around a large man.

"This cabin is off limits," he said. "What are you all doing here?"

Harris fired a single shot and struck the man in the neck. He grabbed at the wound, dropping the stone from his hand to the floor. He gargled, the blood filling his throat, and fell to the floor as Kylie screamed.

CHAPTER 17

LUCAS LOOKED AT THE THREE cubes hovering over them. Another missile streaked by, striking the closest cube. It exploded into pieces and took out the one next to it. "Get out of the way!" Lucas yelled and ran to his wife.

Julie pulled Poly up, as Lucas made his way to them. He grabbed Julie's hand and pulled them away from the falling debris. The loud hum of the remaining cube kicked in and he felt the pull from it just as they made it to the porch.

"Tell me you have another?" Lucas pointed to Trip's rocket launcher.

"I didn't think I'd need more than two . . . that was the last one."

The sound grew, as much of the falling debris started to move toward the remaining cube. Lucas winced and looked to Julie. She held onto his hand and slid along the porch until she hit the railing. Poly fell to the ground and grabbed onto a post.

Gretchen screamed and fell to the porch floor.

"We've got to blank out again," Julie yelled over the loud drone. "It's the only way."

He closed his eyes and tried to think of nothing, but the sound deafened his attempts. The thing pulled on him harder. He tried again. This time, he went to a place of blackness in his mind, ignoring everything around him, until Poly screamed.

He opened his eyes and rushed to Poly, grabbing her floating body. He wouldn't let another one of his friends die.

"Let her go, Dad."

Lucas spun around and spotted Will standing at the door. Wires dangled from his head, and he glared up at the cube.

"Son?" Lucas lifted off the ground.

"I'm going to get into your minds and stop this." Will put his hands on his head and closed his eyes. In a few seconds, Poly fell to the ground, along with Gretchen and Trip.

Lucas pedaled his legs, trying to get back to the earth.

Will opened his eyes with a look of terror. "I can't reach you, Dad!"

Julie jumped to her feet. "Lucas, let Will in your mind."

Lucas looked down at them, now more than ten feet below. The sound of the cube allowed for little other sounds, but he'd heard Julie. He didn't know what it meant, but he tried to clear his mind. It wasn't working. Fear flooded his thoughts. He was going to die and nothing was going to stop it.

Will held his hands over his head again and stared at Lucas, but he didn't feel anything. "I'm sorry," Will yelled. "I can't get into your head."

"No, this can't be happening." Lucas pulled at the air and did every motion, in an attempt to get back to Julie and her extended arms. Tears fell, and he saw her mouth moving, but he'd gone beyond the point of hearing them.

Please, don't let my wife and son see me die. Not like this.

He mouthed the words *I love you* to Julie and Will, and tried to put on a brave face.

She jumped up and down with Poly and the rest, screaming and erratically waving at him. He hated what their last images of him would be.

Not able to watch Julie and his friends in such pain, he turned to face the cube. He found some peace in knowing Will had found a way to protect them from these cube things. But why had it not worked on him?

It didn't matter now. He'd face this fate like he had to face Alice, or Emmett, or Zach; he'd find a way to deal with it.

The cube opened and pulled him into a small black room. When the door closed, the sound stopped and it pressed him against the floor like a magnet might grab onto metal. Lucas felt the metallic floor and smelled the air, a mixture of smoke and ozone. He scratched the floor, and yelled at the horrible machine.

A ball fell from the ceiling and broke open as it landed on the floor; white smoke bellowed out. He couldn't see the walls, or even his own hand, as the thick smoke encased the room. It burned as he finally took a breath, and he felt woozy. The cube's grip never took full hold over him. He rolled to his stomach and tried to stay as low as possible.

Another breath, and the whole cube felt as if it was spinning. He lifted off the floor, floating in the air, as if weightless. Then he slammed against the floor. Groaning, Lucas rolled to his back, clutching his side. He felt his ribs, and a fresh jolt of pain hit him as he grazed them.

The room came into focus as the mist left. With pain, Lucas got to a kneeling position. Prudence had fallen off him in all the chaos and he picked her up, nocking an arrow onto the string. With sheer will, he got to his feet and held out his bow. His eyes burned from the mist, and each breath sent pain into his lungs.

The wall he leaned against opened, and he fell out, unable to grab Prudence in time. The door closed, leaving Prudence within. Smashing his head on his rapid descent, Lucas blacked out.

SUCKING IN A DEEP BREATH, Lucas jolted awake. Struggling to move, and fighting off a headache, he looked down and saw he was strapped to a concrete bed. He pulled at the straps, but still felt the effects of the mist weighing on his every motion. After a bit, he gave in and looked around.

He knew this room. A spitting image of the room that'd held Edith. Concrete walls and floors, with a tube right behind his head.

A clanking sound, as if something was falling down the tube, drew his attention. He tried to crane his head back to see what was coming. He looked up into it and the sound grew louder, closer. Another small stone rolled out of the tube and before Lucas could react, it struck him in the face.

The stone bounced off his face and onto the floor. What had been the purpose of that?

The straps lifted off of him and Lucas sprung to his feet. The stone rolled to a stop on the floor. He reached down and picked it up, holding it up to the light. *Was it supposed to do something?*

A speaker crackled and a woman's voice came across. "Leave your room and head down the hall."

Lucas had heard this before on Hector's world, even the same voice. Edith had emerged from the room right after the announcement. He put the stone in his pocket and headed for the door. A man walked by wearing a military uniform. Lucas stepped into the hall behind the man.

"Hey," Lucas called, but the man kept walking.

A woman bumped into his back and walked around him, heading down the hall.

The voice spoke through the speakers again. "Go to the end of the hall and through the double doors when it's your turn."

Lucas spotted the first person in line, walking through a pair of swinging double doors.

"Stop, don't go in there." He ran past several people, bumping into them to get to the front. He'd seen all this before, but Evelyn wasn't here to stop any of them from their trance.

A man wearing a loose robe disappeared behind the doors, and a woman in a black suit stood at the door, waiting her turn.

"You guys have got to get out of here," Lucas said, but none of them listened. He looked down the line, there must have been over thirty people.

"Next," the voice over the speaker said.

"No," Lucas pulled on the woman, but she slipped through his grip and entered the room.

The same egg-shaped coffin sat in the middle of the room.

"Climb into the container and touch the two stones inside," the voice instructed.

The woman climbed into it. The door over her closed, and a few seconds later, a bright light shot from the cracks.

Lucas grabbed a chair and stuffed it into the door handles of the swing door. He heard the voice commanding the next person to enter, and the door shook as the person struggled to get in. He looked around the room, trying to find something to help him; something to get these people out of there.

A ball struck his neck and he grabbed at it. Turning, he

spotted the man who threw it. It bounced on the floor, and the man followed it, confusion spreading over his face.

"How in the hell?"

"You need to stop this," Lucas ordered. "You can't do this to these people."

"You can't be in here. You should be in line."

"You're not hearing me, man. Stop the zombie line, *now*," Lucas said.

The guy reeled back and threw another stone. Lucas caught it midair, and looked at the black, smooth stone with red lines running around it.

The man stumbled back in shock, bouncing his gaze from Lucas's hand to his face. "Who are you?"

"I'm Lucas, of the Preston Six. I'm here to kick your ass."

CHAPTER 18

THE GLOWING ROCKS PRODUCED LIGHT, but they also produced heat. An intense heat. The freaking place felt like an oven. Kris wiped his brow with his sweaty arm and then went back to holding his broken arm.

The pain wasn't as sharp as before, and after a couple of hours at the bottom of the pit, his arm felt numb. His fingers tingled, and the area where his arm broke had become reddish. Or maybe it was just from the rocks Maggie was heating up to create hand and footholds in the pit wall.

"You've got to stop for a while," Kris yelled up to her. "We're going to cook in here."

Molten rock fell from the hole she worked on. It struck the damp floor and hissed, sending up steam.

"We should have tossed stuff into this hole," Char said, looking up at the door.

Kris had expected help from the outside. Lupe should have heard their cries for help, but nothing had come through the door since they did. He wondered if it had been blocked, or maybe the door's magic stopped them from getting near it. This puzzle, this maze, would be the last thing between them and freedom from another dictator. If they could only reach the next door.

"We need to get to that door," Kris said. He rushed to the wall where Maggie had melted out a few footholds. He held his hand close to the wall in the diminished light, and felt the heat still radiating.

The light dimmed to a soft glow, covering a small radius around the last bits of red on the rocks on the ground. He watched it, transfixed by the visible steam coming off them. Why were they steaming so much?

He moved closer and touched the floor. He had taken it as solid rock, but as he glided his fingers over the damp surface, the water went right back into the spot he dried. "There's water under us," Kris said as he laid down. He put his ear on the rocky floor and closed his eyes. A drip sound, like a drop of water falling into a large body of water.

Char looked at him like he was crazy. "What are you—"

"Shh," Kris said and held out his good arm. He heard another drip. "There's something under this. A body of water, maybe?"

"We aren't far from the ocean, so it wouldn't be too out of the question for the water table to be close," Maggie said. "So what do we do? Having water under the floor isn't exactly going to help us."

She was right. Kris took a deep breath and carefully got to his feet, grimacing with each move. Then an idea struck him. "The water could cool things down for us."

"What do you mean?" Char asked.

"What's holding us back from climbing up through the footholds Maggie's creating?"

"The heat."

"Right. But with water, we can cool each of the holds down in an instant. We can then use Maggie's ladder to get to the next door."

"Even if it works," Maggie said. "We don't know what the next door will hold."

"We're going to die down here if we don't find out, and I'd rather be trying to live than waiting to die." He couldn't see any of their faces in the blackness, but he knew they were coming around to his side of things. "Now, how to get the water out of the floor?"

"May I?" Maggie's hands glowed red, revealing her furrowed brow.

"By all means."

She knelt down and slammed her fists into the rocky floor. Kris moved closer. Her knuckles dug into the stone, like she was pushing them into dough. After a few minutes, she had submerged her arms all the way to her elbows. Then the glow went out and the darkness returned.

"I hit it," Maggie said. The glow returned as she pulled her arms from the holes.

Water seeped out of the holes and created a large puddle. They moved back as the water filled the bottom of the hole to a depth of several inches.

"Keep the lights on. Let's see how far it'll rise." Kris stared at a rock sitting half in and half out of the water, maybe a few inches deep. After a minute, the water didn't move. "Okay, I think that's all it's got. Maggie, let's build that ladder."

She trudged across the water and reached the flat wall below the next door. She looked up at it, then climbed up the few holes she'd already made. Shoving her hand into the wall a few feet above, she started on the next spot.

"Good, Maggie, keep going," Kris said. "Come on, Char, let's get her the water." Kris pulled off his shirt and soaked it in the water. He tossed the shirt up, and she stuffed it into the hole. It hissed and steamed. "Not too long, it'll burn," Kris said.

Maggie dropped the shirt back down to him. Once he soaked it again, he tossed it back up. By the third toss, the hole had cooled down enough. Maggie climbed up and started the next hole.

Over the next hour, Maggie was on a mission, and had made her way up over three-fourths of the shaft.

"Take a break," Kris yelled up to Maggie.

"I don't need one. I'm almost done. Just throw me the shirt."

Kris watched as Char bundled the dripping, tattered shirt around a rock. Kris could have tossed it to Maggie, but the process gave Char a task. He needed something to do, to keep from pacing below, expecting to have to catch her at any moment.

Char tossed the shirt up and Maggie caught it. She stuffed it into the hole she'd created and before the shirt burned, she dropped it back down into the water. Char retrieved it and began the system again.

With Maggie's glow high above them now, the light at the bottom was dim at best. He used his good arm to feel his surroundings. The pain had grown in his broken arm, and the swelling made it feel twice the size. He suspected the bone might have sliced his insides and was bleeding.

"I'm at the door," Maggie called from above.

Kris jerked to attention and gazed up. The area around her glowed red from her one hand. "Don't touch it," he yelled.

Maggie pulled her hand back and looked down. "We need to figure out what this one does, if anything."

"Not you," Char said. "Come down and I'll be the first to touch it."

"Maybe we can just throw some stuff at it and see what happens?" Kris said, shocked that Char hadn't been the one to suggest it. "Maggie, move down a bit and I'll hit the door with a rock."

Maggie scaled down a few footholds and held out her glowing hand to give Kris enough light to see the door. He threw the rock and it struck his target, dead center. Bouncing off, it struck the opposite wall and came back to the bottom.

"You think it's just a regular door?" Char asked.

"I don't know. I doubt it," Kris said. "You hear or see anything weird from there, Maggie?"

She looked over the door. "Just the same kind of symbols the other doors had on them, and I didn't hear anything when the rock hit it."

Kris decided to test it a few more times, each time with the same result. It seemed to be a regular steel door.

Maggie came down and jumped the last few feet.

"I'm going up," Char said. "If anyone of us can handle the effects, it's me."

Kris and Maggie protested, but Char went up the wall, ignoring them.

"I don't like this," Maggie said and got closer to Kris.

He didn't like it either, but Char had a point; with his size and strength, he'd be the logical one to test the door.

"Careful," Maggie called up to her dad.

"Okay, here we go." Char raised his hand and slapped the steel a few times with his palm. "Seems normal."

"Can you open it?" Kris asked.

"There's a hole, I think I can reach it." Char climbed another rung and stretched out. Kris squinted as Char put his finger in the hole.

The door flung open and Char grabbed the wall to keep from falling. A single round rock fell from the opening. Char grabbed it midair and then threw it back through the door.

"Was that a rock?" Kris called out.

"I'm not sure. It was black and shiny. I didn't like the looks of it, so I threw—"

The room above exploded, and a gust of fire and smoke shot from the opening, hitting Char in the face and throwing him backward. His body slammed into the opposite wall and fell thirty feet, to the bottom of the pit, with a thud and a splash.

The front of his shirt had been blown off and his skin looked red and blistered. Blood trickled down his face, and into the water.

"Char," Kris said.

"Dad!" Maggie cried out.

He didn't respond.

Kris put his ear on his chest and heard his heart thumping. "He's alive."

"Dad, wake up." Maggie touched the sides of his face. "We need to get him out of here. He needs medicine."

Kris coughed at the burnt smell filling the hole. "We have to keep moving forward."

"What are you talking about? We are not leaving him here."

Kris knew this would be difficult for her to understand. "We grab what we came to get, and get out."

"Like you know how to do either of those things."

He stood up and met Maggie's glare and then back up to the open door at the top of the ladder. "You can stay here with him, while I check out the next room."

Char coughed, and blood colored his lips and chin. "I'm fine," he said, gurgling and coughing again. "You two get out of here, while I rest."

"Dad," Maggie said. "Where are you hurt?"

He chuckled. "My foot hurts." He grinned with blood on his teeth. "Now, get."

Maggie stood. "I love you, Dad."

"I love you too."

"We'll come right back for you."

Kris made his way to the bottom of the wall, under the door. With a broken arm, it was going to be a Herculean task getting up the wall. He gripped the handhold, and to his surprise, it fit perfectly. He reached up and grabbed the next, using his legs to push up. It didn't take him long to get near the top. His legs burned, but he gripped the bottom of the door opening and pulled himself up into the doorway.

Sliding along the floor, he got all the way in, then turned around to grab Maggie's elbow, careful not to touch her glowing hands. He pulled her the rest of the way into the small hall. She got up, and looked past Kris into the next room.

Kris turned and couldn't believe his eyes.

CHAPTER 19

HARRIS WAITED TO SEE IF any of the purge kids would react to his merciless killing of the man in cold blood. If they made a move, he'd beat them to it. But they all stood, stunned, staring at the dead person laying in the doorway.

The smell of gunsmoke dispersed quickly, with the cold air blowing in from the open door. "He was about to hit you with that stone in his hand," Harris explained, lowering his gun.

"You don't know that," Kylie said. "And you just *killed* him." She looked up at him with fear in her eyes.

Harris kept his gun at his side, and waited for one of the stone throwers to make their move. "Look at the stone he dropped. It rolled near the door there."

With her gloved hands, Kylie knelt down and picked it up. It was black, and she gasped, jumping back. "He was going to use that?" She looked to Wes and David.

"Orders are to kill anyone who comes out here," Wes said. "I didn't think we'd be found this soon. It won't be long before more come."

"Close the door," Gladius said, rubbing her arms.

Wes went to the door and pushed the man's head out of the way enough to close it. Some blood got on his feet. Kylie looked pale and placed a hand on the wall to steady herself. Wes went to comfort her, but she pushed him away.

Hank and Gladius had positioned themselves in the corner of the room, so their backs would never be to the others. Smart.

"I think we should go to this place now," Harris said.

Wes nodded and looked to David. "We all don't need to go. Kylie, you should take them."

"I know the way," Wes said. "I'll take them."

"It takes three of us to control the stone," Kylie said and motioned to the glowing orb.

"We're all going," Harris said.

Wes, David, and Kylie looked at each other, then grouped in a tight huddle and disappeared.

"Shit," Harris said. "I knew I should have killed them when I had the chance."

"You didn't exactly give them a reason to trust you," Gladius said. "You killed that guy right in front of them. Did you see the look on their faces?"

"I know, but *that guy* was going to kill us all. I saved them, and they knew it. I bet this was their game from the start. A plan to stick us here, in hopes we die."

"Maybe. But now what? We're stuck in this cabin. We can't go more than fifty feet outside, without becoming ice sculptures. And who knows if we are even near this supposed base?" Gladius said.

Harris had been in cold weather plenty of times, and knew

this kind of cold would kill them before they made it anywhere. The stick frame building and the glowing ball hanging over the fireplace were the only things keeping them alive.

He opened the door and dragged the man's body inside. Kneeling next to him, he rummaged through his pockets. He pulled out a piece of paper and a sack of stones, being careful not to touch them. He unfolded the piece of paper and read the note.

We love you, Daddy.

Harris crumbled the note in his hand and stared at the ceiling. He couldn't escape the path laid out before him. He didn't know this man laying on the floor, and his family might never know what happened to him.

He didn't know how to break the cycle around him. He'd gone numb to it so long ago. After his first wife . . . something broke in him. But he'd found a way to rebuild his life, and found love again, then she died. Then Compry. He hated himself for not breaking down, even when he saw what Marcus had done to her dead body.

Samantha and Joey's deaths didn't bring sadness, but a weight—a crushing feeling he shouldn't live.

Now, looking at this man, laying dead on the floor, he felt nothing. Even this note from his children didn't send up tendrils of guilt choking his throat, as it once might have.

"I'm going to scout it out," he said. "I think that stone can keep me warmer if I'm by myself."

"We know you're going to go to the place on your own. We're going with you," Hank said.

Smart kids. "No, you two need to use this." Harris picked up the black sack and pulled the tie loose enough to spot the purple stone inside. "This is just like the stones they used to transport us. I think if you picture where you want to go, this will get you there."

"And what, we just leave you out here to die?" Hank said.

"He's right, Vanar sort of needs you, Harris. You remember what MM was without a person like you running it?" Gladius said.

Vanar and MM seemed distant now, like a different life. Since the day he'd taken over the company, he'd poured himself into the work, burying his thoughts into something he could control. And he'd done a fine damned job of it.

By all accounts, the company should have collapsed after Marcus left it in shambles, but he'd managed to bring it back around and turn it into something great. Upon his death, he had standing orders to break up MM into thirty-two different companies, headed by people he knew would do at least a passing job. He had peace in knowing Jack and the rest would take care of it. Plus, if he didn't stop this cube factory, there wouldn't be a Vanar to return to.

"I'm not going to lie to you," Harris said. "I'm going alone for a reason. What I have in this bag, will end these bots. But there are risks and I don't want you guys anywhere near this when it's used." He pointed to the bag on the floor.

"It won't matter much if you get shot in the back," Gladius said.

"Yeah, we're a good team. You're going to need us," Hank said.

"You two are good together. I am a disease to those around me. Travis has been right all along. If I lose you guys, I'm afraid. . . ."

"What are you afraid of?" Hank asked.

Lies spread around his mind, and he squashed them. Maybe that orb had gotten into his brain. "I'm afraid I won't feel anything."

"Harsh," Gladius said.

"When I was a younger man, a long time ago, I did horrible things. I was a horrible person. A young woman changed that, and she became the first person to die because of me. But she wouldn't be the last."

"You're not a bad person, Harris," Hank said. "Not anymore. You've kept us alive more times than I can count."

Gladius looked him in the eye. "My dad told me and my sisters that he didn't care what man we took, as long as we were happy and it wasn't Harris Boone. I spent my whole life thinking of you as some sort of nightmare man and then you showed up at our door one day. You remember that moment, Harris?"

"I do, you tried to kill me."

She laughed. "And surprisingly, you tried very hard *not* to hurt me, and then you *didn't* kill my dad. I started to think there was a man behind the legend. I saw a glimmer of what my sisters must have seen. You're a kind man, Harris, and the circumstances of what has happened is because you've put yourself so far out front, the bullets are missing you entirely. I don't blame you for my sister's death, I blame Marcus."

"Thank you. That means a lot to me," Harris said.

"Then don't go through with this. If this thing has a hundred-mile radius, then let's blow it up right here," Gladius said. "The factory has to be closer than that."

Harris rubbed his chin and found it hard to argue with her logic—if the bag held a bomb. Might as well leave them thinking it is. "It's not a bad idea."

"Good, then set the time on this thing and let's blow this ice cream stand."

He saw that famous Denail spark in her eyes, and it made his next decision all that much easier. "Fine, I'll set the timer and we'll jump out of here." He knelt next to his bag, and fumbled with the keypad and typed in the numbers. "Okay, it's set. Hank, you remember the place we burned to the ground, the one holding the master Alius stone?"

"Yeah." Hank fidgeted and looked at his shoes.

"Good, lock that image in your mind and the purple rock will take us there. We only have a few minutes. Let's do this." They placed their hands in a triangle and Harris held the bag above them. "Here we go."

He dropped the purple rock from the bag, and right before it struck, he pulled his hand back and let it hit Hank and Gladius's only. It melted into their skin.

"Harris, no!" Gladius yelled, then they both disappeared.

CHAPTER 20

EVELYN STARED AT TRAVIS AS she froze time. She wanted to be safe, not sorry. They'd just portaled, and white tiled walls gleamed all around them; the smell of cleaning products filled the air. A row of toilet stalls sat with closed doors and she knelt down to check for feet. To make sure they were in the clear, she opened each door, all empty.

Jackie lay on the floor with her eyes closed, and Evelyn wondered why this would be the place the stone took them. Travis squinted, with a frantic expression stuck on his face. His hand hovered over his hip, in an act of grabbing at his gun.

Evelyn walked over to the door and opened it. The long room looked like a café, with a bar on the right and on the left side, booths ran along the windows, overlooking the city street. It looked like a normal city and a normal café, but that couldn't be further from the truth.

Nearly every person in the café had embers floating above them, and their connections freely flowed from one person to the next. They had jumped right into a den of purge people. This could have been Jackie's drop point to deliver her to the queen, or maybe a sanctuary for purge people like her.

Evelyn spotted an empty booth right next to the bathroom door, and knew what she would do. She rushed back to Travis and slid him along the tile floor, until she got to the booth. She pushed his stiff body into the booth and sat his hands on the table. Next, she took Jackie and shoved her into the booth and sat her face down on the table. A passerby might think she's resting or taking a nap.

She sat down next to Jackie and let time slide back into place. Noises inundated them, with the sounds of conversations, orders being placed, and silverware hitting porcelain.

Travis jerked and looked around. "What the hell?"

"Sorry, I just thought it'd be better if we appeared in the booth, versus a man walking out of a bathroom with a little girl and a passed out woman."

"How did you even get me here?"

"I'm stronger than I look."

Travis looked around the room and one of the waitresses saw him. She raised a finger and went back to talking with the people in front of her. "Don't people notice us just appearing in this booth?" He looked at Jackie.

"You'd be truly amazed at how little people observe their surroundings. People will ignore everything that isn't demanding their attention." A table with a woman and two men caught her attention. She looked again and made eye contact with the girl.

"Hey, didn't even see you come in," the waitress walked up, holding a pen and pad. "What can I get you to drink?"

"Just some waters please," Travis said.

Evelyn nodded and gave a stupid little girl smile that seemed to appease the waitress.

"How about I bring you some chocolate milk to go with that sweet smile?"

Travis spoke first, "That's fine. Thank you."

"Okay, great. Hey, is she all right?"

"Yeah, she's got a sleeping disorder," Travis said.

"Oh, poor thing. I'll get those drinks and take your order when I get back."

"Thank you," Travis said and the lady left.

Evelyn made eye contact with the woman at the far table as she and the two men got up and approached them. Evelyn readied herself to slow down time if needed.

"You shouldn't be here," she said, then stared at Jackie.

"And why is that?"

"This is one of their hangouts. You need to leave before the wrong person comes in and spots her." She motioned to Jackie.

"Who are you?" Travis asked.

"A friend. It doesn't matter, but . . ." She looked outside at a police man walking by. She turned and rushed back to her table before the officer entered the café.

Evelyn watched the uniformed man enter and take off his sunglasses.

Travis leaned forward. "You know, this could be where Jackie intended on trading you. This might be a terrible place to be, I think that woman was telling us the truth."

"I know, but I think it's worth it to stick around and figure out these people. One of them knows where the queen is, I bet. I just have to sort it out."

Evelyn watched the cop take a seat on a stool at the bar.

Jackie's hand moved and Evelyn took in a deep breath, hoping that Jackie didn't burst awake and cause a scene.

The cop sipped on a coffee and looked over to Evelyn as he panned the whole café. Good, a little girl sitting with her dad shouldn't arouse suspicions. She stared at the side of his head and pried into his thoughts. She got pictures, horrible pictures of tortured people. This man hunted people like prey, and didn't see them as any more than that. He knew the queen, but hadn't seen her in a while. He feared her. *Interesting.*

Then a vivid image of Evelyn appeared in his head, a photo of her in the queen's mansion. He wasn't just hunting people, he was hunting Evelyn, and she'd walked right into his bar.

He straightened up and turned to face Evelyn. She turned away, but the damage had been done. He got off his stool, carrying his coffee as he walked, hand near his gun.

"Should I kill him?" Travis asked under his breath.

Evelyn gave a slight shake of her head.

"Good morning, little girl." He ruffled her hair, hard enough to pull some from her head. "I haven't seen you around this café before, you all from out of town?" He sipped his coffee and put on a weak smile.

Evelyn glanced at the table with the girl and two guys. The girl was watching, but appeared not to be willing to do anything beyond that. Good, Evelyn had use of this man.

"We're just passing through, heading to New York to visit an Aunt," Travis said.

"Oh, New York?" he said, stretching out the name. "You know, in this world, its name is New Amsterdam. But I suppose you wouldn't know that." He dropped a stone on top of the table, and Evelyn stopped time; or, at least she tried to. It wouldn't work. She tried to do it again, but nothing changed.

"What is it, you can't change time?" the officer said. "What are you going to do now? Slap me, beg me? I'd like to hear some begging from you."

Evelyn tried again, but something was blocking her. Could that small green rock on the table keep her from slowing down time? How would that be possible?

"Now, why don't you get out of that booth? You and I need to take a little trip."

"She's not going anywhere with you," Travis said.

"Listen, I'm not talking to you, and if you keep your trap shut, I'll just take this little girl and be on my way."

"That won't be happening." Travis slid out of the booth and stood in front of the officer.

"And what is mister fancy pants going to do about it?" The officer flicked a stone and hit him in the neck.

Travis fell back into the booth like a stiff board.

The café stopped their chatter and focused on the cop's encounter with the booth next to the bathroom. Most of them didn't say a word, but moved out of the café and onto the streets.

The cop held a purple stone out in his gloved hand. This was the moment Evelyn wanted. A portal stone back to, most likely, the queen. She begged for time to slow, but nothing happened again.

With Travis out and Jackie a lump on a log, Evelyn knew it would be her against this man. She slid out from the booth and got ready to counter whatever attack this man planned on making against her.

"What makes you so special?" he asked.

Evelyn watched his embers floating above him. Nothing extraordinary about his flow; average, from what she could tell. "If you can't see it, then you'll never know."

"I'm going to enjoy watching you turn for her." He reached for her arm, but Evelyn sidestepped and struck the man's wrist as hard as she could. He reeled back and laughed. "You hit hard for such a little thing."

Ready for the next attack, Evelyn searched for his mind to end this, but got nothing but blackness. How was he blocking her now, when he was an open book only a few minutes before? He grabbed her arm and Evelyn struggled against him, but he was too strong.

He glared at Jackie. "You have her?"

Jackie sprung awake and threw a stone, striking the officer in the neck. Evelyn didn't get a good look at the dark stone but whatever it was, the cop fell to the ground with white foam coming out of his mouth.

"You faker," Evelyn said.

"I just saved your ass. Now let's get out of here, buttercup." Jackie slid out of the booth.

"We aren't leaving Travis."

"Fine." She pulled him up and slung his arm over her shoulder. "That was very stupid coming here."

Evelyn tried to help as Jackie mostly carried Travis to the door. She glanced back at the man laying on the floor. Another waitress knelt next to him.

"Man can't hold his coffee," Jackie said to the hostess and stopped at the door. The woman and two men stood there.

Jackie smiled and hugged the woman. "We don't have time for a reunion, you think you can clean up our mess?" She motioned back to the frothing cop.

"Yeah, it'd be my pleasure to rid the world of that asshole."

Jackie nodded and said thank you as they left the café, stepping onto the sidewalk. She used her free arm to wave down a taxi. The yellow cab pulled to the side of the road and the passenger window rolled down.

"I'm not taking him if he pukes or dies in my car," the driver said.

"He won't do either, I promise," Jackie said and opened the back door. "Come on."

Evelyn helped push Travis to the far side of the backseat and then sat in the middle, between him and Jackie.

"Where to, young ladies?"

"Just get us out of town," Jackie said.

Evelyn grasped Travis's wrist and felt his pulse. "What's wrong with him?" she whispered.

"He's paralyzed . . . temporarily," Jackie added.

"How long?"

"I don't know, depends on how potent of a stone it was. Probably only a few minutes."

The cab driver kept glancing in his mirror as he drove down the road. Evelyn watched a few people walking down the street. None of them had the embers like Jackie. Then, she spotted a couple, holding hands and walking down the sidewalk. Evelyn stared as they drove past them.

"What are you looking at?" Jackie asked.

"You guys don't see it, do you?" Evelyn said as she spotted a man sweeping the sidewalk in front of the bakery store. His embers floated above.

"See what?"

"There's something different about you and the people like you. You have something I can see. Your queen can see it as well."

Jackie groaned. "She's not my queen. I think you're talking about quintessence. It's what gives us our power."

"Is it learned?"

"Nah, we're born with it," Jackie said.

They passed tall buildings and the people on the streets grew in numbers. More people than she'd seen in other spots around this world, and the embers floated above them.

"This is one of your cities, isn't it?" Evelyn asked.

"No, this is their city. We don't come here."

"Jackie?" Evelyn turned to face her and regretted the look on Jackie's face.

"What?"

"I wish I had more time to ask you for your thoughts. And it doesn't help that you tried to kill me, either."

"What are you saying?" Jackie said and Evelyn watched as she fumbled around, looking for her stones.

Evelyn glanced at the cab driver and sent a thought to him, to ignore what was going to happen. He gripped the wheel and stopped looking back. She looked over at Jackie. "So, I'm going to take them."

"What? My thoughts?" Jackie shook her head in confusion.

Evelyn breathed in and stared into Jackie's eyes. They glazed over as she sent her soothing thoughts, much like a leech numbing the area as it sucked the blood. It wasn't the preferred way—it could leave Jackie damaged—but it wouldn't matter. How many lives had these purge people taken?

"Evelyn, stop it," Travis said and touched her arm.

The connection broke off and Jackie slumped in the chair.

Evelyn watched as Travis sat up and put his body between her and Jackie. "You don't have to do this. I don't think these are the bad people. They just want to find their friend. Wouldn't you do anything to help a person you loved?"

"Yes, and I am, right now. So let me get back to it. I was getting flashes about how this whole world works."

"It's not right, and you know it. You can't treat people like they are things, Evelyn."

"She can help me understand them better."

"Not this way. She was telling you everything you wanted to know. Why break her?"

"It's faster."

Evelyn thought of probing Travis's brain and stared at his forehead. The man had always evaded her kindest probes. She found Travis to be such a fascinating person, she didn't want to damage that beautiful mind, so she never probed deeper than his fleeting thoughts.

"Evelyn, there are better ways than this. You need to stay as human as possible. If you start down this road, you're going to end up just like their queen. She sees all life as just a means to her end."

Jackie held her head and sat up. She looked past Travis. "What happened?"

"You passed out," Evelyn said. "You're better now." She gave Travis a look to tell him she wouldn't break Jackie. Then she crossed her arms and went back to looking out the window.

"I don't feel better," Jackie said. "It felt as if you were in my head." She held her hand over her forehead.

"Where are we going?" Evelyn asked as they passed a group of purge people walking down the street.

"It doesn't much matter, we just need to get out of here. That cop back at the café will be sending . . ." Jackie stopped and leaned forward, looking out the front window. "Oh crap."

Evelyn spotted it as well. A group of cars parked along the street, blocked their escape. Half a dozen people stood around the cars.

"Did you tell anyone?" Jackie asked the driver.

"Tell who, what? What's going on here?" the driver asked as he slowed down.

Another car rammed them from behind. "Where are my stones?" she demanded, and held out her hand.

Travis took out a sack and gave it to Jackie. She rolled down her window and tossed a stone, hitting the car behind them. The stone exploded into a large goop that covered the front of the pursuing car. It skidded out of control and struck a parked car.

"What the hell?" their driver screamed. The cab came to an abrupt stop. The driver opened the door and ran down the road, away from the blockade directly ahead.

"Are these your people?" Evelyn asked and made sure she had a bit of her fingers in Jackie's brain.

"No," Jackie said. She told the truth.

"You have another one of those jump stones?" Travis asked.

Jackie looked in her bag. "No, that café one was the last one."

"Make another," Evelyn said.

"It's not that simple," Jackie said and looked ahead. "We've got to get out of this car."

Several of the purge people had left their cars and walked toward them, each of them holding a colored stone of some sort in their hands. Evelyn went to slow down time but again, nothing happened.

"None of them have guns, do they?" Travis asked as he eyed the group walking toward them.

"We don't use them. They can mess with the stones."

"Good. These people get any closer and they're about to get a lesson in lead," Travis said.

The three people stopped, maybe fifty feet away. One tossed a stone at the car Evelyn sat in. It bounced along the asphalt, until it exploded, blowing out the windows of a nearby car.

A warning shot, as Evelyn took it.

Travis gripped his gun and put a hand on the car door. He glanced back and then shoved the door open.

Evelyn couldn't help but smile. How she loved Travis, and kicking these people's asses would be a good way to show him how much she'd grown.

CHAPTER 21

HARRIS KEPT THE ORB DANGLING from his wrist. The longer he looked at it, the more he wanted to. So he reserved himself to quick glances. The glowing orange light seeped into him, spreading over his anger and massaging out his regret.

He thought after ending Marcus, there would have been a great weight taken from him. Marcus had been the architect of so many horrible memories, and the direct result of so much death around him; but with him gone, he felt hollow. He felt as if his sole purpose for so many years, had been to find a way to stop Marcus, to take control of MM and restore peace to the world. He'd done those things, and maybe if he had Compry still at his side, he would have found a hidden spot in the world to live the rest of his life out in ambiguity.

It was the orb talking. He chuckled to himself and snuck another look at it. These weren't his thoughts, nor did he want them to be. He hadn't felt that way in a long time. He found himself staring at the orb again. He shook his head and looked up at the sky. The wind had died down, and the sunrise sent a blue hue over the sky.

How long had he been staring at it? It must have been hours. Blindly, he grabbed the orb with his fist and stuffed it in his pocket. He unbound the string from his wrist and took a deep breath.

The sun brought warmer weather. Stinging cold, but tolerable. A large rock outcropping, layered with a snow cap, stuck out from the ground. A good vantage point to look over the surrounding area.

He climbed the rocks and tested his footing, before standing all the way up. There, he saw it, stuffed down into a valley and surrounded by a large forest, a large white building with no markings and a layer of snow covering the roof. He got off the rock and worked his way toward the building.

As he got closer, he didn't spot any cameras or windows. Working his way around the building, he found a single white door with a keypad next to it. Getting up close to the structure, a humming sound roared loudly, and constant.

The keypad wasn't more than the equivalent of an old ten-key lock, and a joke for his Panavice to break through. He slung his bag across his back and used his Panavice. The door clicked and he turned the handle with one hand and pulled out his gun with the other.

He entered the well-lit hall, closing the door behind him. He thought being indoors might take the edge off the bitter cold, but it couldn't have been much more than a few degrees warmer inside. The sounds though, were more pronounced and defined. The hum of energy came from all directions, and in different degrees.

The hall led to a set of double doors with small windows at the upper third of the door. He stood at the window and peered into the vast expanse of the next room. Beyond the doors, held a massive room, leading far down into the earth. He pushed open the door and winced at the noise.

A cube floated up from below and flew into a square hole at a wall at the far end and disappeared. Then another cube, then another. Soon, a large cube, maybe ten times as big as the small ones, floated up from below and went through a larger hole in the same wall.

He walked the edge of the wall and kept an eye out for humans, but no one came; no alarms sounded. Maybe they figured Ryjack's environment and inhabitants would have been enough of a deterrent. It was brilliant, really. In a world where traveling meant increased chance of death, no sane person would try and make a journey into such a place.

Harris leaned over the edge to get a good look below. He spotted the bottom and a flurry of movement. Carts moved around, carrying loads of rocks and other materials. Still, no people. Everything seemed to be operated on complete autonomy. Vanar could have built such manufacturing, but Marcus kept this sort of thing at bay. He'd always thought once people became a hundred percent dependent on machines, they'd already lost the war. Of course, this was the same person who gave them Orange. . . .

Thinking of Marcus, Harris wanted to take another look at the orb. He resisted, and kept walking toward the doors under the holes the cubes took. He suspected the Alius stone would be behind the wall, with at least one person holding the portal open.

He pushed open the next door and walked toward the circle

in the middle of the large room.

He kept his gun out and pointed at the stone. A man was crouched next to it, and never looked up as Harris approached. The dome around him flickered with pictures, much like a person changing channels.

Then a large crate appeared at the middle of the stone. A mechanical arm rotated out and picked up the crate, bringing it to a large, steel funnel. Stones poured out of the crate and clattered into the funnel. The arm shook out the last stones, then rotated again and dumped the crate into a hole in the floor.

The man at the stone still hadn't noticed his entrance, he didn't think the man had even moved. He wore a set of headphones and stared at the stone, without ever looking up. Harris questioned if the man was even real.

Another cube floated by and a picture of a forest appeared. The cube floated into the circle and disappeared. Then another cube floated in, and a scene near an ocean appeared.

Harris walked around the circle, making sure to stay out of it. He tried to fathom what the man was doing. Taking in what he knew about the stones, this should be impossible; not only was the man holding a portal open, but he was able to change locations without moving his hands.

"Hey," Harris called out, not more than thirty feet away. The man didn't even flinch. "Hey, you, at the stone," he yelled.

The man lifted his head and looked over to Harris. Harris kept his gun trained on him, and was shocked at how bad the man looked. His face was sunken and withered, and Harris had a hard time pegging his age. He could have been twenty-five or seventy-five. His thin hair might have been a light blond or a shade of gray.

"Who are you?" The man croaked out, as if he hadn't

spoken in years.

"I'm the new maintenance guy," Harris said.

The small man smiled and another cube went through the portal and into another world, all while the man gazed upon Harris. "There's no maintenance in this place. Are you here to kill me?" His voice cleared, and the last part of the sentence perked up with hope.

"I'm here to end this place." Harris didn't see any reason to lie to the guy.

"Oh, thank heavens." He looked at the ceiling.

"Do you even know what you're doing?"

"Oh yes, every horrible thing I see never leaves me. I can't forget, as much as I want to."

"How long have you been doing this?" Harris asked and kept his gun trained on the man.

He laughed again, his cracked lips getting stuck on his dry teeth. "As long as I can remember." A large cube went through the portal and Harris noticed no change in the man's expression. "But, you can't kill me. I know, I've tried."

"Is there another distribution center like this one?"

"This is the last functioning center. And if you kill me, they won't have an easy backup person to do what I do."

"Let me put you out of your misery." Harris fired and the bullets bounced off the man's chest.

"I told you, I can't be killed." He looked at the ceiling.

Harris lowered his gun. "Then tell me, how do I kill you?"

"If I knew how to die, you think I'd be here right now? I haven't eaten, slept, or had water for so long, I don't remember what it even tastes like."

"How's that possible?"

"The queen made me a special stone, at least that is what

she called it, but I consider it a curse. It's unnatural to live without dying. People need to die in order to make room for the young." He coughed and wiped his mouth as another cube flew into the portal.

"Can I get you off the Alius stone? That should be enough to stop all of this, right?"

"You can get me off this portal stone as easy as you could detach your penis from your crotch."

"A knife would do the job." Harris stowed his gun and pulled out his knife.

"I wouldn't do that if I was you."

Harris stepped passed the edge of the circle and took one step onto the dirt floor. Something struck him in the chest and sent him flying backward. He slid across the smooth floor for several feet, then rolled over, clutching his chest. Whatever hit him felt like a giant boot kicking him. He struggled to catch his breath.

"I told you not to."

Harris brought his bag between his legs and unzipped it.

"What you got there?" The man yelled over the hum of an approaching cube.

"If I can't get to you, then this will get to all of them," Harris pointed at the cube flying by.

The man's eyes lit up. "What is it, a bomb?"

Harris shook his head and pulled out the shielded box. He used his Panavice to open the first lid. From there, he typed in a code and opened another lid. This particular case shielded any possible signal trying to get in or out. He opened the last lid and took out the small memory stick, containing an evil he thought he'd never see again.

Evelyn had reprogrammed it, weaponizing Alice.

"Is the terminal there?" Harris asked.

"Yes, that's the mainframe. But it isn't anything you can hack into."

"This old lady isn't going to hack into it, she's going to destroy it all."

The man whistled through the hum of a large cube flying by. It reminded Harris of Ferrell. He had to be ten thousand miles away.

The stick holding Alice felt heavy in his hands. He knelt next to the terminal and found the data connection. He hovered the stick next to the port.

"Do it," the man urged.

Hank came to Harris's mind, and he pulled out his Panavice to check to make sure they weren't still on the planet. He stared at the screen and their location. They were still on Ryjack, and close to a place he knew to be a one-way stone. Had Hank led them to the wrong stone? Harris sighed and slapped the Panavice against his waist.

"Losing your balls? Come on, set that thing off before she comes."

Harris couldn't have another one of the six on his conscience, but they should be far enough away, Alice couldn't get to them quickly. Unless she took access of his Panavice and found them . . . He'd have to risk it and have faith in Evelyn's programming.

"I knew it. I knew you wouldn't end this." The man stopped looking at him and got back to his kneeling position at the stone. He looked like part of the stone after a while, holding onto it like he was worshiping it.

Then the humming of the place stopped. The silence was deafening. Harris looked around to explain the silence.

The man at the cube stood up and backed away from the

stone. He looked white with fear and then turned to face Harris. "She's coming. Do what you need to do, now!"

Harris scrambled with the stick and shoved it in. It might take a minute for the thing to load, so he walked away from it.

"She's here."

A woman appeared next to the stone. Harris sidestepped toward the door.

"Who are you?" the woman asked and her voice boomed around the room.

Harris didn't answer, but something told him to run. So he ran toward the door and kicked it open. A row of cubes sat in the air above him, as if waiting in a line. He ignored them and knew he had about thirty seconds before Alice went online. With any luck, the woman would chase him until it was too late.

He got to the rail and looked down into the pit, where cubes were being produced. Must have been hundreds of feet down. Then he felt an object strike his neck. His body jolted out of control and he fell over the railing. *Good, she's keeping up with me.*

As the floor rushed up toward him, he felt another stone hit the back of his neck. None of it mattered anymore, this was the end for him. In the last second of the fall, he witnessed all the machines collectively collapsing. The cubes were falling with him now, and all the different bots went dormant. Alice, beautiful Alice was doing her work.

CHAPTER 22

HANK OPENED HIS EYES. HE hated traveling through that swirling world of freefall. Holding onto Gladius, he looked around. They were in a large building, with rows of metal shelving reaching to the ceiling. Hank let go of Gladius and stepped toward the aisle sixteen sign.

"No, this can't be," he said.

"What? Where are we?"

"Cost Plus."

"Oh my God, is that you, Hank?" A young woman and a little girl came running up to them. "How are you in here? We didn't hear the door open."

Hank blinked hard ignoring the question, glancing back and forth between Mary and the little girl. When Gladius hit his arm to get his attention, he turned to her, eyes wide.

In all of his wildest dreams, he never thought he'd see Mary again, but that didn't mean he never wondered about her. She'd been his first, his only—besides Gladius. He never thought what they did would take hold, not on the first time.

It had been a moment of weakness when Carl had come to them, pleading for someone to lay with his daughter. They wanted a child for her and they'd most likely be the last people they'd ever see. Just the mention of her brother, Peter, being the only other suitor, made him cringe. He couldn't have let that happen.

It had been curious, clumsy, and quick. How could they have produced a child? The thought had been in the back of his mind since they left Mary that morning and she'd hugged him goodbye. But seeing it right in front of him, his *child*, a little girl, he broke down and teared up. He didn't want to cry in front of Gladius, but he couldn't hold back.

"Listen," Mary said with tears building in her eyes. "I don't care how you got in here, all that matters is you are here. You're back. I never thought I'd see you again." Her arms opened and then fell to her sides. She looked like she wanted to be hugged more than any other person Hank had seen in his whole life, but he had to ask the question.

"Is she ours?" Hank asked.

Mary nodded. "Haven't been any others coming by, have there?"

"Wait a second . . ." Gladius stepped to the side and waved her finger between Mary and Hank, then pointing at the little girl. "You're telling me this is your kid?"

"Yes," Hank said. "Mary's dad asked me to try . . . to try and give his family the gift of a child. I never thought. . . ."

Gladius frowned and took in a deep breath. He wanted to comfort her and tell her she was the love of his life—that none of this would change what they had—but her face told him she didn't want his affection at the moment.

He knelt down and faced the little girl. "Hello there."

"Her name is Cindy. Cindy, this is your dad."

She hid behind her mother's leg. "You said he was dead. You told me the monsters outside killed him. You said—"

"I was wrong," Mary said.

Cindy took a step away from her mother and stared at Hank, studying him with her intelligent gaze. "Where have you been?"

"I was tr-trying to protect . . . I was out there." Hank pointed to the outside wall. "If I knew you existed, I would have been here as quick as I could." His chest tightened as he watched his little girl process the information.

She looked from her mother to Hank, and he wondered if he was on some kind of trial. Was he worthy of her affection, or had he done too much harm to come back from? He knew firsthand what it was like to think one parent was dead, and he hated that he'd continued that cycle for another child.

"Did you kill all the monsters outside, dad?" The word *dad* sounded foreign from her mouth. "Is it safe to go outside now?"

"No, it isn't. The monsters are still out there. But I'm here now. I will protect you." She took a step forward and then looked back at her mom, maybe asking for permission. Mary smiled and nodded. Cindy ran to Hank.

He opened his arms and she ran to him, wrapping her arms around his neck. With her secure, he stood and held his daughter. The guilt weighed heavily on him. How could he have been such a terrible person to never have come back here? He knew there was a chance Cindy existed, yet he'd chosen to be ignorant of it— deny the possibility. As long as he didn't know, it wasn't real.

As he held her in his arms and she smiled at him, he knew his whole world had changed. He couldn't let his daughter live on this planet, and stopping the purge people became an even greater priority.

"I've missed so much," Hank said.

"Where have you been?" Cindy asked.

"She's a smart one, just like her dad," Mary said.

Hank couldn't help but smile and hug her again. Eventually, Cindy retreated back to her mom's leg, but locked her gaze onto Hank and Gladius. She'd probably had never seen another person outside of her Cost Plus family.

Gladius cleared her throat. She kept a normal expression, but Hank knew better. The redness in her cheeks and the lines near her eyes told him she was scared and confused. He'd thought about telling her numerous times of his encounter with Mary, but it never seemed appropriate to talk about something that might not have been.

"Let me introduce you to my girlfriend. Cindy, Mary, this is Gladius," Hank said.

"Oh. Nice to meet you." Mary nodded.

"Yes." Gladius put her hand out to shake, and Mary just looked at it, seeming confused. Dropping her arm down, she turned to Hank. "I don't think this could get any more awkward. Hank, did you know you had a child with her?"

"Can you give us a minute?" Hank said.

"Yeah, of course." Mary beamed with a big smile and stared at him. After what felt like too long, she said, "Good to see you again, Hank. Come on, sweetie, let's give daddy a minute with his lady friend."

Hank faced Gladius and took a deep breath. "This is absolutely crazy, I know. You have to believe me, I didn't think she would actually get pregnant. I mean, we only did it once. And the only reason I did it was because her dad came on all strong, with their plight of never being able to find a suitor for their daughter. They wanted the gift of a child, and Lucas and Joey were both attached at the time. I felt bad for them. I wanted to help. It meant nothing. Nothing like I have with you." He bit on his lip and waited for something from Gladius, anything. The blank look she gave him made him fumble for his next words.

Gladius spoke first. "Does this place have a stone near it?"

A stone? He looked around and realized what she meant. "No, it's like hundreds of miles to the south."

"So you chose *this* place, instead of getting us home, so we could maybe help save the worlds. What do you think that says?"

"I don't know. I had the Alius stone in my mind and right when he dropped the stone, I guess I must have subconsciously thought of this place."

"You think of her?"

"Sometimes. But not like that. I'm happy with you."

"I just . . . I don't know what to do with this." She threw her hands up in the air.

"You don't have to do anything. Nothing has changed between us." Hank took a step closer to Gladius. "But you have to know, I can't let my daughter live in this place, this world."

"It might actually be the safest place for her right now. I doubt the queen will ever attack this world, and she has her little factory here."

"I won't leave them here."

"Then *what*, Hank? Are we to adopt a whole new family and put them up in our house? Are we to change our plans of escaping all this? What if we run across another pretty girl who wants a child? Should we galavant around the worlds, dropping your seed for all those needy wombs?" Gladius put her hands on her hips and tears filled her eyes.

He'd never seen Gladius cry. "I'm sorry. I didn't even know you at the time. And it's not like you don't have a history." Hank winced and instantly regretted his words.

"What's that supposed to mean?"

"Nothing."

"Hell no, you tell me right now."

He didn't want to have this conversation. No matter what route he took, he'd sound like a jerk. But she grinded her teeth and glared at him. There was no way out of it. "How many men have you been with?"

"What kind of question is that?"

"I know the answer. It's on Vanar's net. There's a social scoreboard with points and ratings, and you are near the top. I've only been with two women and they are both in this building right now. Not to mention, I've only loved one of them."

"You searched me?" Gladius said.

"I did and I felt terrible afterward. Not because of what I found, but because I did it. But that doesn't matter. I don't care about your past. I only care about the person I have right in front of me."

"That's a lie. If you didn't care, you would've never brought it up!" She growled and closed her eyes briefly. "I hate that I care what you think. I hate that I have a past that isn't like yours . . . but I don't regret it, Hank. Because everything I've done ultimately led me to you, at the exact moment I was ready for you. And the absolute worst part of all of this?" She pointed off toward the direction Cindy and Mary had taken. "This whole situation makes me love you even more."

Hank melted and rushed to her. She met him and they hugged.

He kissed her cheek, then she pulled back and said, "Are there any other little secrets out there I should know about?"

"Just one, and this is a big one . . . I ate the last Snackie Cake at home."

She punched him on the chest. "You better not have. I'm not even kidding." He laughed and grabbed her again. "Now, can you tell me where the hell we are? And who are these people staring at us?"

Hank turned and faced Mary's family. He spotted Mary's dad, Carl, and her brother, Pete. They both looked so much older. Stretching his neck to look around them, he noticed one person was missing.

"Hello, Hank," Carl said. "I didn't think we'd ever see you again."

"Running theme here," Gladius muttered, tightening her arm around his.

"Hello, Carl, Pete."

"Who you have there?" Pete asked.

"This is Gladius."

"Hello," Pete said and waved with a sheepish smile.

"Where's Jenny?" Hank asked, looking for their mom.

Pete looked away, and Mary and Cindy looked at each other. Carl took a step forward and said, "She didn't make it; came down with the illness." His voice cracked and he covered his face with his hand.

"I'm so sorry," Hank said.

"So, what are you doing here?" Carl asked, and glanced at Cindy.

"We were . . . it's actually rather complicated," Hank said.

"He wanted to see if that girl actually produced his offspring," Gladius offered.

"Yeah, there's that."

"Are you staying, Daddy?" Cindy asked.

Hank looked to Gladius and felt himself in a battle of two worlds. Could he explain things without looking completely insane? Could he leave them here, while they dealt with the purge people? What if little Cindy got sick like her grandma?

"I don't think you should stay here, Cindy. How would you like to live in a world where people stayed dead when it was their time?"

"Yes," Cindy said.

"All of us?" Mary asked.

"You know of a place that doesn't have the dead?" Carl said, full of optimism. Something Hank didn't remember seeing in the man the last time they were there. Maybe the death of his wife, or the birth of his granddaughter, made him realize there could be a better life outside of Cost Plus.

"I do, but right now, it's under attack and my friends and I are going to stop it."

"Is Poly around?" Pete asked.

"Yes, she is still around."

"She's hot," Pete said and Mary nudged him. "What?"

"Don't be a sicko."

"Oh, like you and your boyfriend here?" Pete said. "What kind of person has relations with a stranger, only to have a kid? No offense, Cindy."

"That's enough, Pete," Carl said. "Hank, you didn't answer Mary. Are you going to take all of us?"

"I will, but I have to set my world straight first. It might be a more dangerous place than here right now and Gladius and I have a long travel ahead of us to get back home.

Gladius cleared her throat and nudged Hank in his back.

"What is it?" Hank asked as Gladius moved in close to him.

"When I tackled that purger to the ground, I stole this." She pulled out a sack and then opened it. Inside he saw the purple stone, exactly like the one Harris had. "I didn't know what they did until Harris used his on us. This is our ticket out of here. Unless you have another place you want to be on Vanar?"

Hank glanced back at Cindy. "This is amazing. We can get them off this planet."

"I thought you said it was too dangerous."

"That was only because we had to clear through Ryjack to get to the stone. Now we can jump right there."

Gladius shook her head. "I hate to burst your bubble, but didn't you hear Harris? This only works with up to three people."

Pete crossed his arms, but kept quiet. Carl rubbed his thinning hair and gave a slight shake of his head.

The steel roll-up door rattled and the faint sound of groans came through.

Cindy grabbed at Mary's arms, and she picked her daughter up. "Not tonight, you won't."

"I guess you guys are stuck here for a while," Carl said. "I can set up a room for you. We've changed a few things since Cindy was born. We've taken up residence back in the old employee offices."

"No way am I spending the night here," Gladius said. "We should jump now. We can always come back," she whispered.

"I need to see this out. Give me a little bit, please."

Gladius's lips thinned, but she nodded and followed Hank and the rest across Cost Plus.

"Dad," Pete said. "I don't think they plan on staying here long. But, maybe they can help us with our problem?"

"Yes, please, Dad," Mary said, putting a hand on her father's arm.

"Let me guess, you need a second child?" Gladius said.

Mary shook her head and looked at Hank. "We need someone to kill our mother."

CHAPTER 23

LUCAS RUSHED TOWARD THE MAN, stone in hand.

"No, get away from me." The man cowered, keeping his attention on Lucas's hand.

Lucas waved the rock around, thrusting it toward the man. "You don't want this near you, do you?'"

"No, and how can you be holding it? What are you?"

Lucas grabbed the man by the shirt and moved the rock near his face.

"Please, no."

"Just stop this contraption from taking people. End it."

"I can't. It's automatic. I don't have control over it."

"Then why are you here?"

"I'm just here to make sure there aren't any anomalies, like you."

"Then you throw this at them? What is it supposed to do?"

"Kill you. It should dissolve into your skin and kill you. No one can hold onto a stone like that. . . ." His eyes went wide and he scurried backward, but Lucas held him tight. "Are you like the queen?"

"Maybe I am. Now, why don't you tell me how to stop this thing, before I have to use this stone on you."

"I told you, I can't. I swear. I wish I could help you. I don't like this any more than you do."

Lucas let go of the man and pushed him back. "We're going to stop this, one way or another."

"Sorry, kid, but she's going to kill you and there's nothing you can do about it." The man shoved his hand in his pocket and disappeared.

"Crap. Where the hell did he go?" Lucas regretted not killing the man.

After being sure the man had completed a disappearing act, he went back to the machine. There had to be some way to stop it. But there was nothing on the walls, no controls, or levers, or screens to type into. Where was Evelyn when he actually needed her?

The egg flashed on the next person, like a prolonged lightning bolt, and then faded. Something clanked around on the inside and Lucas knew another person had been killed. The door clattered and Lucas ran to it. If he couldn't stop the machine, he'd stop them from getting in.

"Stop it," he screamed at the door, pushing back with his best efforts. "They are going to kill you."

Something struck the back of Lucas's neck and he spun around to see five people standing near the egg, glaring at him. The man had returned with friends.

"See? They don't affect him. They just bounce off."

"Did you use a breaker on him?" A man with a long coat asked.

"No, just some absorbers."

Lucas looked around for an exit. He knew of some stairs beyond the door . . . as long as the building had the same layout as Hector's. But the second he opened that door, the people would flood in.

"You there, boy, what's your name?"

Lucas reached for Prudence, but she wasn't with him anymore. He cringed and pulled an arrow from his back and held it out like a spear.

"My name's Ben," the man with the long coat said. "You should put that little pointer down before you get hurt."

Lucas walked sideways, giving space for the door with a group of people desperately trying to end their lives.

"Don't take another step," Ben said.

"You guys are going to regret the moment you stepped on this planet."

Ben laughed and the men with him shared in the chuckle. "You think we care about regret? You think we want this job? No, we just want you all to lie down, face the facts, and stop giving us a hard time."

"Have you heard from your friends back at the dome?" Lucas taunted, kicking at the foot of the chair holding the door closed. "Oh, that's right, they're all dead. Sorry about that. Real bummer."

"What's he talking about?"

Ben held his hand up and took a step closer. "If what you say is true, then you must know of the little one."

"I do."

"She's all the queen wants. Just tell us where she is and we can be on our way. We won't even kill you."

"She's close," Lucas said.

"How close?"

"Real close. Just check up your friend's ass." Lucas kicked the chair loose and the door flung open, five people collapsed into the room.

A stone flew by and hit the wall in front of him. Green smoke poured from the stone, but Lucas ran through the cloud and to the stairs. His eyes watered from the mist, as he bounded down the stairs, glancing back up to see the men entering the stairwell with him.

He raced down the next three flights and reached the bottom of the staircase. Kicking open the door, he slid to a stop. At the end of the lobby, stood a large group of men and women. One stepped out front, or more like she floated past the people as they gave her space. She looked beautiful, angelic. Lucas couldn't help but stare.

"Hello, Lucas," she said and even her voice soothed him. "I've been waiting for you. We have much to discuss." She appeared directly in front of him and ran the back of her hand across his cheek.

Lucas closed his eyes and felt her smooth skin against his. "Are you—"

"Yes, I am her."

"You're. . . ." He couldn't find the words.

"I have that effect on people. Don't worry, it will all be over soon. Just relax your thoughts and we can have a conversation without words," she said.

Lucas grinded his teeth and let the woman think she had him under her spell as he nodded his head. Maybe it worked on simple-minded people, but living through a grinner bite and being one of the Six, allotted him some powers of his own. "That would be nice," he said.

Spotting the part of her neck he'd attack, he stared at it, gripping the black stone in his hand, waiting for his chance. The crowd behind her watched him, vying for the best view, as if he was a sideshow freak they weren't sure if they were supposed to fear or pity.

She closed her eyes and he felt her mental punch at his head, but it might as well have been against a steel wall. Her eyes shot open in surprise. He seized the moment, slamming the black stone onto her neck. It absorbed into her and she screamed, clawing at her neck.

So that's what it's supposed to do.

Something struck Lucas in the back of the head and he fell to the ground, as people rushed to the queen.

CHAPTER 24

"LET'S DO THIS," EVELYN SAID to Travis, nodding at the group of purge people surrounding their car. She and Travis put their hands on the car door and pushed it open.

Travis led the way and fired multiple shots before she'd even left the car. Jackie shoved by her and threw a stone at the purge group. More purge people through stones from a nearby alley. Evelyn sneered and tried to stop them with her mind, but it didn't work. They were blocking her. She looked at her small hands and equally small body. If she couldn't do the things she could do, what use was she?

"Get back," Jackie said as a stone struck the ground and turned the asphalt road into a black pool of liquid. It smoked and reeked of tar. Jackie pulled on Evelyn and spun her around as she ran behind Travis to the back of the next car. He fired over the trunk at the purge people huddling next to their cars, while Jackie threw another stone high into the sky. It broke open and bits of the stone rained down on the purge people. Screams could be heard and Evelyn eyed Jackie. Was she really helping them?

Doing the things she was doing, meant she'd crossed a line with her kind; one she'd never be able to walk back over. Evelyn grew a smidgeon of trust in Jackie, even if the woman had tried to have her killed. People could change, she had to believe in that.

"They're blocking me." Evelyn tugged on Jackie's arm.

"They probably have a white stone. They'd need something from you to make it work though."

"At the diner, that cop pulled out some of my hair." She felt the top of her head.

"It also means they have some powerful people on their side, if they are able to make a stone like that. We just need to find the person using the stone and stop them, then the block will end."

Jackie looked over the back of the car. "I don't see anyone. But they'll be struggling to hold down a person like you. They're probably in one of the cars." She threw a stone. It flew and struck a car. The whole car exploded, then a brilliant white light shone. Many of the nearby purge people ducked behind their own cars. The white light disappeared, as well as the car it'd struck.

Evelyn looked from where the car had been to Jackie. What could these not do? She tried to slow down time, but she was still blocked.

Travis kept firing. "What's the plan here, ladies?" he asked between shots.

"You need to find this person, and kick their ass," Jackie said. "You can do it with your mind, I bet. Just feel the ground and you'll be able to sense where they are."

"How do you know this?"

"I've seen the queen do it when she wants to find someone. I'm betting you can do the same."

Evelyn knelt down and put her hands on the ground. She wasn't sure what it was, but she felt something; she had a greater connection to whatever it was. Evelyn closed her eyes and searched for the place she couldn't go, to the wall blocking her.

She imagined a 3D world to travel in, seeing the brick walls on all four sides. One wall seemed larger than the rest, but it was purely a construct of her mind. If she learned anything from studying Julie, she knew there would be a workaround, like a back door or a secret knock.

She approached the wall and heard Travis yelling. But it wouldn't matter, soon she'd have her powers back and she'd end all of them.

Closer to the brick wall, she found a crack. Not quite big enough for a finger, but it might as well have been a mile wide. She built her rage to a boiling point, then unleashed a scream at the wall, right at the crack. It blew down, disappearing into the black void. On the other side, a young girl lay on the ground in a fetal position. She couldn't have been more than sixteen.

This girl had power over her, and she couldn't allow that.

She found the girl's mind and then probed into it. She felt a lot of resistance from her, more than the average person, but it was no matter, she got in. The girl covered her head with her hands and groaned.

"Don't worry, I'll make it quick." Evelyn pictured a mind bullet, then stopped. She didn't have to kill. Maybe just disable her. If this simple girl could stop her from doing her thing, than anyone could stop her. A bum on the street might grab her, or some child molester could snatch her up and she'd never be seen again. She couldn't let that happen. Never again. And if they brought up another one of these savants, she'd know how to handle them quickly.

She forced her idea into the girl's head of deep sleep, and then wiped her mind clean, so she couldn't wake up and do this again. Evelyn didn't like being so cruel to a stranger, but she couldn't have a person like that stopping her. She released the girl, and she disappeared in every sense, even her stream of embers; her golden strands of connections to the world, gone.

The shock sent Evelyn out of that world and into reality. Travis and Jackie had dragged her behind another car, further away.

"I killed her," Evelyn whispered to Jackie.

"Sorry, kid. Sometimes, people deserve to die. Time to do your thing, end this."

Evelyn closed her eyes and heard the dull tones of the slowed down world. She stood and walked around Travis. The purge people crowded behind their cars, as bullets struck the doors and windshields around them. A few people hadn't been as lucky, and lay on the ground, clutching various body parts.

A gunpowder smell filled the air as she walked toward the purge people. They didn't see a single gun on them. Were they solely using stones as their offense? A few stones hung in the air. They were heading toward Travis, but she'd make sure they never hit him. She just needed to take care of these people first.

Walking past the first open car door, she touched the man with his arm reeled back in preparation of a throw. A green stone lay in his hand, but Evelyn gave him the thought to pass out and forget everything he knew for the past few months.

She moved around and was surprised at how few of the purge people there actually were. There couldn't have been more than ten, and in a few minutes, she had touched them all. She then went to the alley, where two more men were waiting, and gave them the same sleep command and memory wipe.

Skipping down the alley toward Travis and Jackie, Evelyn felt good about besting these people. How dare they try and take away the thing that makes her special. Those few errant stones floating in the air didn't pose a risk once she dragged Travis and Jackie to the next block. Far away enough from it all but close enough for her to see the stupid men fall to the ground.

She released time.

Travis spun around, taking in his new surroundings. "If you're going to do that, you need to tell me."

"Nice work, girl." Jackie said, eying the collapsing purge people. "You kill them all?" she asked with some hope in her voice.

"I didn't kill them. I just gave them a reason to lay down. And when they get up, they might not know where they are, or what's been going on for the last few months."

Travis shook his head and smiled. "You are a wicked one, Evelyn. I'm glad you're on our side."

"Who said I'm on your side?" She smiled and watched as he took her in with his piercing eyes. The temptation to look into his mind grew, but she looked at the ground and took a deep breath. It wouldn't be right to read him in that way. Besides, he would know. Having a friend in a world was rare for her, and she didn't want to risk losing him.

"Watch out!" Jackie yelled.

Evelyn spun around, only to see the cop from the café standing at the end of the alley, pointing a gun with a large round barrel at her.

She went to slow time as the projectile from the gun came hurtling toward her. Travis pushed her out of the way, and it struck him in the neck.

"No!" Evelyn screamed and fell to his side.

Jackie screamed and threw a stone at the cop. A young man with bright blond hair stepped out from a door. Jackie's eyes went wide as he struck her in the face with a stone. She crashed to the ground and didn't move.

Something struck Evelyn in the back, like two pens stabbing her. Then shockwaves crashed through her nervous system, and she lost touch with the world. Everything seized, as all her muscles fired. She fell to the ground, convulsing. A shadow moved over her, and another shot of electricity raced through her. She would have screamed if she could have, but only a grunting sound left her lips.

"Should have killed me when you had the chance." The cop dropped a stone and it struck her on the forehead.

The world went black.

CHAPTER 25

POLY STARED AT THE SKY. The cubes were gone, and with them, Lucas Pratt.

She wanted to know why these things kept happening to them. They were good people, trying to live normal lives, but the worlds were against them. Maybe the six of them were cursed. Maybe Simon hadn't genetically modified them for Marcus, but for some long con about how much a person could handle and still be a human.

Derek put a hand over her shoulder and pulled her close.

The Preston air blew past them as they stood together on Trip's front porch. Julie sobbed nearby, while holding onto Will. Trip could be heard cursing about how he didn't steal enough RPG's. And Poly openly cried, not just for Lucas, but for all of the days she'd been holding back for Joey.

Leading a simple life at her house, with her mom and

Evelyn by her side, she'd felt like she *might* be able to live without him. But this invasion was too much, and she needed him more than ever.

"Will, we have to get you hooked back up to the radio. All those people. . . ." Julie said.

"Something happened, the power went out." Will pulled the wires attached to his head. "I can keep you all safe, I just couldn't reach Dad. I don't know, he's . . . blocked from me."

"How did you know how to do that?" Julie said as she squeezed him.

"Evelyn taught me."

Julie shot Poly a look.

Poly had felt Will's mind in hers when they were battling the cubes. If it wasn't for him, they'd all be in that cube. She slammed her eyes shut, forcing out the last tears. "We can get to him," she said. "I saw the direction the thing went. We just need to get to the tower before they process him."

"What do you mean?" Trip asked.

"We've seen this before, in another world. They will take him to a tower near here, and do something to him. We were able to stop Edith."

"*Evelyn* stopped Edith," Julie corrected.

"But we have to try."

"I'll go as well," Derek offered, lifting his good hand up. Poly nodded.

Tears fell from Julie's face and then she leaned down to Will. "Can you stay here with Trip to get the radio back up and working?"

"If you're going to save Daddy, I should probably come along. What if those cubes come after you again?" Will said.

"We can handle it, sweetie. You stay here and protect Trip

and Gretchen. We're going to go save Daddy and be right back." She grabbed him in her arms and squeezed him tight.

Poly took in a deep breath. She'd never gotten that one last hug from Evelyn.

"I bet a breaker blew," Trip said to Will. "Think you can give it another go?"

Will frowned and looked back at Julie. "I lied. Nothing broke. I just didn't like getting into so many of their heads. It's not right to know all of their thoughts. I never knew how horrible people can be inside their own heads."

"What are you saying?" Julie asked.

"Nothing. I'll save them for you because I know this is important. Plus, we can't let the queen get any more souls. If she gets any more powerful, Evelyn won't have a chance against her."

Poly jumped at the mention of her daughter's name. "Have you been contacted by her?"

"No, not since she left the planet," Will said. "And I haven't felt her return since."

"Give me a minute with my boy, while I set him back up on the radio," Julie said, then guided Will into the house.

Poly took a few steps away from Derek and glanced at him. He was giving her a look she'd seen from so many men before; his I-need-to-protect-you look. It was so strong, she had trouble keeping eye contact with him. She hadn't been around many non-family-men since Joey died, and she knew she'd never be with another man for as long as she lived. She swore it.

"You have anything else in your goodie bags?" Derek asked Trip.

"Few explosives."

"We'll take some for the road then."

Trip went into the house and returned with a bag of various weapons that Derek and he gushed over, as Poly scratched at the wood railing and stared at the debris in the driveway. She hated waiting. It felt like each second they weren't acting was a second of losing.

Eventually Julie returned, wiped her nose, and kept walking straight to the car.

Poly rushed after her. "We're going to find him and get him back."

She let out a sob. "I know, it's not that. It's Will. He was so cold. I think connecting him to all those people did something to him. I'm not sure I'm doing the right thing here."

Poly cringed at her words and knew her plight well. Being a mother meant putting your kid above all else, but what happened when the waters were muddied and both decisions might hurt them?

"I don't know. Maybe I should take him with us. I mean, those things could come here and attack him."

"I can stay back," Derek said. "I may only have one arm, but I can stop any of those stone-throwing bastards from getting to your son."

Julie shook her head. "No, thank you, but we have to give up on this notion we are in control. Things are going to happen and there isn't a thing we can do to stop them. I trust that Trip and Gretchen are going to protect him with their lives."

Poly got into the car at the same time as Julie, taking the driver's position. She looked over to her friend and glanced back at Derek. The truth of the matter was, if Will had any of the powers Evelyn had, then he wouldn't need protecting. In fact, he'd probably be the one to save Trip and Gretchen's lives when it came down to it.

"He's going to be okay," she said. It sounded simple, but Julie nodded and wiped her nose again.

"Just go before I lose it."

Poly started the car and drove away. She wasn't exactly sure where she was going, but the next town over was much larger, and was the direction the cube had been going.

"You going to Lakeford?" Julie asked.

"Yeah. It's the only big city around here."

"I was thinking of the same thing." Julie didn't say another word for a few minutes, but kept fidgeting with her Panavice and looking out the window. "You think he's still alive?"

"We have to believe he is. He'll be fine. Lucas is smarter than he leads on."

"I suppose." She sighed. "Do you think it's too late for this planet?"

Poly knew exactly what she meant, because she and Julie had seen it firsthand what happened to a world sent into chaos. "We'll fare better than Vanar; we have a shorter distance to fall."

POLY HAD BEEN TO LAKEFORD many times, and she knew the tallest building was the courthouse, at maybe ten stories. Now, right where it used to be, stood a thirty-story structure with a blinking green light. The purge tower.

"You think Lucas could be in there?" Julie asked.

"I do," Poly said, as she slowed the car down and headed straight toward the tower.

Cubes flew in and out of the structure, but the city itself felt quiet. No one walked around, no one was being sucked into the sky . . . and then Poly saw someone.

"I think Trip's radio is working again," she said as they passed the man laying on the sidewalk. Soon, many more people lined the sidewalks, or sat in their cars. All had their eyes open, blankly staring at nothing.

"Will's doing it," Julie said. "It's working. I can't believe it, but Marcus might have saved some people."

"Don't ever give that guy any credit," Poly said between clenched teeth.

"Evelyn told me about him," Derek spoke up from the backseat. "She told me how Zach was his puppet." He shook his head in disgust. "I only wish I knew you people before you killed Marcus. I would have done anything to get my hands around his neck."

Poly thought of the moment Joey killed Marcus. That one moment, where she'd simultaneously gained independence from her oppressor and lost her husband. She'd do anything to get one more moment with him. She didn't give a damn about revenge anymore. She just wanted to help those she loved avoid the pain she felt—the utter loss.

Putting the car in park, she looked to Julie. "Okay, brainiac, what's the plan? That thing have guns like back on Hector's world?"

Julie stared at her Panavice and looked up. "Yes. It has less floors than Hector's, but everything else appears to be the same. Give me a second and I can turn off their defenses." Her hand flew around the Panavice screen. "Derek, get ready. If anyone looks like a threat, shoot them."

"Okay," Derek said and pulled out a rifle from the bag Trip gave them. "When we get to the base of the building, let me take lead."

"Fine, we can direct you from behind," Poly said. "Just don't get all commando on us."

"They're down," Julie said as she gazed up at the tower.

Poly took a deep breath and drove the car near the base of the building, keeping an eye out for the green light from the upper floors. No cubes had flown by since they'd arrived, but Poly had a bad feeling. Like she was being watched.

Derek got out of the car first, with Poly and Julie coming up behind him. They followed him toward the building, and stopped at the front door. "Once we're inside, we're on their turf. Meaning we shoot first, okay?" Derek handed her a gun. "You know how to shoot, right?"

"Yes." Joey had taught her, but she didn't like them.

"Stick close to me."

"Okay," Poly and Julie said in unison.

Derek pushed the door open and moved inside. The lobby didn't have a soul in it. He moved around, checking the blind spots before coming back to them.

"The stairs are over there," Julie said and pointed to the door at the back wall.

Just then, the door opened and a man stepped out.

"Lucas?" Julie rushed up to him. "Oh my God, you're okay."

"Of course I am. Where have you been?"

"Right where you left us. I figured the bastards had already torn you apart."

"No, I escaped," Lucas said. But didn't make eye contact, choosing to look at the floor instead.

"You okay?" Julie asked.

"Yes, I just miss our son. Where is he?"

"Back home."

"They did something to my head," Lucas said. "I think something hit me. Can you tell me where home is?"

Julie touched the back of his head. Lucas stared out the window as she ran her hand through his hair. "You got a nasty bump back there. Does it hurt when I touch it?"

"No, I'm fine. I missed you."

She took a step back. "I missed you too."

"Have you seen Evelyn? I can't remember where she was last either."

"They're both very far away, Lucas. You know this."

"Tell me where our son is," he said with a raised voice.

Julie backed away from him. "I'm not telling you."

"Tell me where Evelyn is."

Poly put her arm around Julie and answered, "No."

"If you don't tell me, they are going to kill me."

Julie covered her mouth and shook her head. "What did they do to you?"

Lucas winked. When Julie moved closer to him, he shook his head and she stopped. Poly watched on with confusion. He seemed weird, and now he was acting weirder.

"They're watching. Run," Lucas whispered. "Run!"

The door swung open and a woman walked out. "I didn't think that compulsion stone worked on you. What did you do, put it in your pocket?" she said walking up to Lucas.

Derek fired a bullet, and it bounced off her like it had hit a steel wall.

The woman glared at him. "Don't do that."

"This is their queen," Lucas said.

Poly's jaw dropped and she stared at the woman. She didn't think she'd actually see the person behind it all. She looked ordinary, with straight brown hair, maybe in her thirties, but she moved with a confidence Poly had become familiar with. Travis had the same kind of swagger.

"You are such an interesting person," the queen said, studying Lucas. "I've never seen a person resist stones like you. Do you know what makes you different?"

"I guess I'm just special."

"No, you don't appear to have the gift. The smart thing to do would be to kill you, but I'd like to study you for a while . . . see what's making you so unique."

"You can't have him," Julie said.

The queen regarded them, as if for the first time. "Some might say I'm lucky to stumble upon one of the *Six*, as you call yourself, but I don't believe in luck. The universe wants me to transcend. It provides what I need, and what I need is Evelyn and your son, Will. Combined, I believe I will have enough to move to the next step." She smiled and looked to the ceiling.

"You're batshit crazy," Poly said. "We won't let you take our children."

The queen narrowed her eyes and stepped closer to Poly.

If the queen had a shield, then there might be a way around it. Marcus's shield had a workaround and Poly kept many different types of blades on her, made of materials from the exotic and weird. If she could get close enough, she might be able to test them out.

A pain shot into her brain and she felt as if another person was in her head, excavating. She dropped the blade in her hand, as memories swirled around in her consciousness—thoughts of Joey and Evelyn. She slammed her eyelids shut and grinded her teeth. The pressure lessened and she focused on pushing the intruder out, but it felt like moving a boulder. She bared down and yelled, pushing the presence out of her head.

The queen looked stunned. "You're her mom."

In one quick motion, Poly threw the knife. The queen didn't move and it struck her in the shoulder, narrowly missing the intended target, her neck.

Shocked, she grasped the thin blade and pulled it from her shoulder. Blood trickled out of the wound. "How did you do that?" She blurred, then reappeared near the door.

Poly knew she'd just moved through time like Evelyn did. She searched her person and found all of her blades were gone. Julie's Panavice wasn't in her hands anymore, and Derek had been disarmed.

"Twice today you have attacked me and succeeded." She dabbed at her shoulder and looked at the blood on her fingertips. "I won't let that happen again. I see your last text to Will, but it won't help him. I know where he is now. It's only a matter of time. The rest of your family will come for you, and eventually, I'll have you all."

Poly stared at the wacko standing in front of them. It'd be a cold day in Hell before she ever gave up her daughter.

"I'll even let you see what I do with your children, since you've given me such trouble. You can watch them help me take my ascension. It's something to be proud of, really. They will be the final ones to push me to the stars." She looked to the ceiling with her hands held high.

"If you think we've hurt you," Poly sneered, "wait until Evelyn and the others get ahold of you."

The queen laughed. "You think you hurt me? Nothing can hurt me. And soon, the entire galaxy, and every version of it, will be at my command. You and your band of ordinary people will be nothing but a blip in my endless life."

"I'd rather you killed us than have to listen to this garbage," Lucas said.

"You're the most interesting of them all. I may keep you," the queen said, then turned to Julie.

Julie grabbed at her head and fell to her knees.

"Stop it!" Lucas yelled, and jumped on the back of the queen.

Derek rushed to the queen as well and swung at her, striking her in the stomach.

The queen grunted and threw Lucas into Derek. She laughed and pointed at them. "This is fun. No one ever dares to attack me." She adjusted her shirt.

"You're a lunatic!" Julie screamed.

"Yes, well . . . I'm afraid I'm going to have to end this little show now. We've set up a not-so-nice place for you. Some of your friends are already there. Something about you three," she pointed to Lucas, Julie, and Poly, "in the same place, is energizing. I'm interested to see if the effects amplify with more of you."

Poly raged and pulled at the spaces where her knives should be. She was still upset about missing the first time. But what could they do now? The woman could control time, she had a shield on, and she'd taken all of their weapons. With a quick glance to Julie, she knew they were screwed. Her eyes were wide with fear. Poly knew the feeling. Someone was hunting their kids now, and that kind of fear overwhelmed you, until you couldn't breathe.

"Maybe we can make some kind of arrangement," Poly began to say, before she felt something strike her hand.

A purple stone soaked into her hand and she fell. The world swirled around her, and soon, her feet hit something solid. She teetered on the bar she was now standing on, and looked down at her feet. A lattice work of metal bars ran underneath her and continued up the walls and over her head, encasing her in a cage of steel. Below her, a metal chute ran into a dark hole below.

"Poly, is that you?" a man called out.

She whipped her head around and in the cell across from her, sat Harris in his underwear. Poly looked down and saw she was in her bra and panties.

Lucas and Julie appeared in another, then Derek. All in the

same stage of undress.

"Great, they got a bunch of you." Harris plopped down on his steel cage and it rattled through the rest of them.

The door at the end of the catwalk running between the cells opened, and the queen walked down it. "Sorry the accommodations are so poor, but we built this on a moment's notice. It will serve its purpose though, as will you all."

CHAPTER 26

HANK STARED AT THE DEAD woman, who used to once be Mary's mother, Cindy's grandmother, and Carl's wife. Mary was the only person that stuck around when they came to this holding cell for their turned mother.

"That's a grinner?" Gladius said and whipped out a knife.

"Just end it," Mary pleaded and ran away.

Jenny staggered and knocked into a chair. She fell to the floor and kept crawling, growling as she moved.

"So crazy," Gladius said. "You think she has any human left in her?"

"No," Hank said. But as he looked at Jenny, he couldn't help but feel for her and her family. This was his kid's grandma. "My real question is, why did they stuff her in here?" Hank hadn't killed a person he knew before, and while he could simply stomp on her head, he hesitated, choosing instead to move Gladius to the other side of the room.

Jenny got back on her feet.

"Can I kill it?" Gladius asked.

"Sure. That thing will kill us both, without remorse or cause. It will rip our flesh off and eat it until it can't eat anymore."

Gladius threw a blade at Jenny and hit her in the neck. "Ooh, look at that black blood. I don't think it even slowed her down. Fascinating."

"It has to be a head shot," Hank said, his blood pressure rising with each step Jenny took.

"But it's not like she poses any real threat. We could just keep walking around the room and avoid her."

"No, these things are too dangerous."

Gladius groaned, then threw another knife. It stuck into her head, causing her to face-plant onto the carpet. "We should leave," Gladius said, reaching down for her knife.

Cost Plus might have been a great place to live on Ryjack, but it wasn't a place to raise his daughter. He turned and faced Gladius. She pulled her knife from Jenny's head and wiped it on Jenny's shirt.

"So gross," Gladius said. "I mean, you told me what these things were, but to see it live, it's just crazy. I wonder what else Marcus spread throughout the worlds that we don't even know about. All the more reason to get off this planet as fast as we can."

"I can't leave her here."

"Really. You want to bring your bastard family along for the ride, to Earth . . . the place that has a full blown *invasion* happening?"

She was making good points, but none of that mattered to Hank. "I know, but I can't. I *won't* leave her."

"Why? You gave them a gift and now you want to take it back?"

"It's not like that. Once I saw Cindy, I knew, I just knew, I could never forget her for as long as I lived. I can't explain it."

Gladius closed her eyes as she crossed her arms. "I'm trying, Hank, I am. But I'm struggling. It's not like you to do what you did. This is a lot to take in all at once."

"Mary was my mother's name," Hank tried to explain.

"What?"

"I don't know, but when I heard her name, I thought it meant something at the time. I thought of my past and how much pain we endured. I saw it in all of our parents' eyes, and I thought, if I can bring a little bit of happiness into one family, how could I not?"

"I get it. You always want to help and I love you for it, but both of our worlds are no safer than Ryjack at the moment. Earth and Vanar may not even be around, if we can't beat this culling queen."

The door burst open and Mary rushed in. She looked as if she had something to say but stopped and stared at her dead mother on the floor. "Is that . . .?"

"Yeah, I'm sorry," Hank said and regretted not covering the body.

"You have no idea how happy I am." She walked closer to him. "Since she died, my dad's lost it." She glanced back at Gladius. "If you're wondering if I want to go with you, I do." She nearly squealed at the end.

"Why not? The more the merrier," Gladius muttered.

"My dad won't like it, but we all need to go. We need to leave this place. I think just being here is messing with him, making him worse. It was the place he built with my mother, and now it's all just a reminder of everything he's lost."

Gladius sighed and rolled her eyes. "Even if we wanted to,

those purge kids said this portal stone could only take a maximum of three people. That leaves me, Hank, and one more."

"Portal stone?"

"We don't have time to explain all of this," Gladius said. "Bottom line, this stone can take us wherever we want to go."

Mary turned with big bright eyes, gazing at Hank, causing a pit to form in his stomach. "You could have gone anywhere and you chose here? You were thinking of me."

"I, uh. . . ."

"Listen, Mary, you're not hearing me," Gladius said. "This stone only takes three, and we only have one stone left. We can't take all of you, even if we wanted to."

"Take Cindy then. Peter and I can find a way to make it there. Just give us a map, something we can follow and we'll meet you there."

Peter stood at the doorway, staring at his dead mother laying on the floor. "Holy hell, you got rid of her. Thank you so much. You know how hard it is to sleep with that thing in the same place as you?"

"Peter, I told you to watch Cindy."

"Oh, Dad took her."

"What? Where?"

"I saw him heading toward the pharmacy," Peter said.

Mary jogged out of the room and pushed past her brother.

Hank rushed after her and glanced back to make sure Gladius was following him. "You think something is wrong?" he asked Mary.

"I sure hope not."

They rushed past aisle thirty-two and made their way toward a large glass window with red lettering spelling out *Pharmacy*. Mary put her hand on the door and shook the handle. She paced near the glass, and then Cindy and Carl came into view. Cindy sat on the floor, playing with a coloring book and a doll. Carl held a gun and kept pacing behind her.

"Dad, open the door."

Carl walked closer to the glass and pointed at Hank. "I refuse to let this man take my granddaughter."

"He's not just any man, Dad," Mary said. "He's her *father*."

"He wasn't ever supposed to come back, that was the deal."

Mary turned to Hank. "Did you tell my dad that?"

Hank rubbed his chin. "I don't know. We were living day to day back then. Still are." He wondered if Carl posed any real threat to Cindy. Though, if Carl showed one sign that he might hurt his daughter, he saw several objects nearby to break down the glass and force entry.

"Did you want to come back to see me, or just a curiosity to see if . . . you know, what you did to me took hold? Did you ever think of me?" Mary asked.

"Maybe we should concentrate on Cindy," Hank said.

"He's not going to hurt her," Mary said, putting her hands on her hips. "If anything, I'm more worried about my dad's safety."

Hank didn't blink as he watched Carl pace. He kept shifting his hand on his gun and touching the trigger. "Is that gun loaded?"

"Yes, he went outside and got some supplies a few months back. Mainly, he wanted that gun. He sleeps with it." Mary hit the glass. "Open this door."

"No, he's going to take her away from us," Carl said. "I saw the way he looked at her."

It wasn't easy for Hank to hide his expression of urgency in wanting to get Cindy off this planet, but he didn't want to break up a family either. First things first, he needed to get Cindy out of that room and contain Carl. If it weren't for Carl's kids looking on, he might have already subdued the man physically, but they had seen enough in their lives. Carl was right though, he was going to take Cindy, one way or another.

"Do you want to raise another kid in this place?" Hank asked. "Look around you."

Carl's pace slowed, but he kept moving and tapping his gun.

Hank continued, "If you let me take her, I can bring her somewhere safer. I can provide a home for her."

"You speak as if you would just take Cindy. Why wouldn't you take Mary or Peter?"

"I can't. Not now, but I will come back and get them all, you as well, Carl. There is a place that doesn't have the dead banging at your door."

Gladius huffed, only loud enough for Hank to hear. But her words from earlier echoed in his head. Bringing them back to Earth wasn't exactly safer, but he had faith in his friends, in Evelyn. They would find a way to stop the purge, just as they had found a way to stop all the other people who stood in their way.

"So we are just to accept your magical appearance here, and let you whisk our child away, without a real explanation of where you're taking her?"

"Yes."

"Then my answer is no. And I don't care if there are a thousand dead things outside, I want you gone, *now*."

"Daddy, no," Mary said.

Carl lifted his gun and pointed it at Hank.

"Lower the gun, Carl." Hank didn't think the glass separating them would do much to slow the bullet. He pushed Gladius back and away from him.

"You can't have her, I won't let you." Carl grinded his teeth in a snarl, then jerked his hand back in pain. His fingers extended and the gun fell to the floor. He looked back at Cindy as she stood behind him, holding out her hands, staring at him through the tops of her eyelashes. "What did you do?" he asked, and fell to his knees.

"I won't let you hurt my dad," Cindy said.

"No, tell me it isn't true," Hank said and moved to the glass. "I was hoping. . . ."

"She can do stuff when she gets mad," Mary said.

"Why didn't you tell me?" Hank asked.

"I didn't want to scare you away." She looked at the floor and swayed.

Hank watched as Carl fell to the floor in a fetal position. Cindy lowered her hands and Carl rolled onto his back.

"Just what we needed," Gladius said. "One is trouble, two are dangerous, but if we get three of these near each other, it will be downright scary."

"What are you talking about? Are there others like her?"

If Cindy was anything like Evelyn, she'd be considerably more powerful than just messing around with an old man. She would be controlling this entire place, and probably all the grinners outside as well. No, Hank knew Cindy was something different. Much older, but with only a smidgeon of the others' powers. Hank's real question was, what would Evelyn think of Cindy? Just one look at Will and she'd turned on him, saying he would end them all.

The extra complications added to an overtly complicated situation to begin with, and Hank second-guessed his decision to take her to his world. She might be safer here, away from Evelyn, and maybe even Will.

Hank shuddered at the idea of what Evelyn would be like when she reached the same age as Cindy. Maybe they could hide her from Evelyn? "There are two others. Remember Joey and Poly, and Julie and Lucas?"

"Yeah."

"They had kids."

"Cindy could have friends near her age? They would be like cousins."

"Sort of."

"I still want you to take her. Even if it means I won't see my baby girl for a few days. Just tell me where you're going."

The pleading in her eyes tore at Hank's heart. If he couldn't bring them both, then should he even bring the one? Separating mother and daughter; it wasn't right. And what if something terrible happened back on Earth? Either way, the odds weren't in her favor.

Mary held her hands together, near her chest. Hank gazed at her and her youthful face. She didn't have the innocent look he might see in most young women—he doubted anyone on Ryjack would have that look—but she did seem further away from his age than the last time they met. Shorter as well, if that was possible.

It didn't much matter because what had happened, happened, and Cindy was the result of their encounter. He still couldn't get over it. He had a daughter and she was standing a dozen feet away.

Ignoring the looks of Mary, he pushed at the locked door. The urge to get to his special little girl swelled up in him. Maybe the shock of it all had worn off and the true emotions were settling in. Whatever it was, he wanted to hold his daughter. He wanted to pick her up and see her smile.

The door opened and Cindy stood there, looking up. "I didn't hurt him too bad. He might have a headache and a sore wrist."

END OF THE SIX

He swooped her off the floor and held her high above him. Her hair dangled down her face, as she giggled at the activity. It felt stupid to have so much love for someone he'd only met a few minutes earlier, but there it was.

"I'm getting you out of here. Would you like that?" Hank asked.

Cindy looked perplexed and Hank set her back down. "Mom, are we leaving?"

Mary knelt down to Cindy. "I'm going to be right behind you, but your daddy is going to take you away first. I promise, I'll be coming for you as soon as I can." Cindy's eyes watered and Mary brushed back her daughter's hair. "Don't cry. I'll see you again, real soon."

"Oh, for the love of God, I can't take this," Gladius spoke up from the hallway. "Hank, you take your family to the stone. I'm not sure how you're going to explain to them that we travel between worlds, but go for it. I'll find my own way and meet up with you. I have a bajillion times better chance of making it than Mary. No offense."

Hank paused and wished he hadn't. It gave Gladius the idea he might contemplate leaving her behind. He looked over to Carl as he still lay on the ground. If Cindy could do that to her grandfather, what might she do to someone whom she didn't like? "I'm not leaving you."

There wasn't any question in his statement, but Gladius took it as if there was room in it.

She jumped on his response like a coiled spring. "Why not? You don't think I can take care of myself? Or do you think I might be jealous of this whole insta-family thing you got going on here?"

"I never said—"

"I'm perfectly fine with this magical appearance of your

family. No problems at all."

"Gladius, please. I'm not going to leave you here."

"Then what will you do? Send little Miss here across the grinner infested earth to try and reach the stone, which she will have no idea how to work, and it wouldn't matter if she did because it wouldn't work for her?"

"You don't know that."

"I do. You think she's been tinkered with? Her daughter, maybe, but her, no. You send her out there and it's a death sentence. The only path that makes sense here, is for you to take the mother and daughter, and I'll make my own way."

Hank rubbed his chin, feeling a day's growth on it. The fact she was mad at him, made his gut hurt. The idea of leaving behind his daughter seemed as impossible as leaving Gladius behind. "Mary, I swear, as soon as I can, I will come back and get you, and your brother, and dad as well." Mary opened her mouth and raised her finger, but Hank rushed over her with words. "There isn't any other way to do this. And this way, we can get Cindy to a place of safety."

Gladius cleared her throat and looked at the floor.

"He's not lying, Mom," Cindy said. "The best option right now is for them to take me and for you to stay here until we can get back." She reached her hand up and grasped Hank's.

Carl groaned and rolled onto his side.

"We should leave now. He won't be pleasant soon," Cindy said.

Mary rushed over to her and grabbed her in a big hug, tears falling from her eyes. She turned her gaze to Hank. "You swear on her life, you'll come back for us?"

"As long as I am alive, I will find a way back here," Hank said, and knew he would find a way, even if it meant getting them all out through the wasteland of Ryjack.

"Mom, I'll be fine. He's going to protect me now. We can stop worrying," Cindy said.

Mary smiled and wiped her wet face.

Gladius approached with the stone sack in her hand. "We ready?"

"Yes," Hank said.

"You better concentrate on the location this time."

Hank nodded and they formed a hand triangle with Cindy. Hank caught Mary's eyes as he felt the stone hit his hand. For her, he concentrated on getting them home. If they still had a home to get to, that was.

CHAPTER 27

EVELYN'S FACE BOUNCED OFF THE carpet. Her body jostled around. She opened her eyes and quickly assessed her situation. Carpet floors, rattling noises, tires moving over a road. She was in a trunk of a car, and worse yet, someone was blocking her abilities. She tried to move, but her arms were restrained behind her back and tied to her feet.

The car bounced again and her head struck the steel underside of the trunk. The car engine roared, and she felt the momentum of driving forward with great acceleration. She'd pay attention to any turns and road conditions from then on. The car veered to the right and the drone of tires on pavement turned into the crunchy sound of tires on dirt.

Over the next twenty minutes, Evelyn pulled and tugged at the restraints, resulting only in cutting her skin on the cuffs.

The car stopped, then shook, as the car door slammed shut.

Shoes shuffled across the hard packed dirt. Evelyn made one last effort to get loose, but failed. She resorted to playing dead, and closed her eyes.

The trunk lifted open and the bright sun flooded in. She felt the heat on her skin and the light shone through her eyelids. She stayed as still as a corpse. A hand touched her and shook her, but she played out the ruse.

Two hands moved to her back. She listened as the restraints loosened and the person pulled her from the trunk. She struggled with the urge to slip time and ruin these kidnappers, but the blackout person was still around. She'd have to bide her time and search them out in the darkness.

Where are Travis and Jackie?

"I know you're awake," a man said and she recognized his voice from the diner. "You can stop pretending, it won't matter. We'll block you out until you're delivered to her."

At least now she knew her destination, her captor, and one or more blockers.

She opened her eyes to see the cop holding her like a baby. She couldn't use her demure size to fool this man, but everyone had their weaknesses. With her hands still tied behind her back, she wiggled her wrists, trying to find a way out of them.

"There's those pretty eyes."

"Why have we stopped?" She gazed at the desert beyond.

"This is the final destination for you and your friend."

"Where is he?"

"Still unconscious in the back of the car. Apparently, you have a resistance to stones he doesn't share. You are the most interesting little girl I've ever encountered." His black shirt felt rough against her face and the stiff buttons poked against her arm. Two pin holes sat on his breast pocket, probably where his name badge would normally sit.

"What did you do with Jackie?"

"The blonde? She's on a no touch list. Probably back to her plotting and scheming. God I hate those kids."

She frowned and looked up at the man. He had one of those faces that'd seen too much sun. His brown hair held tufts of gray, though the man didn't look much older than his late thirties.

The person blocking her must be in the car. Controlling her breathing, she closed her eyes and went into the world between worlds. The place she last found her blocker. Then it winked out and she snapped back into reality.

"We saw what you did to the last girl. There are precautions in place this time. We don't want to lose our precious cargo. The only drawback is portal stones don't work, so we've got to do this the old fashioned way."

In the heat, her wrist sweated and she continued to work on her restraints. Just a bit further and she might be able to dislocate her thumb. "You won't make it out of this alive," she warned.

He laughed. "None of us will. We all die."

"She won't though, will she?" Her thumb caught up on the edge of the handcuff, and she pushed it inward, trying not to show any pain or strain in her face.

"May she live forever," he said and looked to the sky.

Evelyn pushed until she felt her socket pop. Then she yanked her hand out of the cuff. The cop still looked to the sky as Evelyn straightened and stiffened her finger and sent it into the man's neck. She felt the esophagus and pushed her finger through, collapsing the man's windpipe. His warm blood poured over her hand and trailed down her arm, but she kept digging and squeezing, until he dropped her to the ground.

The warm sun shone brightly on the cop as he stumbled

backward and tripped over a rock. He grabbed at his neck, gurgling and spurting blood down the front of his shirt. Falling to his side, he stopped moving.

The gross feeling of another person's blood on her skin made her feel the need for a thorough wash down. A gust of wind swept up some dirt and sand, collecting on her sticky hand. She reached down and wiped it as best she could on the bottom of the cop's black, pleated slacks. A gun stuck out from just above his shoe and she pulled it out of its sheath. A small revolver of some sort, maybe a .38, with the bullets in it.

Walking toward the car, a young girl's head popped up from the front seat—maybe fourteen. Then Evelyn spotted the same girl in different clothing pop up and stare at her.

Twins.

Evelyn sighed and remembered the twins back on Earth, and at the queen's house. She'd handled them, and surely she could handle another set of twins. They must have held some kind of extra power. Maybe they could join forces and create a super stone-making person. The thought of it made Evelyn laugh. If they had any chance against her, they should have taken it while she lay unconscious in the trunk.

If Travis wasn't in the backseat, she might be tempted to blow holes through the car, or light the whole thing on fire. But she needed two things: to get rid of these twin girls, and to make sure she had a way out of the desert without walking what might be a hundred miles.

She rolled her thumb around until she got it to pop back in place. "Get out of the car and I won't kill you." She held the gun up and the girl ducked back down. She fired a shot, bouncing it off the front windshield. They screamed and the door opened. "Thank you. Now stop doing whatever it is you are doing to block me, and walk into the desert and don't look back."

The twins walked away from the car. Their long, black curly hair waved around in the wind. Dropping a white stone on the ground, they stopped and looked at her. Evelyn felt the world come into focus. The wind, the heat, the sounds, all became amplified. She wondered if she had just experienced the world as a common person would—dull and lacking the colorful sensory receptions everything had to offer. The twins' connections and embers floated around them.

"Where do we go?" one of the twins asked.

"Can't you people jump around?"

"They won't give us portal stones," they said in unison.

God, she hated twins; something creepy about genetically identical people. "The cop was meeting someone here, so I'm sure they can help you if you wait around long enough."

They both looked at the cop laying in the dirt. She assumed they would be disgusted, but they seemed indifferent at his gruesome demise. "Are you going to kill the queen?"

"I'm going to try. Now get out of here before I change my mind about you two."

The girls sneered but walked away. Evelyn darted to the car and opened the back door. Travis's foot slipped out and she climbed into the car. Cradling his head, she sighed. These damned stone people and their powers. She hated the idea of such a race existing. They could do so many things with their ability that she couldn't understand, yet. If she couldn't beat these people the way she wanted to, she might have to resort to doing things she didn't want to do.

Hopping into the front, she started the car. Doing a U-turn, she eyed the twins. They were a few hundred feet away, their gazes following her as she drove away.

Another problem with her small body . . . cars weren't built for little girls. She split her time between looking over the steering wheel, and pressing the gas pedal. She didn't have time for this. Stopping time and running would be faster, but she just didn't have it in her. Plus she didn't want to leave Travis behind.

The flat road stretched out to the horizon, and she knew where she needed to go. The trip was undetermined, but the destination wouldn't be. She'd only hoped the mutants had come through for her. If they did, it'd be a straight trip to the queen. And once she got ahold of that woman for a second time, she wasn't going to let go until she ended her.

CHAPTER 28

HANK STOOD AT THE EDGE of the circle. The forest around Preston had healed, for the most part. Charred branches and fallen trees were still prevalent, but it all made him smile. The silence. The sunlight. Had his friends already won?

This portal had been a thoroughfare of invading cubes. Now, a blue jay was squawking.

"Daddy, is this home?" Cindy asked.

"Yes, it is."

"And there's no dead people like Grandma around?"

"Nope, this planet doesn't have such dangers."

Cindy let go of his hand and turned in a circle, looking up at the sky. A small round rock landed near her.

Hank squinted and gazed at the green stone, as it broke open. A cloud burst around them. "Cindy!" He grabbed her and pulled her away from it. But two steps later, he felt the toxins bringing him to his knees. Hank fell down and watched as Gladius and Cindy fell next to him.

He hadn't been in his world for more than a minute with his family, before getting them all killed.

"HANK, WAKE UP."

He knew that voice and he bolted upright.

"There you are, big man. I knew if they caught me, you'd have no chance," Lucas said.

"Lucas?" Hank got to his feet and looked at the cage surrounding him. In the other cages nearby, he spotted Lucas, Julie, Poly, and another man who seemed familiar, but he couldn't place. One of his arms looked to be cut off, with bandages wrapping the appendage. Harris sat in a cage to himself and raised his hand in a wave.

Next to him, Cindy and Gladius stirred awake.

"What happened, Daddy?" Cindy asked, and four heads whipped around to look at her.

"Whoa, hold on a minute. Did she just call you *Dad*?" Poly asked.

"Yes—"

"Did you and Gladius get trapped in some kind of time rift?" Julie asked and then a terrified expression filled her face. "How long have we been in here?"

"Everyone, this is Cindy. You might remember her mom, Mary, from back on Ryjack."

Lucas looked confused and then his eyes went wide. "You sly dog! No wonder you wanted to take the first shift that night."

Hank tried to keep his face from going red, and failed miserably. "Yes, but only to help them. I didn't even know

Cindy existed until just recently. And when I found out, I couldn't leave her on Ryjack."

"Way to go, *Daddy*," Lucas said. "Save her from Ryjack, only to bring her here."

"Where is here?" Gladius asked.

"We're in her prison," Harris said and got to his feet. "The queen is rounding us up like sheep and stuffing us into these corrals. I'd hoped you two could escape this. And congrats on the kid, by the way."

"Thank you," Hank said. "So how are we going to get out of here?"

"It's impossible," Julie said. "I've looked at every angle, and they all lead to us being stuck right here."

"There's more of us still out there. So, there's hope," Hank said.

"How much did it take to get you in here?" Julie asked.

"We were ambushed right as we landed inside the portal circle in Preston," Gladius said. "I didn't even see our attacker."

"Exactly," Julie said.

Hank frowned and studied each of his friends. How long had it taken for them to give up in here? No place, no matter what Julie stated, was impenetrable. They could find a way, they just needed to figure it out.

The door at the far end of the line of cells flung open, and a beautiful woman stomped down the steel floors, sending vibrations through the metal framework. Hank glanced at his friends as they scowled at her.

"You've got to be kidding me," she said and covered her mouth. "There is another of you?" She stared at Cindy. "Not as brilliant as the others, but . . . wow, you sparkle."

"Go to hell," Poly said.

Hank pushed Cindy behind him.

"One or two more and we can be done with this. They should be here soon," the queen looked back at the door. "You know, with all of you in the same room, there is a much stronger glow emanating off of you. This last one, Hank is it? Amplified it." She tapped her chin. "Very curious, you lot."

"What do you want with us?" Hank asked.

"Nothing more than the souls of your children." She smiled. "Doesn't *that* sound wicked?" She raised an eyebrow, then rolled her eyes and groaned when she didn't get a response. "None of you understand the gift you're giving. When I complete my transformation, there will be no more pain, suffering, or plight. I will be able to control all and be all. You said 'Go to Hell', but I aim to make this plane of existence Heaven."

"You're crazy," Gladius said.

"You know, at first I underestimated your lot. I mean, we've plowed through worlds with way more tech than you, but I've never seen anything biologically like you in all the worlds. So I did research and while it was very difficult to figure out your history, I gathered from the different worlds you all bounced around on, that you were invented to defeat me. A man named Marcus Malliden seems to be behind it all. Is he still alive?"

"We killed him," Poly said.

"Pity. And what happened to Joey and Samantha? You all started with six."

"They were killed by Marcus," Julie said.

"Interesting, and the humans on your planet were able to block out my collectors. Do you know how?"

Silence.

"I can make you talk."

"How are your collectors doing now? Do they like their new master?" Harris asked.

"Your little bit of tech may have destroyed my reclamators, but it all matters not. I have no use for them, once I collect what I need from the children."

"Evelyn is smarter than you and you know it," Harris said.

She chuckled. "She might be smarter, but I'm wiser. She's a little girl. Now that I know her tricks, she won't get past my protection."

Poly walked to the edge of her cell, getting close to the queen. "She's smart enough to know not to come here. She will break you in a way you won't see coming."

CHAPTER 29

KRIS HAD GONE THROUGH SEVERAL doors now. Each brought some sort of pain or difficulty, but the last room held something he couldn't have prepared for. A miracle.

"Tara, is that you?" he asked.

His first wife stood in the circular room, with her back turned to him. Her long, wavy brown hair and bracelet gave her away. He'd given her that bracelet as a wedding gift. Made from a band of silver and sapphires. Nobody in the tribe wore such jewelry, but Tara loved it from the moment she saw it.

She looked over her shoulder and Kris fell to his knees.

"That's not Tara," Maggie said.

"Yes, it is. She's been brought back to me." Kris extended his arms and walked toward Tara.

She turned and faced him, extending her arms.

Joy filled Kris's heart. Then he felt hands grabbing his

shoulders. Maggie was trying to stop him. She didn't want him to be happy. He fought with Maggie, shoving her to the ground. He would apologize later. First, he needed to embrace his wife.

Maggie grabbed his broken arm and yanked at it.

He screamed and raised his hand at Maggie, then stopped. *What am I doing?* She held her hands up, ready to defend. The trance-like feeling of seeing his ex-wife left him. He turned to face the woman, but no one was there. Just an empty room. "What do you think that was?"

"I don't know. A projection of some kind. Did you see my mom?"

"No."

"I didn't think so. I bet if we went up to them and took those hugs, we'd be dead."

Kris shook his head and rubbed his hurt arm. It still stung from Maggie ripping at it. He helped her off the floor and apologized for his behavior. She accepted it, and they moved toward the circular room.

"Freaky stuff. It must be some kind of magic," Maggie said.

"I don't believe in magic, but I believe in the capabilities of man. Whoever set this place up, doesn't want the wrong people to find what's hidden here."

"We have to be close. I don't even see another door in the room up ahead."

Kris gazed at the circular stone room. It had a stone chest in the middle. The contents had to be what they were looking for, but how could he trust anything so easy for him to open and take?

"You think it's in there?" Maggie asked.

"Something is in there and I doubt it's pleasant." He walked to the box and stopped a few feet in front of it.

A stone lid, about an inch thick, sat on top of the stone box.

The lid had an engraving of a circle with symbols all around it. Some were masked by a layer of dust. He bent down and blew off some of the dust and one of the four symbols lit up with a green light.

"What'd you do?" Maggie asked.

"Nothing, just blew on it."

"What does it mean?"

"I don't know. These kind of symbols were on the doors as well."

"Should we just try and open it?"

"I don't know. I've got one useful arm. You think you can get the other half of this?"

"Yes," she said and Kris heard the urgency in her tone. They both knew they didn't have long before something terrible would happen to Char.

"Only live once, might as well leave with no regrets," Kris said and stood next to the lid. "You ready?"

She nodded and stood next to him with her hands still blazing. The stone lid would absorb it, but he also thought if this didn't work, she could melt it down.

"Okay, lift," Kris said.

They both pulled on the small edge of the stone. Maggie's hands burned hotter and another symbol lit in a bright red. "What the heck?" she said, stopping her efforts to look at the new symbol.

"You see that? When I blew on it, the green one lit, and when you got close with those hands, the red one lit. How much you want to bet water lights up one?"

Maggie's face brightened and she ran back to the end of the hall. "Dad, can you throw up that wet shirt?" In a few seconds, she had the shirt and rushed back to the stone lid. She squeezed the shirt and a few drops of water struck the lid. Another symbol lit up blue.

"Only two more symbols left."

"These are elements," Maggie said, pointing at the lid. "Earth. The next one is earth, I bet. Is there any dirt?"

Maggie went to the floor and rubbed her hands on the stone. Not seeing anything but rock, Kris went to the walls and then to the ceiling. Each inch seemed to be carved from solid stone. A small stone lay on the floor and Kris picked it up. A rock was made of the earth, maybe it would work.

Hovering over the stone, he dropped the rock onto it. It bounced and then rolled off the edge. Nothing lit up.

"Worth a try," Maggie said.

Kris patted his pants pocket and felt a lump. He plunged his hand inside and felt a small pile of sand. Sand was earth. It had to work. Grabbing as much as he could, he held it over the lid and poured it out like an hourglass.

Another symbol lit and he brushed off the lid to look at the final symbol. A spear holding up a heart, like a demented cupid. "What do you think?" Kris asked.

"Blood?"

"Maybe." Kris remembered a sharp rock against the wall when he searched for dirt and went back to it. Using the back of his hand, he scratched the rock until he had a trace of blood running down his hand. With fresh blood, he ran back to the symbol and let a drop hit it. He stepped back, and watched as a spike came out of the symbol to the height of a few inches, before receding back into the lid.

"What the hell was that?" Maggie asked.

"I think it wants more." Kris looked down at his hand. It had already scabbed over, and the flow had ended. He cut up his hand until the blood gushed once more, then placed it over the symbol. The spike rose higher and produced tiny needles around it, much like a cactus. Kris tried to maintain the blood coming from his hand, but he felt dizzy and cold.

He sat down and wrapped his hand up with material from his torn sleeve. The spike retreated back into the stone. "I don't think I have enough blood in me."

Maggie sat down and let her hand go out. In the darkness, Kris listened to her breathing, and stared at the four lit symbols. He had to be missing something.

"This sucks. I'm going to check on my dad," Maggie said and turned back to the pit.

Kris hesitated, hoping for a last second inspiration, but nothing came.

They made their way down the ladder. Maggie jumped from the last few footholds and landed in the water. "Dad?" She shook him and looked back to Kris.

His heart sank and he prayed the big man wasn't dead. Not now.

"Dad. Wake up." She pushed on his chest and Char raised his head and opened his eyes.

"You get the treasure?" he asked.

"Not yet." Maggie wiped her nose. "God, I thought I lost you there."

"Still here." Char coughed and in the dim light, blood trickled down his chin.

"Dad, you're bleeding."

"It's okay."

"No, it's not. We need to get you out of here."

"Get what we came for first, *then* we can start thinking about getting out of here."

Maggie kept her glowing hands back and put her face on

her father's chest.

Char petted her hair and looked up at Kris. He shook his head and then looked down at her. Kris understood the meaning and would take care of Maggie as if she was his own. He fought back tears and turned to look back up at the door.

"Don't even think about it," Maggie said.

He didn't know she'd been watching, but she'd probably thought the same thing. How much blood would it take to open the box? Kris thought he knew the answer, but didn't want to say it out loud. And everything in him told him the only way out of this place was to open that chest.

"Think about what?" Char asked.

Maggie went on to tell him about the symbols and she rushed over the heart one with a couple sentences.

"It's going to want a whole lot more than the blood anyone is willing to part with, is my guess," Char said.

Kris agreed. "Aye, I think you're right on that."

Char nudged Maggie back and then rolled over onto one knee.

"What are you doing? You shouldn't be moving," Maggie said, holding out her hands as if she'd need to catch Char at any second.

"Nonsense, I think a third set of eyes is in order. A fresh perspective," Char said and got to his feet.

"You can barely stand. How do you think you can make it up the shaft?"

"Piece of cake. I'm stronger than the average person, you know." Char eased his way over to the wall of the pit and put his hand in the first slot. "Stay back, just in case."

Kris didn't need the warning, but Maggie took a few steps back to give her dad some landing room, in case he needed it.

"Be careful," she said and looked to Kris. "I don't like this."

Char pulled himself up the first rung and then quickly made work of the next four with only a few grunts. In under a minute, the big man pulled himself on the upper platform and disappeared into the hall.

Kris nudged Maggie. "Go on up."

"I'm coming, Dad." She rushed up the latter and Kris followed right behind her.

Char lay at the end of the hall, propped up against the wall and looking at the stone.

"You okay?" Maggie asked.

Char nodded, but then went into a coughing fit.

"We need to get him out of here," Maggie said.

"Did you notice the door we came through?"

"What of it?"

"It's clearly a one way door. The only way out is forward. If we can't figure this last symbol out, we're all going to die down here."

Char again willed himself to his feet and stumbled toward the stone. "Listen, it doesn't take a rocket scientist to figure out the symbol. It wants a spike through the heart. It demands a life."

"But what if it doesn't want that?" Maggie asked.

"I'm not sure how much longer I have, my dear." Char gripped the sides of the chest the symbols sat on.

Kris felt his heart pounding. He knew what Char was about to do. "No," he said and used his fast arm speed to push Char aside. In the same movement, he smeared blood across his chest and hugged the lid, placing his heart right where the symbol was. The spike came up and pierced his chest bone, his blood soaking into his shirt. He ignored the screams from Maggie and held tight onto the stone lid, as her hot hands tried to pull him off.

In his final moments, he knew Char would pull through. The last thing he wanted was to see Maggie lose another parent.

He didn't have any kids of his own; probably didn't have the right stuff to make them. Many mutants were that way, which made Char and Maggie all the more special.

He thought this would be the part where he died, but that wasn't so. Not yet, anyway. It hurt like hell and he held back a scream of his own, as Maggie yanked on his shoulders. She couldn't see it, but he was far too gone to stop. The damage had been done.

Next, hundreds of needles stuck into his chest cavity and the thing pulled at him. Tears fell from his eyes as the spike retreated. He slid off the chest and looked up with his last seconds of life, to see the edges of the lid crack open and emit a brilliant light. Maybe this was Heaven calling to him, but at least he knew he'd just sent his friends home. That had to count for something. Maybe some of his sins would be forgiven now.

MAGGIE PUSHED AGAINST KRIS. "WHAT did you do?"

But he didn't answer. He wouldn't be answering another question ever again. The man lay dead at the base of the chest.

Her heart pounded and she stepped back, as the lid on the chest lifted.

"Careful," Char wheezed.

She slid her feet across the stone floor, daring a peek into the open chest. She cringed as she looked into it, expecting a spear to shoot out.

Nothing. No weapons or booby traps. All it contained was a simple box that lay at the bottom. She briefly panicked, thinking the box would demand another sacrifice, or even worse, it would be empty and Kris's sacrifice would be for not.

"You think it's in there?" Char asked.

"I don't know, but there's only one way to find out." She reached in against Char's protest and lifted the box out. Not much larger than the jewelry box Char had carved out of a solid block of wood for her thirteenth birthday.

Maybe this box would give them their final freedom. Evelyn had shown them this promised world. A world without prosecution or judgment, and the freedom to make it as they saw fit.

The idea seemed too big and she took a deep breath, feeling as if she was drowning. Kris would have been the spearhead of this transformation, but now he lay motionless at their feet. She felt the tears building and held them back.

She sat the box on the floor and lifted one hand to give her more light. With her other hand she opened the lid.

Char peeked over her shoulder. "What are they?"

"I don't know, but I do know this is what Evelyn will want."

Inside, sat four stones. Two color shifting stones on each end. Hues of white and black, mixed with deep reds and sharp yellows. The colors moved as she moved the box.

The other two stones sat in the middle of the velvet lined insides. They were purple, with identical yellow markings.

"What do they do?" Char asked and then coughed.

"I have no idea." She looked at Kris and then to the ceiling. No exit had opened, and nothing had changed. They were still trapped.

"Look," Char said and pointed at the lid.

Maggie tilted the lid and saw the gold engraving above each stone. Over the two color-shifting ones, sat a single letter over each, an *A* and an *M*. In the middle, it showed a hill with a door in it, and a tower with a circle around it.

"That looks like the hill we just came in," Maggie said and studied the picture. "What do you think it means?"

"Maybe that stone takes us to these pictured places, like the Alius stones."

"That's crazy."

"The person who made these stones probably made the Alius stones as well. I don't think it's farfetched to think they made a portable version."

They debated for several minutes before Maggie conceded to the idea. "What do you think we should do?" she asked.

"We should touch it at the same time."

Maggie nodded and lifted the box with one hand. She neared her pointer finger to the stone and waited for her dad.

"If this doesn't work. . . ."

"Save it. On three. One, two, three." She pressed her finger on the stone at the same time as her dad. The world fell from under her, and as she entertained the idea she'd died, the world firmed back into place, and they both appeared outside the enclosure.

She laughed and closed the box. "We made it!" She jumped and hugged her dad.

They stood on top of the same hill they'd entered. A few of the mutants had made a campfire below, and several structures had been built for makeshift tents and toilets.

"Hey, up there!" one of them yelled as he noticed them on the hill.

Maggie and Char waved below. Then it struck her, Kris still lay down below; dead, but without a proper burial. She wanted to rush through the maze once again to pull him out.

"He's where he belongs," Char said. "Don't let his sacrifice be wasted. That box represents a new beginning for us. We are going to finally have a real home."

She bit her lip and looked down. Somewhere, deep underground, lay Kris. She kissed her fingers, then touched the ground. "Thank you."

"I was supposed to be the one to lie on that spike. Not sure why he did it," Char said, before he coughed blood into his hand.

"You better not die on me now."

"Never." He wiped his mouth. "I hope it was worth it." He pointed to the box.

"We need to get this to Evelyn," Maggie said.

"You think this will truly be the end of it?"

"I have to believe it will."

CHAPTER 30

EVELYN PARKED THE CAR NEAR a tree and turned off the engine. Reaching into the backseat, she shook Travis.

He moaned and lifted his hand, but didn't regain total consciousness. She didn't need him to be fully functioning, but she surely couldn't leave the man in the middle of China.

"Travis, wake up." She shook him again with vigor, and he opened his eyes.

He sat up, rubbing his head. "What happened?"

"I just battled with that sheriff guy and some creepy twins."

Travis nodded as if he understood, but Evelyn doubted it. The man was a grade *A* bullshitter. The politician in him shone through more times than not, but she'd come to admire him for it. He'd been gifted limited ability, yet still accomplished so much.

Evelyn often wondered what her history would be like once she reached Travis's age. Dark images usually swirled around in her imagination when she did. Her young mind kept hope for the human race, but what would happen when she'd seen too much?

"Where are we?" he asked.

"We're still in China."

He looked out the windows and at the forest surrounding them.

"Don't worry. They don't know I'm here."

"You get us next to a stone?"

"Yes."

"Where's Jackie?" Travis asked.

"They said she was untouchable and let her go; whatever that means."

"Good. We need to get back to Earth. We need to find the others and help them."

"This is where we're going to split up," Evelyn said. "The next steps are things only I can do."

"What about your family?"

"Most likely, the queen has them at this point. Worst case, she's killed them. But I don't think she'll do that."

"You don't know that."

"No, but I don't believe she would kill the only bait she could use to lure me in."

"Some things are unpredictable. You don't need to do this alone. You could have left me in the back of this car, rode the stone out of here and never looked back, but you woke me."

"It was the right thing to do. Regardless, the next part of this could go bad for me—bad for all of us—and people like you are going to slow me down. There will be no time to hesitate, not when so much is on the line."

"Going alone is a mistake, trust me."

"I do trust you," Evelyn said and gazed at the floor mat. "It's just, the queen is more like me than you. She'd crush you like a tsunami moving through a wheat field. I have to do this alone."

Travis frowned and slid to the edge of the backseat to get closer to her. "I know what it's like to be alone in the world; to think you are the only one who can do what needs to be done. I've been there at one point and it nearly killed Poly and Julie. When I became president of Vanar, I knew I'd have to work with many people to get the job I needed done. People I thought might hurt me. . . ."

"Like Harris?"

He nodded. "People like Harris, and many others. I formed a team, and together, we brought back Vanar. And yes, you were a big part of that team."

She felt more like the entire team. She'd reprogrammed their net, got Orange flowing, trucks moving, and turned back on the power plants. She'd done more for Vanar in a couple months than Travis's team could have done in years.

"I see in your eyes I'm not getting through to you," Travis said. "So, I must demand to go with you. They are my friends, not to mention my own daughter is involved in this. Plus, you'll need me at some point. You'll need to learn to rely on us. You are not alone in this fight."

"You don't get it." Evelyn willed her voice to not crack. "I was right there when my dad pushed himself too far. I was too young then, too trusting. I let everyone help me, and look at what happened to my dad."

"Marcus killed your dad and there's nothing any of us could have done to stop it. You're going to have to trust me on this. Bring your family in, bring the Six in . . . you are going to want them all to help you get rid of this queen."

Evelyn sat back in the front seat and tapped the door handle. She could easily bounce into her slow-mo and leave before

Travis could say anything else. Friends and family made things harder. The emotions tied to them, the feelings. . . .

She sighed. "Fine, you can come with me."

"Good. Where are we going?" Travis asked.

She hadn't wanted to bring him to the planet she'd found for the mutants, as they would see it as a breach of trust, but the man was persistent. Besides, maybe he was right. She might actually need them.

"We need to pick up something from the mutants; something I hope they've collected by now. Then, we make our move on the queen."

Travis didn't push her to what that might be and she was grateful for it, because she wasn't entirely sure what it'd be at this point.

They made their way to the nearby stone and Evelyn had Travis turn his back to her as she typed in the code. In the last moment before the jump, she stilled her time, allowing her to control the jump point.

Above them, a dome of air stood, holding back the ocean that was waiting to crash down if she let time slip. She could have told Travis before they left, but she didn't want the man freaking out on her and questioning what would happen. That would have wasted minutes. Better to just jump and apologize afterward.

She pulled Travis's body toward the edge of the collapsing wall of water and took a deep breath. Pulling him into the warm waters, the pressure pushed on her, popping her ears. Going underwater wasn't something she'd done much of, but she found she didn't need to swim up for breaths of air. In her slowed time, she could stay underwater for a long time. She hoped it worked the same for Travis as well.

Once she got to shore, she struggled to get his large body

out of the water and halfway onto the beach. Breathing hard, she released time.

"What the . . .?" Travis jumped up as a wave came up around his legs, and he spun around.

Evelyn patiently waited for him to come to terms with his new location. "You okay?" she asked.

"We're in the ocean. What in the hell?" He turned in a circle once again, and stopped to look at her. "Where's the stone?"

"It's best if we just keep moving. This is why I wanted to go alone."

"It's *in* the ocean, isn't it? You pulled me out."

"Can we go now, or do you need to keep asking questions?"

Travis wiped the water from his face and adjusted the blade at his hip. "Lead on, princess."

They walked through the thin forest of palm trees scattered among the sand and rocks. Evelyn had scouted out the place, right after she'd learned of it in the queen's mind.

Making her way toward the hill, she saw the door had been crushed in by what looked to be a giant boulder. And this was why she'd used the mutants, not just for their talents, but for their ingenuity.

"There's people down there," Travis said.

Evelyn walked along the worn trail the mutants created, and smelled the campfire and cooked fish. If she'd been by herself, she'd have slowed down time and studied these people before making herself known. But Travis, with his stomping feet, had probably already alerted them.

She walked past a small hut, then another. A person walked by and dropped a load of rocks she'd been carrying, when she spotted Evelyn.

"She's here," the girl yelled before running away.

In a matter of seconds, Maggie came running up to her, holding a wooden box. Evelyn's eyes widened as she gazed at the box.

"You're here?" Maggie said. Her eyes looked puffy and red, as if she'd been crying.

"Is this . . .?"

"Yes, we were able to get it out of that cave."

"Hand it to me." Evelyn wasn't sure what the treasure would be, but whatever was in the box, meant the world to the queen, and now she had it. Maggie held out the box and Evelyn took it. "Did you look inside?"

"Yes, just a few stones. But one of them teleported us right out of that cave. Well, it teleported some of us."

Evelyn looked into the eyes of Maggie. "Who did you lose?"

"Kris. He died for us. The magic holding this box demanded a life."

Of course it had. And Kris was probably the only person in the whole mutant village capable of keeping them all together. Without him, Evelyn figured the odds of them surviving had just decreased tenfold. Maybe another leader would emerge in his absence.

If Evelyn could, she'd spend more time helping them . . . but first things first. She needed to get to her family, defeat the queen, and tie up loose ends. "I'm so sorry. He was a good man."

She kneeled down and opened the box. On each side, sat stones, with initials engraved above them on the lid. "Allie and Mark," Evelyn whispered to herself. She didn't know how it could be, but they were in those two stones. The third stone intrigued her and she looked back up at Maggie.

"You used one of the portal stones?"

"Yes, to get out of there."

"Then I wonder where the other one goes?"

"Look at the picture," Travis spoke up. "I'd bet it's to an Alius stone."

She frowned and had to agree with him. It did appear that way, but it also could send them to the queen. The idea of her being on this planet didn't seem plausible, but the planet was a big place, with many hiding spots. The queen could have a hundred locations around the world, and it'd take Evelyn a regular human's lifetime to find them.

In all likelihood, this stone was probably a shortcut to something the queen had planned out. She must have assumed she'd be the person to collect these stones, making the portal stones her escape options.

"Are we free now?" Maggie asked. "Is this truly the end for us?"

Evelyn stood and looked up at the girl. She might be the one to take over the mutants. She certainly had the guts, and maybe even the intelligence for the task. "This is your planet. I've brushed over it and found no evidence of man. You can do with it what you want. You are free."

Maggie's eyes watered as she looked past Evelyn. "We can never be truly free with those stones in existence. At any point, a Marcus could emerge from the ocean and rule over us."

"You choose who rules over you."

"You could rule over us," Maggie offered, sounding hopeful.

And there it was. A request for her to stay with them. Not that it wasn't enticing, but there were more things to do other than the simple life of world building. Maybe, at some point in time, she'd check back with them and see if they were keeping together, progressing. If Evelyn learned anything from all the history she'd read, she knew they were human and prone to all of the standard weaknesses of greed, hate, jealousy, and rage.

"You don't want me. I may be a mutant, but I don't belong here."

"The tribe is choosing another leader tonight."

"Good. Move forward. Think big and act small. You will have your time."

"Will we see you again?" Maggie asked.

"I don't know." Such a complicated question. If Evelyn had more time, she might have talked with this young woman at length, to maybe even try and persuade the tribe to elect her as their leader.

Evelyn knelt over the box. "Travis, give me your hand."

"Why?" he said as he extended his hand.

"We're leaving."

Maggie hurried to speak. "Thank you for giving us a second chance at life."

"And thank you for getting these. It might be the only thing to save our worlds." She held Maggie's hand. "I'm sorry about Kris. I will make sure his death is honored through my next action." She let go.

Evelyn pulled Travis's hand down and made him touch the stone at the same time she did. Their feet landed on firm ground and she gazed at the nearby structure, in awe of what laid beyond. "You've got to be kidding me."

It struck her then, that there would be no end as long as the Alius stones existed. She'd have to change her plans once again.

CHAPTER 31

TRIP DROVE HIS OLD CHEVY truck down the dirt road, far from Preston. The sky had once been crawling with those damned black cubes, but in a blink, they were gone. It didn't stop him from checking every few seconds though.

Will said Evelyn had probably wiped them out with some kind of computer virus, but she hadn't mentioned it when she contacted him to send him the meeting location.

"How much farther?" Will asked. The boy sat between Trip and Gretchen. The bumpy road made him bounce around and grasp the dash from time to time.

"Not far," Trip said and checked his rearview mirror.

Minter drove his old mustang behind him. Seeing the car sent a tinge of regret through Trip. It reminded him of the day he convinced all his friends to meet Isaac. If he hadn't brought his friends, maybe none of this would have happened. Or maybe, this cube invasion would have played out the exact same way and they would've been defenseless against it.

A fierce bump sent Will into the dash. He held out his hands and narrowly stopped his face from smashing into it. He glared at Trip.

"There." Trip pointed ahead, to an imposing mountain of granite.

Will leaned forward to get a glimpse of the peak. Trip checked the Panavice to make sure this was the place. Evelyn had confided in him that everything may not go as planned, but she had backup plans. A little prepper in the making.

"Is this the place?" Will asked.

"It sure is." He pulled his truck near the base of the wall and drove over the grass and around a fallen tree. Then parked.

Minter, Karen, Beth, Opal, and Rick got out of the Mustang and gazed up at the mountain.

"It should be back here." Trip led them past the fallen tree and around a section of rocks jutting out of the ground—all as described by Evelyn. From there, he found the cave entrance.

A small tunnel led them to the familiar shape of the dome. An Alius stone sat in the middle.

"What makes this one different?" Beth asked, walking closer to the stone. "It's a master stone, but . . . wait, look at these lines on the side. I've never seen that before."

"Evelyn said to come here. She gave me a location and said we needed to wait for her first. She'll meet us here."

"I'm not going anywhere without my kid," Rick said.

"Same here," Beth added.

Trip sighed, knowing how they felt. "Evelyn said they'd be on the other side."

"Why don't we go now then?" Minter asked.

"Yeah, we're just supposed to wait here, while our kids are probably fighting for their lives?" Opal said.

"Evelyn planned this out. I think we should give her the benefit of the doubt."

"Look at you all, glowing like stadium lighting in here," a woman said. Her voice moved around the dome and they all had their weapons out, looking for the person behind the voice.

"Show yourself," Minter said holding out his gun.

A round rock rolled on the ground, then lit up with a bright white light. The woman appeared at the corner of the dome. She glided across the floor, staring at Will for much of the time.

"So beautiful," Rick said.

"I can't believe you fell for it," the woman said, then changed her voice to sound just like Evelyn. "Trip, I want you to gather everyone and meet me at this location. It's very important. Can you do that?" She laughed.

"She's going to kill us," Will warned.

Trip knew the boy was right, and he'd been the one to lead them to their deaths.

EVELYN AND TRAVIS STOOD NEXT to the massive rock outcropping. She thought Will might have spotted her on the way into the cave, but he'd made no motion to the fact. And when the queen popped into existence at the mouth of the cave, she knew this was the end.

She'd intercepted the transmission from the queen to Trip, but this turned out to be a blessing. It got all of her friends together in one place.

"You sure about this?" Travis asked.

"Yes."

"You're putting everything at risk."

"If I lose, we all lose together. Either way, it will end today."

"Your last encounter with her didn't go well."

"This time I know what she is." Evelyn walked around the rock, making her way into the cave. Gunshots blasted and she rushed inside.

"Did you kill her?" Karen asked.

The queen lay on the ground and most of the parents formed a wide circle around her. Evelyn thought against all hope, it was over before it even started. But the queen's embers and connections still floated around. "She's still alive," Evelyn said.

Everyone turned to face Evelyn and Travis as they stood at the entrance to the dome.

"Evelyn?" Minter asked.

She walked in with authority. "Get up. You don't fool me."

The woman on the ground laughed and floated back to her feet. "This is better than I could have ever hoped for. Just look at the two of you. And with the third, I am now certain this will be the end . . . well, for you. It's a new beginning for me."

"Third?" Evelyn asked.

"I didn't think you knew of her. I could read as much from the others."

What could she mean, a *third*? Evelyn pushed aside the distraction and focused on the queen. "It ends here."

"You're close, it will be ending soon. But only when I say it's over. You people have given me a remarkable amount of trouble for some rubes."

Evelyn glanced at Trip and then scanned over the rest of the parents. "This isn't a group of rubes, these are some of the greatest people I have ever met in my life. Now, I want the rest of them. Where are Poly, Lucas, and Julie?"

"Let's not forget about Hank, Gladius, Harris, Derek, and little Miss Cindy."

Evelyn frowned at the list of names. "You have everyone I care about. I guess we're even."

The queen laughed, then froze as she saw the wooden box. "Is that . . .?"

"Yes."

"Impossible. How did you get it?"

"It doesn't matter."

The queen disappeared and Evelyn was ready for it. She stopped time, and there, a few feet in front of her, stood the queen holding a stone. "Stop," Evelyn commanded.

The queen stood still and shook her head. "You can't have those stones. Those are mine."

"Who would put their own daughter in a box?" Evelyn asked.

"You don't understand. I had to hide her from all of this."

Evelyn shook her head and took a few steps forward. "Don't forget, I've been in your mind. You're scared of consuming her. Your daughter is something of a special person, a powerful person. She would have helped you reach the next level, wouldn't she?"

"You don't know what you're talking about. I put her in there to protect her."

"I saw into you. I know your fears . . . what you might do to her."

"Give me that box."

"You give me everyone I care about, and I will do the same for you."

"Or I can just take those stones and kill you here and now, along with everyone you care about."

Evelyn opened the box and turned it so the queen could see

the contents. "Kill me, and you will never find them."

Her gaze darted around as she searched the empty box. "What did you do with them?"

"There are so many worlds."

"No. This I will not stand for. You're going to tell me!"

Evelyn felt pressure in her head, as the queen pushed in with her mind. Evelyn tried to block her, but the rage the queen held pushed past her first wall and pierced into her brain. She panicked at the immediate intrusion. With all her strength, she pushed back, yet the queen was stronger.

I need you, Will. She projected the thought and wasn't sure if he would hear it, or if he did, would he even had the ability to help her. But she was desperate. If something didn't change, the location of the stones would surface and then everything would be for nothing.

Then she felt it, a hand on hers. Will by her side. It was as if she had another person to push back the crushing weight. Together, it became almost easy to repel the intrusion.

The queen huffed and scowled as she paced. "You can't keep her from me."

"Give me mine, and I'll give you yours," Evelyn repeated, gripping Will's hand tight.

The queen looked around at the parents and then at Will. "Don't you understand what you're doing? The two of you alone could stop the death of billions. With my consumption ends. I evolve into something so marvelous, the heavens themselves will be in my hands. I won't need stones to travel. I will be everywhere."

"You will fail," Will said.

Evelyn glared at the queen. "You need to leave Earth and Vanar alone. Do what you want with the rest."

"What about the one with the gifted people? You sent them there. I sensed it in your mind. They got the stone from the chamber, didn't they? Are they like you? There are many of them."

"No, and you are not to go near them."

"You act as if this is a negotiation. Tell me where to find those stones, or I'm going to start hurting people."

"You've hurt enough. Now bring my family here and I will tell you where your daughter is."

"Fine, we could go round and round, but in the end, it's just not worth it."

"And if you don't come back with my family, I will use this stone on myself." Evelyn held a white, crystal-looking stone.

"Where did you get that?"

"I am the only person in all the worlds who knows where they are located. If I use this, that memory will be gone."

The queen stopped and took a deep breath. She took her hand out of her pocket, and for the first time, looked unsure about her next step. "I'll bring your friends here, and then we can discuss the matter of my daughter and her boyfriend. Deal?"

"Deal."

They released time and Evelyn shushed the parents from asking questions, having them clear the room instead. All they needed to know was Poly and the rest were on their way. She was getting them back. They heard the stone hum.

"She's going to come back with backup," Trip said.

"No, she won't," Evelyn said.

"How can you be sure?" Beth asked.

"She doesn't see us as a threat. We're like ants to her. Annoying, pathetic ants that are ruining her perfect picnic." She turned to face the group. "Listen, what's coming next might require action from each one of us, if we have any chance of stopping her."

"We'll do what we can," Minter said. "For Joey and Samantha. We owe it to them to see an end to all of this."

"Yes, you're right. For Dad and Samantha," Evelyn said feeling the weight of everything pressing down on her.

A small hand wrapped around hers. "I'm here as well," Will said. "I can help. I can do the things you can do."

"Will, I have a special stone for you to use when the moment comes. Can you do that?"

"Yes, of course."

Evelyn handed him a stone wrapped in papers. "Just touch it and everything she and I can do will be equalized."

"Won't we be vulnerable as well?"

"Yes."

The stone room hummed and Evelyn walked back in, seeing Poly, Harris, Trip, Julie, Hank, Gladius and a new addition to the group, Cindy. She studied the girl. Similar face to Hank, but no sign of Gladius's DNA. Who had Hank fathered a child with?

Poly ran to Evelyn and nearly tackled her to the ground. Keeping an eye on the queen, she embraced her mom. When the queen's mouth hung open in awe, Evelyn took a step back, curious to what she was seeing. The connections. The golden strands increased by tenfold and she too became lost in the beauty of it. They swirled around in a maelstrom, as everyone greeted and hugged their loved ones. It was almost overwhelming. She met eyes with the queen and thought she saw a flash of humanity. A glimpse of the love she probably had for her daughter.

That's when the queen dropped a stone.

"Will!" Evelyn screamed. But it was too late.

The stone burst in midair and the wave spread over the group, freezing each person in place. Evelyn could move her eyes but nothing else. She stared at Will's hand, his fingertips at the edge of his pocket. If he could get to the stone, then maybe they had a chance.

The queen didn't say anything at first, choosing instead to look above the group.

"Evelyn, do you know what I just used? A stone so exceptionally rare and difficult to make, I saved it for a time such as this. There may never be another stone like it ever again. Feel privileged you brought it out." The queen said. "Now, get on your knees."

Evelyn knelt, but not under her own power. All the rest did as well. They were in a row, facing her like a group waiting to be slaughtered, and that is exactly how Evelyn felt. She'd led them to this fate and she wasn't even able to put up a good fight.

She struggled against the stone's control, but with each attempt, it pushed her back with the power of a bulldozer. Had she really underestimated the woman once again?

"I could make you all kill each other right now, and let the victors live with the knowledge of what they've done. It would be fitting to the amount of trouble you've caused. Do you think I like to get my hands dirty with affairs such as this?"

Panic filled Evelyn, not for fear of her own life but at what her hands, her mind, could do to those around her.

"Evelyn."

She perked up, ready to spill her own guts, or anything that would be commanded of her.

"I could ask you the question right now and end this game, but would that teach you a lesson? Do you think it would be fitting for me to let you off so easily, when you have killed my people, ruined my entire reclamation process, and even stolen from me?"

"No, I wouldn't," Evelyn said, even as she tried to keep her mouth from moving. The shock of the words spilling from it felt much worse than her body moving. It meant she'd give this woman all the information she wanted, all she had to do was ask.

"Evelyn, pick one person in this room and kill them."

Evelyn stood and walked in a straight line. She tried to stop it, screamed at her body to stop, but nothing impeded her progress. A marionette of murder, and she a mere puppet. The strings floated above her, hidden as much as her own connections.

"Go on," the queen urged.

Evelyn stopped and regarded the young girl. Not much taller than her, and she not only had a resemblance of Hank, but she had his eyes as well. Her hands raised and she brought them around her small neck, grip tightening. Cindy gurgled as she fought for breath.

A tear streamed down Evelyn's face as she tried with everything she had to pull her hands from the girl's neck. Helpless, she watched the girl's face change from a pale white, to a dark shade of red, as the blood and oxygen stopped flowing.

"Let her go," the queen said.

Evelyn immediately released Cindy, leaving her gasping and sucking in ragged breaths.

"Can't have you killing one of the specials," the queen said. "Pick another, but not Will."

Evelyn walked to the nearest adult and saw in his eyes the fear. Lucas Pratt, kneeled before her. Her hands felt small around his neck and she squeezed hard. Her strength never matched her size and she knew the sick truth; she had plenty of force to stop the air from getting to his brain. Much like Cindy, his face turned a sick shade of red.

Lucas whispered something. She struggled to hear it, but it sounded like, *get ready.*

Before she could register the words, his bulging red face changed to one of determination, and he grabbed her with both arms. "Now, Will!"

Will shoved his hand in his pocket, and Evelyn felt the wave of freedom crashing over her. She took her hands from Lucas's throat, and the room echoed with gunfire.

She tried to slow time, but she felt the block working. It'd happened. Will got to the stone. She scurried to her feet to get a look at the queen. She lay on the floor, bleeding from multiple gunshot wounds.

The queen held a stone in her hand and it dissolved into her skin.

"Stay back, she took something." Evelyn was quite certain of the stone she'd absorbed, because she should be dead by this point. She only hoped the queen had another of them on her.

POLY HELD HER THROWING DAGGER and rubbed the green etched dragon on the steel. Compry's mark. She'd never forget the person who'd helped her master the skills of the blade. Staring at the top of the queen's head laying on the dirt floor, Poly took a step closer. She would end this woman's life.

"Mom, stay back," Evelyn said.

The queen stirred and lifted her head off the dirt. Some of it stuck to her face as she got to her knees. *Impossible.* They must have shot her twenty times, and Poly had stuck her with several blades. Despite these wounds, the queen got to her feet, blood trailing down her face and chest. Her lips turned up in a grim red smile, blood smeared over her teeth.

"Almost got me on that one," the queen said. "But you've failed to notice, I cannot be killed. You've only succeeded in pissing me off." She winced, then her eyes widened. "Blocking stone. Who has it? Will?"

Lucas pushed Will behind him, as many of the parents formed a circle around him. "You don't have power over us anymore."

"You think I've shown all of my tricks?" She dashed to the stone.

Everyone rushed at her, and Poly threw her blade into the queen's back. More gunfire erupted, but it was too late. As they tackled her to the ground, the stone hummed.

CHAPTER 32

THE BARREN LANDSCAPE SPREAD OUT in all directions. The cold seeped into Evelyn's bones and her body felt light as she moved. She knew the feeling of an inhospitable planet, and rushed to the stone.

She typed in the code and knew at the very least, it would make the queen think of what she had, and maybe what she could gain from cooperating with them. Maybe she could get that glimmer of humanity back in the queen's eyes.

The stone hummed and the world changed again.

This was the place the second stone from the box had brought her and Travis. This was the place where she saw the queen had planned a future.

"Get off her, but keep hands on her. Will, you stay way back."

They climbed off the queen, still shaking from the frigid, barren world. Another few seconds and they'd all have been dead. The queen's plan all along, she was sure. But the meaning behind this action was startling. The queen was willing to abandon the idea of harnessing Evelyn's power, in order to preserve herself.

"Lift her up," Evelyn said.

"You can't do this to me," the queen said and fought against Trip and Travis holding her arms.

Lucas snickered and shook his head.

"You think this is funny? You are the freak that stones don't affect. I should have known you and your freak offspring would be immune."

"Shut up," Evelyn said. "And look around you."

A large statue of the queen stood near the stone. She pulled one last tug at Trip's grip and then stared at the statue of herself and the underlying city below. A vacant city, with gleaming architecture and clean streets.

"Why did you bring me here?" the queen asked.

"I wanted to remind you of what you want out of all this. I wanted to remind you of your daughter." Evelyn reached into her pocket and pulled out the color shifting stone holding her daughter.

"You had it on you the whole time?"

"Yes. She is what you are doing this all for. A mother's love for her daughter is strong. You can see that as much as I can." Evelyn looked to her mom and knew some of those connections over her head were meant for her. She felt them. She knew the queen had to see them as well. "Family is what it's all about. Not this quest for galactic domination, or whatever it is you are hoping to achieve through taking me and Will."

"You think it's that simple?" the queen shot back. "You think I can just turn it off and move on with my life?"

"It can be. It *has* to be," Evelyn said. "Because for you, it's over."

"You see, that is where you are wrong," the queen said with a wicked smile.

Evelyn faced the queen and spotted the stone rolling on the ground. The stone cracked open and an explosion blasted out from it, sending everyone to the edge of the circle.

"I knew you'd tell me where she was if I gave you enough rope to hang yourself with. Now give me the stone."

Evelyn gripped the stone tightly and got off the ground. With her free hand, she brought a second stone out and held it close to her daughter's stone.

"No! Don't touch them together."

Evelyn held the stone back. "So you know what will happen if I do?"

"Yes."

The one would extinguish the other and they'd both be gone forever. "Then stop this. Stop all of it."

"I *can't*." She grinded her teeth. "You think if I could I wouldn't stop this?" A tear fell from her eye. "It controls me. It demands me to complete this phase and move to the next. I am powerless against it. I am it, and it is me. "

"Then you have my pity," Evelyn said and nodded to Travis.

From behind the queen, Travis stabbed his sword into her chest, then moved the blade up, slicing through the top of her shoulder and cutting the queen nearly in half. Blood poured down her body and pooled on the ground. A glazed look came over her eyes and she swayed, as if only staying up by instincts. They wouldn't have much time before she healed, and Evelyn doubted she'd have another chance at surprising her.

Running to the stone, she typed in another code, a last resort, and hopefully the final resting place for the queen. Evelyn looked out at the beautiful city this woman had created for her daughter, and felt disappointment welling; she hadn't been able to get her to see what was really important. She wasn't sure if the queen was completely gone in her mania to evolve, but she had to be on the edge. She pitied her daughter and hoped the girl never woke to a world where her mother still existed.

"Here we go," Lucas said.

They jumped again. A place of history for the Six; where Evelyn's dad nearly died twice.

"You took us to Arrack?" Julie asked.

Arracks appeared from the rubble of the building around them.

"I've made arrangements and helped the Arracks. They have agreed to do this. I don't expect them to be able to hold her for long, but it may give us the time I need. Will, give them the stone."

Will handed one of the Arracks the blocking stone and Evelyn was highly doubtful the Arrack with many necklaces would be able to hold the queen for long. But Evelyn didn't need long, and as soon as she got away from the blocking stone, she'd have plenty of time.

The queen finally fell to the ground and the Arracks rushed into the circle. Everyone grabbed at their weapons, but the Arracks ignored them all, except for Evelyn. She'd grown to know these people over time, and had helped them to develop their world. Helping them, and asking for nothing in return, but this one moment she thought would never happen. She only hoped the queen wouldn't take it out on this wonderful civilization.

"Take her, Durraz," Evelyn said. "You know what to do."

The Arracks pulled at the queen's body, wrapping it up and carrying her over to Evelyn. She searched her body and pulled the two stone sacks from her before nodding and letting them take her away.

Durraz stayed behind as the rest took the queen over a debris pile and away into the unknown. "We have your promise?" the Arrack hissed.

Evelyn took out the small key and handed it over to Durraz. He took the key and gripped it firmly. He nodded and then ran off to catch up with the others.

Evelyn sighed and faced the group as she typed in the code. She held the stone sacks in her hand and was too nervous to look inside them. Everything depended on their contents. "We're going home."

They jumped and the group looked confused. They were back to where it all started, the master stone room under the mountain. Evelyn had wished to bring them all back to Preston and be done with it, but the world demanded her to complete a few more tasks before the end of it all.

"I need you all to leave the room. I have places to travel and time is not on our side."

They grumbled but left, and she typed in her first code, slowing down time just before the jump happened. She needed all the time she could find.

"WHY ARE YOU GIVING ME these?" Jackie asked, staring at the two stones in the box.

"Because I know you can help them, and maybe they can find a way to finish where I failed," Evelyn said.

Jackie teared up, as Wes, David, and Kylie crowded around her in amazement. "We can finally bring her back to us. I just knew that bitch had hid them."

"I'm glad I could give you this gift. And now I must go."

"Evelyn?" Jackie said and Evelyn turned back to her. "Sorry

about trying to kidnap you and stuff."

Evelyn smiled. Under different circumstances, she would've enjoyed getting to know this girl better. Slowing time, she ran back to the stone. A few more places and she could bring this to an end, once and for all.

CHAPTER 33

JULIE KEPT ON AND ON about how this stone with three lines on its side wasn't marked on any map, while Poly paced. She was beside herself, waiting for the hum of the stone and the return of her daughter. She wished she would've sliced the queen up into tiny pieces. Let's see her heal from that.

Will stared at the stone as Lucas and Julie held onto him. "I'm glad we're here. One more minute of being in the minds of the world and I'd have gone crazy." He looked up at his mom. "Do you know what people have hidden in their heads, their thoughts, their dreams, and desires?"

"We all have them."

"That's what I was afraid of." Will crossed his arms. "They make me sick," he mumbled.

Poly felt a hand on her shoulder and turned to see her mom. "Was it this hard when I left you behind?" she asked, thinking of the first time the Six had left the world.

"Yes, but it was a comfort knowing you had Joey and the others with you."

Poly closed her eyes and thought of her husband. His smile. His arms tightening around her. She gripped herself in a hug, scared to think of the life she had ahead of her without him. If something happened to Evelyn, she'd truly be lost.

Travis came up behind her. "I'm here for you, no matter what."

She turned around and hugged him. The man had been with her every step of the way, always there to lend a hand or offer his support. And she'd never thanked him. But true friends didn't need to be thanked. He knew how much it all meant to her.

For the next couple of hours, the group talked about old memories, and some of the mood lightened—even a few laughs were shared. With all of them in the same place, it felt magical. Much like the moment when they'd found Joey on that bridge on Arrack. They were meant to be together; together, things made sense. The whole world outside the dome was in total chaos, with families missing loved ones, and the entire power system down, but with all of the people she loved around her, she felt optimistic. Maybe a future wasn't just a continuous lineup of miseries.

Hank has a kid! Poly couldn't believe it. She might not approve of Hank doing what he did with Mary, but it had created such a beautiful life, and she adored Cindy from the moment she met her.

Could this be the end? The idea of it actually being over sent chills down her spine.

The stone hummed, causing the white noise of multiple conversations to go quiet. Poly backed away, nervous and excited.

Evelyn appeared next to the stone. She glanced up at Poly,

then looked back at the ground.

"What happened? Is it over?" Poly asked.

"Almost, but there is something I have to tell you first. I lied to you, and I am sorry."

"What do you mean?"

"About Dad. I led everyone to believe he'd died because I thought a glimmer of hope would be a cruel thing to dangle above your head."

"What are you talking about?" Her heart raced and she stepped toward Evelyn. Why was she talking about Joey right now? Lucas asked a question, then Hank. Poly couldn't hear what they were saying over the thrumming of her heartbeat in her ears.

Minter and Karen grasped hands and stepped closer, holding onto one another for dear life.

"Please, let me finish. This is important, and I don't have much time." Evelyn put up her hands to stop the group from talking over one another. "As I grew up, I learned to see connections between people." She smiled as she looked up and around the room. "I didn't know this when I kept Dad's body at the same hospital as you, Mom. And as a result, you felt him. In a subconscious way, you and he were reaching for each other. While everyone around you told you he was dead, you still felt him. I realize now, this connection nearly broke you, and I am sorry for not getting you off Vanar sooner."

"What—are you saying he's he alive?" Poly focused on her daughter's lips, waiting for an answer.

"I put him in a state of suspended animation. I thought maybe, in a hundred years or so, I'd find a way to bring him back. But the more I studied, the more I knew there was nothing I could do."

Poly's heart sunk and tears filled her eyes, the pain of his loss flushing over her once again, as if for the first time. She had thought she was crazy at the hospital. But she *had* felt him. "Why are you telling me all of this right now?"

"The purge people . . . they don't use technology like we do. I learned they use what they call *quintessence* to create these stones in a form of alchemy. That is when I realized they might have what I was looking for—a cure."

Poly's eyes went large, and she heard Julie gasp.

Evelyn looked at the clock on her Panavice and stepped away from the Alius stone. She talked quickly. "He's not all back yet, but Mom . . . he's going to be here in a few seconds."

Poly's mouth hung open and she stared at the stone, body shaking. She felt at once numb, and as if every nerve ending were pinging with excitement. It hummed and she sucked in a deep breath. "You didn't." She held a hand over her mouth.

Joey popped into existence a few feet in front of her. She froze in shock, tremors consuming her body. Then she stumbled toward him and grabbed him, touching his face and his arms. "Joey?" When he nodded, she threw herself into his embrace; his weak frame couldn't support her weight and they fell to the ground.

"Poly?" he said in a whisper.

Hearing his voice sent chills over her body. "Yes, yes. It's me." She clasped the sides of his head and held tight. "Joey." He felt cold and the look in his eyes had changed. As if something was missing. "Are you okay?"

"I don't know. What happened? I can't remember much."

"It may take time," Evelyn said.

"I will spend a lifetime telling you whatever it is you want to know." She kissed him and felt pure joy as he kissed her back.

"Son," Minter cried, kneeling next to Joey. Karen dropped to her knees beside them in hysterics.

Poly looked up at all the loved ones around her. They all held each other and stared at Joey in shock; all except Travis, who stared right back at her, tears in his eyes.

Poly got off Joey and helped him to his feet.

"How did you do it?" Julie asked Evelyn.

"I think they call it a life stone," she said. "It's one of the ways the queen can't be killed."

"I don't care how you did it." Poly bent down and hugged her daughter. They could finally be a family again. The people who'd hurt them for so long were out of their lives. Sure, the world would be a mess, but it didn't matter, now that she had Joey and Evelyn in her life.

"There is something else I need to tell you. Something I need to tell *all* of you," Evelyn said, backing up to address the group. "The queen will come back here. She won't stop. Which is why I must ask you all to make the hardest decision of your life. Right here, right now." She walked to the stone and Poly thought she saw tears in her eyes.

"This," she pointed to the Alius stone, "is the door that has kept our worlds together. I spent some time inside the mind of the queen. The knowledge the woman had of the worlds...." she looked at the ceiling. "Somehow she knew that this stone was special, she built a house around the one on her planet. But more importantly, she knew how to destroy it. All the stones are linked in a way, but this is the master link, none of the others can exist without this one."

"You're going to destroy the stones? All of them?" Julie asked.

"Yes."

"There has to be another way," Travis said and looked at Gladius.

"I could go over all of our options, but they all end with the queen winning, and we don't have the time. She could pop back into this room at any moment, and we will not be as lucky the second time around."

"We can temporarily seal the stones, or put up defenses," Hank suggested.

Evelyn closed her eyes and shook her head. "She will get past them. She knows our tricks and I have no more of them up my sleeves. Once she gets here, we won't be able to stop her. She will finish what she started. The only option we have is to shut the doors forever."

"Can't she just make more of the Alius stones?" Harris asked.

"She didn't make them."

"What?" he said in shock.

"She *discovered* them after she evolved into her current form," Evelyn said.

Harris rubbed his chin and stared at the Alius stone. "Then we have to decide where to be when these stones are destroyed."

Poly's staggered back and grabbed ahold of Joey. She could say goodbye to Harris and Travis if it meant this would all be over. She didn't care where she went, as long as she had her husband and her daughter. They could go back to living their boring lives. Nothing sounded better.

"We'll stay in Preston," Trip said and the rest of the parents nodded in agreement.

Poly nodded and knew the answer for all of them, but a couple split between the two worlds. She turned and faced Hank and Gladius.

CHAPTER 34

HANK'S HEART POUNDED IN HIS chest as he held Gladius's hand, blankly staring at the stone.

Mary popped into his mind and he shook his head. "First, I need to get Cindy's family before this happens. They're traveling to the stone in Ryjack as we speak. They should arrive tomorrow."

He could hear Joey asking Poly who Cindy was. He'd have to make introductions soon.

"I'm sorry, Hank, but we don't have time." Evelyn looked stressed. "I have the queen contained, but it's not permanent. In fact, she could be free at any moment. If I had my choice, I would have destroyed the stone already to banish her there, but I had things to complete first."

Hank wouldn't accept no for an answer. "You can get them for me. You can move as fast as light."

Evelyn took a deep breath and closed her eyes. Hank didn't want to push the little girl, but he also couldn't leave them on Ryjack for the rest of their lives. He'd made a promise; one he intended on keeping.

"I can bring them back," Joey offered.

"If you even *think* of doing that, I will bust your kneecaps," Poly said.

Hank blinked hard and focused on Joey once again. It was weird seeing him alive. His best friend . . . back from the dead. He couldn't wait to have some time with him, to tell him everything that'd happened while he was gone.

"We're risking everything if I go and look for them." Evelyn sighed.

"Please," Cindy pleaded. "If I could do what you do, I'd go after them myself."

Evelyn clenched her teeth. "Fine. I hope they are worth the risk."

"Thank you," Cindy and Hank said in unison.

Gladius pushed Hank back to the edge of the circle and glanced at the group. "What are we doing?" she whispered.

"With what?" He watched as Evelyn blinked away.

She slapped his shoulder. "Where the heck are we going to be when those stones come down?"

"Oh, I didn't. . . ." He stopped from saying he didn't think they would go anywhere but Earth, but then he caught Travis staring at them. He knew exactly what that man would want. He would want his daughter and hopefully, one day, his grandkids on his planet.

"This could be our chance to get away from all of this," Gladius said. "You know this won't be the end of things. Just look at Evelyn and especially Will, and. . . ." she hesitated.

"And Cindy," Hank finished.

She bit her lip. "Yes, Cindy as well. You think this world is a better place than Vanar?"

"No, I don't. And I can't ask you to lose your family," Hank said. "But I also can't ask you to leave me here. I can't live without you . . . so if you need to go to Vanar, I'm with you. But Cindy comes too. Her family as well."

"You're serious?" Gladius asked.

He felt sick to his stomach, but knew what his answer would be. "Yes. I don't want to wake up without you; I also don't want you feeling regret about where we are. I want you to be happy."

"And what about your happiness?"

Hank glanced at his dad and his friends. They had already proclaimed to be staying on Earth. As much as it hurt to leave them, he'd do what he had to, to make sure Gladius was happy. "I'm with you, wherever you may go."

Gladius hugged him and Hank had a feeling they were going back to Vanar. He wasn't going to have that conversation with Joey. The idea of not having them in his life seemed as implausible as leaving Gladius, but there it was. There would be no possible way to ever see his friends and family again.

Hank and Gladius walked back to the group, already in conversation.

Julie nodded and said, "We're staying in Preston." She held Will's hand.

"I have my best friend back," Lucas said, wrapping his arm around Joey. "You couldn't tear me away from looking at this beautiful face." He pinched Joey's cheek.

"And you have a *family* here. . . ." Julie supplied.

"Yeah, of course . . . but dude, just look at Joey. He is real. How the freak is that possible?" Lucas said. "And hell yeah, we're staying on our planet. Can you just imagine all the looting we can do right now?"

"You're an idiot," Julie said.

POLY THOUGHT SHE KNEW THE answer, but had to ask. "Travis, where are you going?"

"I have to go back to Vanar. That world needs me as much as this world needs you." He stepped closer. "It's going to break my heart to never be able to see you again. I thought with Joey gone, we'd form a tighter connection, but I wanted to be patient for you. I figured we'd have all the time in the world to find each other, but like many things in my life, I was a fool."

"You aren't a fool."

"I am," Travis chuckled and hugged her. He kissed her on the corner of her mouth and then stepped back and whispered, "You have your man back with you now. You tend to him. Love him with that amazing heart of yours, and I will cherish the brief time I got to spend in your light."

Poly felt the tears building again. She couldn't believe she was losing another man in her life. "I don't know what to say. I feel like we never had a real chance at getting to know each other."

"I think it's for the best this way," Travis said and hugged her again. He pushed her back. "You'll have a scar to remember me by."

"I'm still holding you to our deal about Harris."

"I think we'll be fine."

"I'm going to miss you, Travis." She hugged him again and then let go, rushing back to Joey's side. Harris was deep in conversation with him when she approached.

"I will miss you all," Travis said to the group. "If it wasn't for you guys, I'd still be a playboy, running around the streets of Sanct. Now, I have a world to look after." He faced Harris. "What do you say, Harris?"

Harris kept his hand on Joey's shoulder. "I'm thinking maybe Vanar would be better without me."

"The fact you are even questioning that, means you need to come home with me," Travis said.

Harris eyed him with suspicion and let go of Joey. "Without me, you'd have no opposition. You'd have total control over everything."

"What's the fun in that, old friend?"

Harris laughed. "Not much. But if I do go back to Vanar, things are going to be very different for me."

"You do what you need to do."

Harris pulled Poly closer and motioned for Hank, Julie, and Lucas to join him and Joey.

They huddled together in a tight circle. "I need to apologize to you kids."

"For what?" Joey asked.

Poly wasn't sure how much he remembered. She wanted the man alone to assess him, and much more.

"I will admit that early on I used you to get to Marcus. I manipulated you for my personal cause and as a result, I am responsible for Samantha's death, and until recently, Joey's death."

"If you didn't save us the day Isaac came to collect us, then none of us would be standing here," Julie said.

"I'm not so sure about that, now that I know what Marcus's long game was. I think I may have hurt more than helped, and for that, I am sorry."

Joey put a hand on his shoulder. "You may not have known what would unfold, but you gave us the chance to fight for our friends and family, to get our lives back. You brought us closer than we ever thought imaginable. We should be thanking you. And I will always think of you fondly."

"This will be a goodbye then. I will have trouble thinking of a life where I can't see any of you, but I will try and honor you by changing my ways."

"We'll miss you," Lucas said and hugged Harris.

"I didn't say anything about missing you, Lucas."

He laughed and pulled back. "Oh, crap, I need another Prudence before the door closes. They can't make that stuff here."

"Shut up," Julie said. "You can get your stupid bow earth-made and like it." She hugged Harris. "You can honor me by finding happiness, Harris."

"Thank you. I will try."

Hank stayed quiet and hugged Harris before moving out of the huddle and back to Gladius. Poly felt as if he was hiding something, and she couldn't even begin to imagine saying goodbye to the big guy.

"I can't believe this is goodbye," Joey said.

"The feeling is double for me, Joey. I've said goodbye to you more than I care to count," Harris's voice cracked. "You take care of them all. They need you more than you know. And no more dying this time around."

"I'll try. I seem to be a danger magnet." They hugged and Poly started crying. She couldn't stand more people leaving her.

"Come here, Poly." Harris pulled her in for a hug and whispered into her ear. "You are the glue of the group, the heart, the soul, and one of the most amazing people I have ever had the honor of getting to know. You have to promise me one thing."

"What is it?" Poly asked.

"Don't let this change you. You have Joey back now, and I want you to find that joy in your heart again. Don't block it out;

share it with them all. They will need it in times to come."

"I will," she whispered, but wasn't quite sure what he meant.

The stone hummed and Evelyn appeared with a few people Poly never thought she'd see again. The awkward kid, Peter, had turned into a young man. Mary as well, had become a woman. Carl seemed frozen in confusion as he looked around the dome and the people occupying it.

"Cindy!" Mary yelled and ran to her daughter.

CHAPTER 35

EVELYN STOOD NEXT TO THE stone and watched as her family and friends embraced and shared their last words with one another.

She only wished it all could stay the way it was right in that very moment. Smiles, tears of joy, and the strongest group of connections she'd ever witness in her entire life. If she could, she might have frozen time right then, just to sit and stare at the tapestry of her life. But there was a lady out there who wanted nothing more in the world than to take this all away from her.

"It's time," she called out. "Harris and Travis, are you ready?"

"Yeah," they said in unison.

"We're going as well," Hank said.

An explosion of outcries filled the air.

"What?" Gladius responded over the din.

"I thought we were going to Vanar?" He appeared dumbfounded.

"I never said that. You really think I would take you away from the Six?"

Hank stood there, staring at her in disbelief. "I don't know what to say. Your father. . . ."

Gladius walked over to her dad and hugged him. They spoke to each other for a while and embraced one last time. Running over to Hank, she had tears in her eyes, but a wide smile.

"This can be a new start for both of us," she said. "But don't think for one second I'm not going to get my Snackie Cakes factory built."

"I love you."

More tears flowed as they all said they're goodbyes to Harris and Travis. If the queen somehow made her way back to them in that very moment, she'd be blinded by a glorious sight. Their connections roared around them like a river of golden strands. She knew she'd never see such a sight of love and friendship for the rest of her life, and it made her sad to think she had hit another peak, and all before her second birthday candle had been blown out.

"We really must hurry," Evelyn said, feeling the stress of impending doom.

They all left the dome, leaving Harris and Travis alone to make their final jump. Evelyn listened for the stone to hum, then she walked back to the entry. They followed closely behind her, but she stopped abruptly and turned to face the group. She was about to speak, when she felt opposition building from one person in particular.

"Evelyn is taking me," Will said.

"I didn't say that," Evelyn said and tried to graze Will's mind for information, but he blocked her from his thoughts. She'd taught him too much. Made him do too much. And now they would all pay.

"You're taking our son from us?" Lucas said and reached back for a bow that wasn't there. Julie glared at Evelyn.

Evelyn didn't want this to be messy. "I won't lie to you. Will saw things that no human should, while hooked up to the machine. I knew this might be a possibility and it's one of the reasons I had Will do it for me. I've felt a change in him."

"What are you talking about?" Julie asked. "You said it was safe."

"Safe for him physically, but seeing into the minds of all those people. . . ." She shook her head. "Their darkness, their depravity. It's more than any one person can handle, and I've seen his destiny from the moment he was born. I said he would kill us all and I wasn't mistaken. He will play with them at first, by using the bug Marcus implanted on the world. He will want to tap into it, manipulate the world as he sees fit."

"The people of this world could use some guidance," he said defensively. "You have no idea what's in the minds of the people out there."

Evelyn sighed. "I was afraid you might feel that way. Did you know the purge people had many wonderful and magical stones? And then they had some downright nasty ones. I can't make them, but I can use them, and I have a few I took from the queen's supply with me right now."

"Is that a threat?' Will said and Julie and Lucas flanked him.

"It's a gift." Evelyn produced an opaque stone that looked like a round diamond. "This is going to help you get rid of the memories of what I taught you, what you saw in all those people. This is going to make you safe, make you whole again."

"No, I'm not unlearning what I've learned. The things you taught me . . . I won't let you use that on me."

"If you are thinking of touching one strand of hair on his head. . . ." Julie said, pointing a finger at her.

"I am only giving you your son back; to undo what has been done to him."

Lucas looked at Will and then back to Evelyn and she spotted the struggle in him. He had seen the change as well. Maybe even felt it.

She hated dealing with a special person like herself. Hiding behind words became difficult. She stared at the white stone with pink flakes on it. Will turned sideways and held his fists up. This wasn't going to be easy, but if this stone worked the way she thought it did, then he wouldn't remember any of this happened.

She took one step closer.

"I told you," Will said. "I'm not letting you do this."

"Then you might as well kill them now," Evelyn said. "I saw this future of yours since the moment you were born. This," she held up the stone, "can change that course."

Evelyn felt the pressure in her head and a heat down her spine. Will was attacking her mind. She froze from the pain and stared at Will. Had he grown more powerful than her? Impossible. Another step and she felt a fire blazing. She stared at Will. Sweat formed on his forehead. The fire wasn't real, but he was sending the information to her mind, making it feel very real. She slammed her eyes shut and tried to push him out of her mind, but she couldn't grab him. Every thread she pushed at slipped by.

She tried to take another step but fell to the ground and groaned. Joey and Poly rushed toward her.

"No, stay back," she yelled and was happy to see them obey.

"Stop it, Will," Poly cried.

The Alius stone sat just a few feet from Evelyn's hands, but she couldn't move. After all she'd been through, this was how she'd die? She knew Will would be the downfall of them all, but she'd been sure she'd stop that fate from happening.

"Please, Will." Evelyn groaned. "Stop it."

"You don't think I knew what your plan was from the start? When you first met me and projected your thoughts into me, you didn't have the discipline yet. I even knew you'd hoped the purge people might kill me in your mighty dome you built."

Evelyn cried out and rolled on her side.

"Stop it," Joey said and moved toward Will, but Lucas held him back.

She didn't want her parents to see her die and she reached for her slow motion, but it failed her. The memory stone fell from her hand and rolled onto the ground.

"You're hurting her," Poly said and a few parents moved toward Will as well.

Evelyn slipped in and out as the pain overwhelmed her, and his intrusion into her mind deepened. Then it came to her. Memories. She had enough in her head to fill several lifetimes of knowledge. She let go of all of it. The pain, the pressure, the resistance against his attack. She let it all go. She felt the flash flood of information pouring from her and she rolled back as Will staggered. He grabbed at his head and yelled. He'd know everything now, if only for a moment. Her endless knowledge she collected over the many years of slowed time.

She reached for the memory stone, but Julie snatched it off the ground first with a piece of cloth. *No!* She had failed.

Will fell to his knees as the information flooded him.

Julie looked at Evelyn, then ran to her son's side. She placed the stone on his neck and he collapsed to the ground.

Evelyn, sweaty and exhausted, rolled onto her back and

stared at the domed ceiling.

"It better work," Julie said.

"It will," Evelyn said and felt the pressure lessen. With Will out of the way, she only had one more thing to complete before the end of it all.

With all her strength, she rolled over and kneeled next to the master stone and felt the three lines etched down the side. She would use this stone as a link between all the others. Evelyn knew how to destroy it, and she had the queen to thank for the information. It had been sitting there in her mind.

It killed her to think of not being able to explore the worlds, the people, and the environments. But she loved her family more than gaining knowledge. And who knows, there was probably something bigger and badder than the queen herself—like the creators of the Alius stones. In time, their planet would've likely been decimated by whatever monsters could come through the stone.

She gripped the sides of the Alius stone and closed her eyes. Flowing her thoughts into the stone, she found the three strands dangling into the earth, connecting the Earth's currents to all of the worlds. In a way, the stones had a network of connections quite similar to humans. The only way to sever them all was to cut them at the root, and the rest of the system would collapse.

She only hoped what was held in the queen's mind was right. Her body floated in the void between all the worlds. A blackness surrounded her, and the golden strands ran deep into the darkness below. She reached down and she squeezed her grip and yanked hard. They wouldn't release. Next, she pulled at the strands with her mind, using her hands as a reference. They still didn't break. She screamed and placed both hands on the strings, pulling with all her might. Two broke loose and fell into the blackness below.

The last string brightened and hummed with power. Maybe someone, somewhere was using the stone and she panicked that maybe the queen was moving around; maybe she was back in the dome, killing her family.

The last string vibrated in her hand and she felt the power of it. Infinite power. The queen had ideas about what might happen if it broke, terrible ideas like the worlds exploding, but Evelyn didn't think so. She wrapped the strand around her hand and pulled again.

It twanged and pulled her back, sucking her deeper into the darkness. She heard voices running along the string like a record player recording the etched sounds of existence. Images plowed through her mind as she screamed and pulled at the strand, trying to break the last thing keeping her family from being free.

Then she saw it. The face of the creator. An ancient image of a woman, threading the strands between the worlds, creating the stones. The woman seemed familiar in a way, then the strand hummed again and she felt the immense power. The image disappeared. The string tightened around her hand and pulled her down again.

If Will hadn't just drained her of all her energy, she might have been able to break this last one. As it was now, she just wanted to give up.

"Evelyn?"

She opened her eyes. Cindy floated next to her, or what looked like Cindy. More of a ghostly image of her body, as she shimmered in and out.

"Cindy, what are you doing in here?"

"I knew you needed help."

"I can do this." With Cindy watching she gave another

mighty pull on the string. She plunged into the darkness again, leaving Cindy floating way above her.

Cindy appeared next to her once again. "This time, we do it together."

Evelyn nodded and Cindy reached down and took the string in her hands.

"Use your mind. I think that's what gives us the power," Evelyn said and Cindy nodded.

Evelyn closed her eyes and thought of her dad and mom waiting for her to return. She thought of the queen, who was probably making new stones and getting ready for a major retaliation.

"Now," Evelyn said and felt part of the string getting pulled by Cindy.

She poured everything, her love and hate, into this last pull. If it didn't break, she knew she'd plunge into the darkness below and never be seen again. Cindy groaned next to her and then she felt the release, as if they were pulling on nothing.

"Let go," Evelyn said.

The string flickered as they let go, then fell into the darkness with a few last bursts of light.

Evelyn felt the push back to her body and she fell back onto the ground. She couldn't move. She could barely breathe and as she lay there, she watched the stone crack and then break apart.

They'd done it. The stone was gone; every stone would be broken now. No one, anywhere, would be able to get to them now. They were free.

EPILOGUE
ONE YEAR LATER

HARRIS STOOD BEHIND TRAVIS, OVERLOOKING the streets of Sanct. In the last year, he had dissolved MM and split it into thirty-two companies. Some failed with the split, while others skyrocketed—the way a free market should work. He gave up on holding onto the power, and for the first time in a long time, felt as if something wasn't crushing down on him.

Travis waved to the enormous crowd and they cheered. Over the last year, Travis and he had spent a lot of time together, rebuilding Vanar, and making the tough choices. In the end, Travis remained president and even brought in Harris as an advisor.

"Thank you so much for making it to our first annual day of celebration," Travis spoke to the crowd. "The day our oppressor turned off the power and lit our world on fire."

Thunderous boos spread over the crowd.

"I know, I know. But it was also the day our world came together, in a united front, to rebuild and reform all of those broken ties. And we can stand here today and proudly say that we've succeeded."

The crowd cheered even louder.

Harris chuckled and thought of the little girl who'd came into their lives like a whirlwind and saved the day. He wished for Poly and Julie to be standing up here with them. He could only imagine what the crowd would do if they showed up.

The Preston Six had become something of a legend. Most of the people figured they died in the moments after Marcus cursed the world. Others said Travis had them cryogenically frozen, so they'd could be revived if the world ever needed saving again. That one made Harris laugh the most, even though they had a building that could do just that.

There wasn't a day that went by without thinking of the kids. When he thought of Joey, his heart sank each time. Evelyn somehow brought him back from the grave. It felt almost unnatural to him and he often thought of Compry. Could that stone have brought her back from the abyss? Had he been impatient and cruel when he killed off her grinner body without so much as a second thought? Or what about Ryjack?

He twitched at the need to use an Alius stone and see his friends once more. Even the vast expanse of his own world felt small now. He felt confined to a cage he'd never be able to escape.

The only relief from his confines, was in the form of the company he'd kept under his command. Stowing an endless amount of money into his space program, he couldn't wait to see what civilizations he could discover. There were worlds out there, he knew it. Marcus had hated the idea of space travel, but for Harris, it felt like the next choice, the next adventure.

The crowd quieted to Travis's calming hands. "We have a lot to be proud of, but there is more work to do. . . ."

Harris drifted off as Travis went into his rehearsed political speech. He'd heard him speak so many times now, it felt as if they all blended together into one optimistic tapestry of hope, thankfulness, and remembrance.

"He start talking about Poly yet?" Katana asked.

"Not yet," Harris said and took her hand in his. And here he thought he'd never love again. But against all odds, there she was, sitting next to him, looking as beautiful as anything he'd ever seen. She looked just like her mom, Maya. Which he was grateful for because he didn't like the idea of looking into Travis's eyes on cold nights.

"You tell him yet?" Katana asked.

"I was going to save it for after the speech." He felt the ring on her finger.

"How do you think he's going to take it?" Katana asked.

"Well, he's the one who introduced us, so I think he's going to be okay with it." Harris had come to think of Travis as a brother, or at the very least, a great friend. They'd been through hell and back together, and lived to tell about it.

"I heard he went dancing last week. And even picked up the sword again."

"That's good to hear." Harris knew Travis had had intentions with Poly, but the world didn't work the way you wanted it to sometimes.

"Oh my *God*, is that a ring?" Douglas leaned over with his fingers tapping his lips. "Let me see it!" He caressed her hand, then looked to Harris with a raised eyebrow. "For the richest man in the world. . . ."

Travis glanced back and witnessed Douglas fondling the

ring on his daughter's hand. He stared hard, then looked at Harris. He pulled the mic from the stand and motioned for Harris to come next to him. "I want to introduce a man who needs no introduction, Harris Boone, my future son-in-law."

The crowd roared more than any previous cheer. Harris stood next to Travis and took in the mighty crowd.

Travis leaned in to whisper to Harris, "Anything happens to Katana and I won't honor any deal Poly and I have." He squeezed Harris's shoulder hard and then waved to the adoring crowd.

He'd make sure Travis never had to break that promise with Poly.

JOEY WALKED NEXT TO THE car, carrying the small cooler under one arm. Poly jogged around the other side and pulled on his hand, dragging him up the front stairs and onto the porch of his parents' house. Bull rushed out from under the house and greeted him. He knelt and petted his old friend, who wagged his tail and licked his hand.

"Good to see you, buddy," Joey said.

Not everything had come back to him when he'd woken up on that cold slab in the basement of the hospital, but he had a vivid memory of his old dog. It seemed like so many years ago now that they went off into that forest together, starting the entire adventure.

The front door flung open and Lucas jumped onto the porch wearing a pointy birthday hat. "I thought I heard you guys out here. You're late."

Poly winced at the words and Joey gave her a sideways look.

"Or," Lucas continued, "have you two been out here sucking face the whole time?"

"We just got here," Joey said.

"Though the car ride here *was* fun," Poly said.

"Oh, you crazy kids. Get in here." Lucas grabbed Joey around the neck and pulled him into the house.

"How'd the sleepover go?" Poly asked with a bit of nervousness in her voice.

Lucas smiled. "Those three kids," he shook his head, "I can't understand half of what they are saying anymore. They just live on those Panavices. So, in other words, they couldn't have been any easier."

"Oh, good," Poly said.

Joey wanted to see his little girl's face, and looked through the window trying to spot her. An odd thing, having a gifted child who was so advanced, holding a solid conversation with them became difficult. It felt easier to just let Evelyn explore her gifts, but maybe that was because he had his own. Not that he'd ever use them again.

They entered his parents' house and eighties rock played through his dad's stereo. Evelyn, Will, and Cindy stood next to the stereo and stopped the music. They took out the cassette tape and passed it around, studying it. Minter walked up to them and took the tape, giving them a quick explanation of the different metal filaments that aligned in such a way the heads in the stereo picked them up and converted it into audible music. Their three faces lit up with fascination.

After a night filled with laughter, presents, and birthday cake, they settled into groups. Poly grabbed Joey's hand and they walked off to the back porch for some night time air. Even though he and Poly had moved just outside of town into their own small house, this place always felt like home.

"Samantha kissed me here," Joey said.

"You trying to get me jealous?" Poly nudged him in the side. "I miss her as well. She had such a fun, infectious way about her."

"Like gravity."

"Yeah, she drew you in."

Joey thought of the time he'd spent with Samantha in the amusement park. He almost wanted to thank Marcus for giving him those moments with her. They'd gotten to know each other on so many levels, and even though he was never in love with her, she still meant the world to him.

"The sky is so beautiful now," Poly said and Joey looked up into the night sky, so many stars gleamed. So bright in fact, the power would be turned off after ten.

"Power curfew should be kicking in."

"Yep, the kids must be hacking the system again."

"Should we stop them?" Joey asked.

"Nah, let's just have one night with the lights on."

The world had gone haywire, as one would expect, after surviving the *alien invasion*. And with their resources crippled, many of the cubes and structures still lay dead and scattered all over the world. The governments, fresh off the near-apocalyptic Cough outbreak, struggled to get a handle on a second world-wide recovery.

Trip had become something of an expert to the growing underworld of preppers, and went into the business of helping people prepare for the next calamity. He and Carl had become good friends, and ended up partnering in the endeavor, with Peter tagging along.

Joey loved taking Peter and Mary out. Everything they saw brought such a wonder to their eyes. Joey only wished he could have shown them what the world had looked like before the invasion and the Cough.

With the school systems in shambles, Poly had started teaching some of the local kids in one of the classrooms in the school that wasn't completely ransacked or burnt down. While she busied herself with feeding young minds, Joey spent his time down at the gun store. He mostly did it just to keep busy, but he also liked to handle all the different guns.

Minter and Rick led the rebuilding effort in Preston and nearby towns. They'd done such a good job that in a few months, the new school would be opened. Beth and Gretchen had formed a Planting for Life foundation and taught the people of the new world how to garden and grow their own food. Opal started a program teaching self-defense, and even drew in some celebrity types with her amazing knife skills. Poly would even stop by from time to time to offer a hand.

Julie, Lucas, and Will stayed in Preston as well, but Julie used one of the few Panavices they still had to create some wealth, magically distributing it into needy people's accounts. The news reporters called the anonymous donations a digital Robin Hood.

Lucas and Will spent a lot of their time driving to different areas, and offering their help to get power back up, or just handing out food and seeds. Lucas fashioned another bow, but still muttered about missing Prudence. *It has to be in one of those cubes,* he'd say. The more Joey thought on it, he wondered if Lucas and Will were just on a major hunt for his missing bow.

The three wonder kids spent a lot of time together, mostly working in effort to make the world a better place. And with ZRB, the company Evelyn still owned, they seemed to be doing that in spades. Joey never asked too much about what they were doing, as somethings were better left unknown.

Poly touched his arm.

He folded her into his embrace and they gazed out into the night. "What's up?"

"After a year, I still have to check and make sure you're real."

"I'm real." He smiled and kissed the top of her head.

The back door opened. Julie, Lucas, Hank, and Gladius joined them.

They stood quietly for a minute before Gladius said, "Oh, I got the latest test batch today. I even have a couple left over."

She pulled a cellophane package from her pocket. "My freaking Snackie Cake factory finally got it right." She opened the package and bit into it, looking as if she would melt with ecstasy. "So good. This world's going to go insane over these, if I decide to let anyone else have them."

Hank smiled and hugged Gladius. "The factory can make tens of thousands a day. You can only eat so many."

"Says you," Gladius said and took another bite. "You guys have got to try these." She pulled out a couple and laid them on the railing.

Lucas took the next package and wolfed it down. "That's amazing," he said with a mouth full of Snackie Cake.

"I know, right?"

"I have an announcement as well," Julie said. "I've perfected Orange. Well, I should say I did it with the help of our own wonder three."

"What?" Gladius eyes went wide and Joey thought he saw tears welling. "Thank you so much," Gladius said. "You know, you guys can drink it as well. We have the same genetic markers. You can all live for a long time."

"I guess," Joey said.

"When I said I'd marry Lucas for life, I wasn't counting on a *forever* kind of life," Julie said.

Lucas huffed. "You couldn't handle all of this for that long anyway. We'll just get all old and wrinkly together." He snuggled up against her in a hug.

"Stop it." Julie playfully pushed him back.

"Speaking of surprises," Lucas said and let go of Julie. "Hank and I got something from the old school. A birthday present to all of us, if you will." They both darted off the porch and yanked a blanket off what looked like a rickety table. Carrying it onto the porch, they sat it down with big smiles stretching across their faces.

"A table?" Gladius asked.

"Not just any table." Lucas pointed at a marking.

"Is it . . .?" Joey rushed to the scribbling they'd made so long ago. His finger rubbed along the etched letters. The bumps and lines stood as a reminder of a day when they still had Samantha, and the world had felt so big. A happy time, filled with the innocence and free thinking of young teens.

"Thanks, guys," Poly said and moved her fingertips across the letters. "This is so special."

Hank hugged Gladius and whispered into her ear.

"Hey, since we're all old and responsible now, I think we should go to the lake and do some nighttime swimming, in the nude," Lucas said.

"Sure," Joey said. "Well, except for the nude part. But a trip to the lake sounds nice."

"Let's go! Hank, you have to row the boat. I'm not wasting all my money on gas when I have a trained ape on hand."

"You better run. . . ." Hank chased after Lucas and into the house.

"Kids." Gladius sighed and went into the house.

Julie walked up next to Poly. "Remember the time when Samantha stuffed bait fish into Lucas's sandwich?"

Poly smiled. "Yeah, that was funny."

"I say we pay Samantha a little homage tonight. You guys down?"

"Yeah, we're down," Joey said.

"Okay. I better catch up to them, I don't want Lucas driving there."

"Sure, we'll meet you at the lake," Joey said, then turned to Poly as Julie went back inside.

Poly turned to face him with tears flowing down her face.

"What's wrong?"

"I'm scared."

"Of what?" Joey asked. "Marcus is gone, that queen lady can't get back to us, we have a family now, and a solid place in which we can live. It's our time to be happy."

"That's what I'm scared of. For so long, we ran from chaos and calamity, only to charge headfirst into the unknown danger. And then, Joey . . . you were *dead*, and crazy alien queen was after our daughter. And now . . . well, now look at us." She motioned back to the laughing parents as the kids pulled a cassette tape apart to study the remnants. "Our daughter seems happy. We seem happy."

"Then what's to be scared about?"

She wiped her face. "I can't shake the feeling it isn't going to last. And worse than that, I don't want to lose that feeling. I'm letting myself slip into this reality of safety and comfort, which will only make it worse when it's pulled away from us once again."

Joey pulled her in for a hug. It killed him to hear his wife's fear to be happy. He wanted to suck all the pain from her and put it on his own shoulders. The idea that she'd spent so many months thinking him dead weighed on him.

"Listen, we have each other, we have Evelyn, our families . . . the new little one," he touched her belly, "and we have happiness. There is no reason to squander the good days in dread of bad ones that may never come. Let's live in this moment, and if something changes down the road, we'll deal with it then."

He bent down and found her lips for a kiss. She kissed him back and hugged him hard.

"You okay?" Joey asked.

"Yes," she smiled and kissed her finger tips, then rubbed them along the etched letters of *The Preston Six*.

THE END

Made in the USA
Middletown, DE
10 July 2020

12440759R00166